Attack Of The Moon Cows

RODNEY MILTON

Published by RODNEY MILTON, 2023.

This is a work of fiction. Similarities to real people, places, or events are entirely coincidental.

ATTACK OF THE MOON COWS

First edition. July 3, 2023.

ISBN: 979-8215626252

Written by RODNEY MILTON.

This Novel is dedicated to Philip Cross who had a cow called Holly.

I would like to thank my editor Geoff Nelder for helping me get this novel up to muster.

I would like to thank my cover artist Rebecca Martin for her wonderful cover art.

I would like to the Left Field Creative group in Chester for their help and support especially Peter Hurd and Lewis Martin.

I also like to thank the Chester Nanowrimo group for creating a fantasticall creative atmosphere during the creation of this novel

Chapter 1. Beer stains and Bull-lords.

Grassy greeting groove kits, let me introduce myself. My handle as the young folks used to say is, Holly, milk-bound star-child, sometimes known as the merry, mooing, cud-muncher, or even the moon marching, freedom mother. When I'm letting my funky rainbow dance horns down to a rock-and-roll frenzy they say, 'look a ... funk-powered, super-chilled, bright-eyed, boptastic ... barn wrangler, I really dig that funky cat.' Of course some cruel haters mutter spiteful things about my sense of rhythm and trauma caused by watching my sweet style in local nightspots. It's best to ignore those bitter spite cats. Haters are going to hate, besides I've never been successfully sued for damages based on any negative effects of my groove. I always settle strictly out of court for stuff like that.

You peeps look like you're pleasant enough so it's fine and freaky if you just call me Holly, keep it chilled and informal you know.

If you're concerned this is another of those pesky Moby Dick tributes let me assure you nothing could be further from the factual. Never had any issues with whales nor do I socialise with those who do, I am cool whale wise. I only mention it because I know a lot of folks are totally sick to the wisdom munchers of all that Moby Dick related stuff that's around at the moment, I know I am, I mean eight films and then twelve seasons of the television series were just a bit more than this humble cud chomper can handle, and let me tell you cats I am capable of handling a heaping helping of heavy shit, like crazy avalanches of it man.

You know I'm thinking maybe in your universe everyone hasn't gone Ahab crazy, if so you're probably sitting, mouth agape, demented drool dribbling from the corner of your snarling and confused lips. What is this loon cat rambling on about, is she a bat loop or high on fairy juice? Well I am sorry if that's the case dude cats, you'll have to bear with the old Hol-meister, it's just in this reality Moby-white-whale shit is all over the shop, we, are figuratively drowning in the stuff. My advice, don't let it happen to you.

Holly you're saying to yourselves, that's a freaky name, what's the deal? It's a girl's name right? The sort of thing you'd call your third pet cow after you'd used Buttercup and Fancy-free, naturally.

Well here is the big news flash for you folks, I am indeed of the female persuasion and a bovine to boot, check out my udders they aren't no strap-ons that's for sure. Hey I didn't say you could touch them, keep your dirty hands to yourself. I have enough trouble with those cold-handed, dirty-minded farmers always trying to milk me. They don't like it when you try and milk them, no sir. Although there was this one guy, but that is a whole other story indeed, best to stick that one the back burner I like to call deep denial, a very disturbing incident and no mistake.

I live in the Fun-filled city of San Francisco with my life, love and business partner, Vincent mean martini Moochuckle. He's cool and funky like myself, as well as being a fellow bovine. While I am an extremely broadminded hippy right on cat, I do have my limits. Interspecies romances are a step too far for me, sorry if that causes offence but I am the bovine I am. Not that I haven't had offers from humans of all genders, my oh my yes, apparently there is something about my super-dextrous tail, rainbow horns and big brown eyes that give all manner of humans that frisky farmyard feeling.

What is all this in aid of, if it's not whale related then what is this bleating bovine's story you're asking? Don't blame you if that's the case, quite understandable.

You know a few years back we had that trouble with the mad moon cows causing all sorts of trouble? You may have lived through those dark days if you're from our reality or you might have suffered night terrors from the dreams we transmitted across the multiverse to promote this book, hope you weren't too traumatised by them. Hopefully they intrigued you enough to seek out a copy in either the noble spirit of idle curiosity or as part of your therapeutic regime. Perhaps you watched the film, which is nonsense by the way. Heavens to Hendrix groovers you may have even read the heavily censored accounts in the blogs from those involved. Well, none of them will give you anywhere near the full tale.

I am one of the few that really knows what went down in bad-trip, moon city but until now it was all top secret and I could not moo a word. Finally, I am told I can write an uncensored account of the whole damn story, warts and all. Here it is folks for the first time a genuine first hoof account of what went down. Why don't you kids Kick back, chillax and give those tired disco feet a warm and bubbly foot bath while you let this funky book give your brain the soapy, steamy-mind-funk it deserves.

I will grant you some stuff I didn't see myself but I got the lowdown from those who were there or in a couple of cases those who interrogated them, using genuine advanced interrogation techniques. Not that I approve of that sort of thing but sometimes you have to get your gossip and general damning confessional slander where you can. Am I right cats? Am I right?

It all started with the international American moon-base. It was a freaky place, America claimed it was theirs and the rest of the world thought everyone owned it but let the Americans pay for running it. They went through a phase of letting any old crazy college kid work there mainly to cover the nightshift which none of the proper astronauts wanted to do.

Hence this night (Tuesday I think, isn't it always a Tuesday, what's with that anyway?) the guy running the night shift was crazy, joker and eternal frat boy Larry (for you international readers frat boy is American for idiot).

'Look lively my little pledge-lings,' squelched that lanky, wired-up-to-the-streetlights young chap as he bounced for joy in the beer-sodden captain's chair.

Oh bounce, bounce, bounce, went the buttocks, splash, splash, splash went the beer.

'Piss right off,' went young Davey as he tried to sleep on the floor.

'That's not the attitude David my lad,' scolded Larry with a wag of his finger and the most gleeful little snigger you ever did see. 'If you want to join the, Lunar, Mooning, Alpha, Wasters, you boys will have to buck your ideas up and suck up my beer, from my seat that is. Come on my boys, roll up, roll up.'

'No one wants to join your stupid, made-up fraternity, Larry,' crunched another young fellow tucked up all cosy beneath a nearby console as the potato chips, liberally sprinkled across the carpet during the early evening merriments now disintegrated in great numbers as the sleepers dreamed restless dreams and struggled to find comfortable spots to slumber.

It wasn't just salty snacks that littered the floor that night, oh no my little blacklight beauties no they were just the primer coat, layers of greasy meat, cheese and splashes of both the bodily and beverage kind laid a thick strata of youthful grime. On top of that was a generous spread of crusty and full-bodied odour oozing, socks, undergarments, and food wrapping. Finally for the piece de resistance, came a delicate sprinkling of freshly shorn beer cans, now empty of libation but dripping with potential.

The day crew would naturally complain quite bitterly about the mess and the deeply ground-in salty patterns, some said you could get as high as a paisley proud peace park Paula, if you sniffed those streaks just right, they didn't do anything for me though groove cats so I can't verify that.

Larry's wasters left their marks on most of the adjoining corridors as well much to the fury of the base commander.

'But it's art you ignorant fool,' Larry would announce with a grin into the red snarling face as the big hands gripped him hard by his sticky shirt shaking the unrepentant young man up and down like a rag doll.

'If your father wasn't General Jones and I didn't have an irrational fear of people thrusting irascible skunks down the front of my britches', the General had a reputation for doing exactly this kind of thing to his enemies, 'I'd whup your ass out that airlock and into orbit before inviting every nation in the world to use you for target practice.'

'Well he is and you old chum are a philistine,' Larry would say before dropping to the floor. With a grin and a bow Larry would stalk off to his quarters to rest and ask his father once again to either arrange for him to return to Earth or at least despatch some high spirited skunks to make his time on the moon more entertaining.

Larry's fraternal lunar lair contained many pungent odours groove cats, sweet beer and sour scents of young men their lives liberated from the oppressive shower- filled constraints of polite, nasally-sensitive, soap-addicted society.

Young women also worked the night shift as you might expect but their admittance to Larry's inner sanctum was rebuffed by a choking fog of giggling, misogyny.

'For gods sake what is wrong with you people, it fucking stinks in here?' was a phrase gasped by women at the door to the command room so many times it had passed into cliché long back in the mists of lunar time. This legend and the ever popular, 'you need to see a doctor/dentist/psychiatrist/pest controller, Larry that smell/rash/urine colour/thing coming out of your nose, isn't normal I think you're contaminated,' flowed over Larry and his, lunar mooning, alpha wasters like a dancing queen sailing over a funky vodka-slicked nightclub floor heading for her waterloo.

'Don't snooze out on me fellas, no one sleeps on a pirate ship, I need stimulation here,' but those wasted wasters could only reply with a gentle snoring serenade.

A dedicated few sat at their stations trying hopelessly to defeat fatigue and do the tasks actually assigned to them. It was these brave souls that Larry took aim at now as he spun the command chair around and around, one piece of stale food or other rubbish flying through the air missing each and every one of his targets.

'Piss off Larry, you demented knob squirrel,' muttered one of the dozing crew as one then another of Larry's sweaty moon boots bounced of the view screen and hit him full in the face.

'Don't make such a fuss,' shouted Larry leaning forward, a empty beer can held tight in his hands ready for its maiden flight. 'I wasn't even aiming at you. I was trying to get one of them freaky moon creatures; if I can wind them up enough perhaps a few will come out onto the surface and do an angry dance. Provide us all with a bit of entertainment.'

Larry continued to frantically pelt the view screen with empty beer cans in a vain attempt to taunt any moon creatures out onto the surface where they might take the edge off the crushing boredom that swirled dully around his senses. He had dreamed, in the days before coming to the moon, of excitable, green-skinned, moon women blessed with oversized mammary glands and strong desire to hear his exotic earth accent whisper tales of freedom and of the kissing.

All he found were serious-minded professional women who gave Larry and his stinky sock puppet, Mr Pew, a wide berth. 'You shouldn't discriminate against poor Mr Pew,' Larry would yell down corridors at the many women who pushed the dirty, reeking sock away from their faces before walking away as fast as dignity would allow. 'He's got a medical condition common amongst the sock people, it's often fatal you know. What sort of person shouts abuse at a poor sick sock, probably on its last legs,' Larry would continue with a giggle edged with sadness for the poor humourless losers that surrounded him.

Some women told Larry where he could stick Mr Pew. 'What a great idea,' Larry would reply and do as they suggested. This only added to the sock's potential to cause distress. Most of the female crew eventually just carried jock repellent spray to ward off Larry's greasy intentions.

Larry had also been baffled by the lack of beer and takeout available on the moon, his stocks smuggled from Earth a month earlier were dwindling fast and he faced the horror of spending the rest of his stay sober, something Larry really could not face.

Despite these disappointments he had been cheered on by the reaction of the crew to his continual practical jokes. By the end of his first week he had received no less than seven death threats and had found posters depicting his decapitated body in his locker everyday with the words, 'die you annoying freak.' Larry's heart was truly gladdened by this reaction, in fact the growing tidal wave of frustration and pure hate was the only thing that kept old Larry sane, it was almost like being back at college.

Suddenly, to Larry's delight the face of fellow night-shifter Boomer appeared on one of the communication screens, he was dressed in his space suit and sitting in the driving seat of the moon rover vehicle.

'Moon base control, come in,' said Boomer keeping things formal and professional even though only crazy Larry was listening. 'I am taking the lunar rover out for a spin, think I might check out that strange and totally creepy cave system we all saw yesterday, unless it's going to upset the big cheese and his apple core of trouble.'

Larry started to giggle and rub his hands together before licking at his last stale slice of pizza. As his stock of takeout pizza dropped to the critical point he had taken the radical step of restricting his experience of pizza to licking only. This strategy had made his present piece of super cheese pepperoni last three weeks. Any mould or maggot related issues were quickly resolved by exposing his pizza to the harsh lunar atmosphere, 'better than bleach,' said Larry who planned to bottle and sell it as a disinfectant when he got back home. Well either that or patent the idea and sell it to some billionaire or multinational for crazy money.

Anyway Larry was happy, Boomer his absolute favourite victim had made contact and it looked like he was about to do some crazy arse shit which would entertain Larry no end. 'This is moon base control, go knock yourself out Boomer old chap, the apple cart is stable and this big cheese is happier than a teenage boy in a Jacuzzi full of centrefolds. Why don't you get some pictures while you're down there? We're all getting sick of looking at ore samples around here. I haven't got anything else to look at now that the new President's feminist supporters made me dump my porn stash into space.'

'Yeah that was a real shame,' said Boomer taking the moon rover out onto the surface. 'I hear her husband likes a bit of the old hot action porn when no one else is looking and then there was that film he made with all those cow girls covered in jam and honey, what was it called, The sweet ass lasso, or some sort of nonsense. No one stopped him releasing that. I guess its one rule for the big shots and another for the little guy, isn't that always the way?'

'You got that right, Boomer buddy. If he was stationed here the dude would be assigned his own personal bikini model to bring him coffee and put mints on his pillow if you catch my drift. While hardworking Joes like you and me get the bums rush, right. You know they even stopped my movie nights, who'd ban a fellow doing something innocent like running a movie night?'

'You projected those porn films onto the moons surface, people on Earth could see them, what did you expect to happen, Larry?' said the crew member who had just been knocked in the face by the sweaty moon boots.

'Listen pal this is a private chat between me and my mate Boomer here,' snapped Larry. 'It doesn't need your negative attitude, 'besides they were all specially selected to be tasteful, posh arty European stuff, you know with couples painting their houses, drinking fancy coffee and talking in breathy French accents about feelings before getting down to the flatteringly well-lit action, nothing seedy about it. I was just trying to give those werewolves something to howl about. I mean the moon's just so boring, the same look night after night, my plan would have spiced things up a whole lot,' yawned Larry.

Now that bored astro-cat, Boomer, bounced his moon buggy right across the moon to those little old hills in the distance hoping for a little adventure, crazy Larry egged him on, until the hypnotic movement of the moon buggy caused Larry to slip gently towards the land of nod.

After tormenting the beings that populated his subconscious dreamscape for a while he was suddenly kicked furiously back into the world of wakefulness. 'I was only resting my eyes Miss, honest I wasn't asleep,' muttered Larry, as an urgent excited voice shouted from the speakers.

'I've found a cave system moon base control,' yelled Boomer over his radio.

'Hey is that you Boomer old fruit? You've found those creepy caves? Well that's funky man. Grab that camera and get on in there.'

'Are you sure I should go in alone? It might be better to wait for back up, protocol and all that.'

'Now don't go wimping out on us Boomer, protocol is for sad losers who iron their socks on a Saturday night, now get that camera and get exploring. You've got us here backing you up old buddy if some freaky Lunarian leaps out at you.'

Boomer started to explore those crazy lunar caves, looking for excitement and adventure. Sometimes man you need to be real careful what you wish for in case it comes and bites you in the ass.

'Wow, this is weird man,' said Boomer in growing excitement, 'I am seeing all kinds of freaky runes, like the moon men of legend wrote a message or warning for any unsuspecting visitors or innocent and naïve wanderers. There are pictures too, freaky creatures looming over me.'

'Sounds great Boomer buddy,' said Larry, 'keep on going perhaps you'll meet a moon man and he'll tell you what it all means. Don't forget to take plenty of pictures now bud, we need all the stimulation we can get over here.'

Larry turned off his mic and laughed twirling his fingers next to his head in the classic that guy is crazy, hand dance.

'Don't worry; I'm taking loads of pictures. This stuff is wacko crazy in old school beatnik style,' said Boomer breathless with excitement.

'Yeah Boomer, I am sure it is totally trump tramp crazy.'

'Wow this is beyond Freaks-ville; I am seeing an actual shiny metal door made of real actual metal. I'm going, I'm actually going through, oh man this is like a molten roller coaster ride with bad trip Magoo.'

'Yeah that sounds great, just keep on trucking Boomer buddy,' said Larry suppressing the fit of furious giggles that danced in every fibre of his being.

'I am man, oh wow I am going through some sort of internal airlock now, it's incredible, the beings who built this place must have been really advanced, like far future, oh man I am in a huge room and it's full of all kinds of pictures, all over the walls. They all have these real freaky beings in them, like cowmen or something. They all have huge devil horns and demonic glowing eyes. I think they might be watching me,' said Boomer an almost hysterical tone building in his voice as the radio began to fade and crackle.

'Just keep going buddy, sounds like you're having a fine old time,' said Larry who was leaping ape like around the control room while beating his contorting features with a large foam hammer.

'There is a row of huge cryogenic suspension chambers, my god they're massive. Whatever is in them, they must be some kind of giant monster things. I am moving around the front of the first one. I am trying to see through the clear panel in the front, it's full of fog all swirling around. I can see a shape behind mist but it's not clear enough to tell what it is. Wow I think it must be an alien moon beast, I wish I could see it better.'

'Try pressing some buttons, perhaps it will open up and you can get a better look and those all-important pictures you promised us,' said Larry now in a full ape suit lolloping around the control room roaring at his colleagues in the guise of a fabled moon monster.

'Hang on, what if it's dangerous,' said Boomer the fear in his voice only matched by the fading crackle of the radio. 'If it's dangerous and comes back to life we could all end up drowning in a ton of killer alien cow shit.'

'Calm down Boomer buddy, get a grip on yourself. You're perfectly safe, things in cryogenic chambers don't suddenly wake up when you open the door, they take hours to revive. You just need to open it up waft away some of that misty shit and get your shots quick and close the box right back up again. Real simple Boomer pal, unless you want to run away like a big girly wiener rabbit, loser from wimpington the capital wimpsburgland. Because you know in the movies the loser wimps get killed first even when they run away, monsters like to eat wimps and they can just follow the yellow trail losers leave behind when the piss their girly pants.'

'Hey, Larry, I'm no loser wimp. If you think it's safe I'm going in. I trust you. Wow I'm going to make first contact; I'm going to be a goddamn hero. Samantha McBride will wish she had gone with me to the senior prom instead of laughing in my face and calling me a sad loser freakozoid. I bet she calls me up straight away begging me to make sweet, sweet, bouncy, kitchen table love to her and perhaps her cute sister Jacky too. Oh Samantha, yes I forgive you, let me stroke your golden hair.'

'Now don't get side-tracked Boomer buddy, they'll be plenty of time to get bouncy over your lost love later, get on in that chamber,' said Larry turning off the microphone to let the squealing laughter spring forth from his gurning lips as he rolled around on the floor bashing his fists about in an excited manner.

'Okay, okay, I'm pressing the buttons. Wow it's opening up, I'm wafting away all the mist, I can see it clearer now it's some kind of huge bull beast,' gasped Boomer, 'my god it's hideous. My camera is in position, getting some good shots here man. Shit, I am sure the thing moved, ahh, noo.'

Boomer's transmission ended with a scream, a violent gurgle and loud crunching noise over the Ever-crackling radio and then silence.

Over at lunar command everyone in the control room was looking pretty freaked out as they listened to Boomer's final desperate dying gurgle.

'What the hell was that about?' said nervous Pete the paranoid radio operator who thought every bit of static was something either alien or human plotting his personal doom.

The only one who did not wear a stunned and generally freaked out look was Larry who took his demented gurning grin and other odd facial contortions round the room, doing a mocking dance in front of each crew member in turn as they just stared at him.

'The look on your faces, old Boomers had you over. Well done old Boom buddy I didn't think you had it in you. He fooled all of you, but not me, no sir you have to get up pretty early in the morning to fool the old Lar-meister yes in deedy, cock a doodle doo.'

'What are you saying Larry?' said the crew member known as freaky Phil (so called for the amount of times women called him a freak when they heard one of his crude chat up lines), as he knocked Larry's extended middle digit away from his face.

'Well Phileep my cheesy little chap, I will tell you and the rest of the sweet and innocent rubes in the room what just happened. Very simple Boomer boy's overactive imagination that's what. He scared himself to death imagining a big scary monster with snapping fangs and slashing hooves in those caves. He probably wet his knickers and ran for the rover like some panicky wet-bottomed man-child. He'll come back saying he escaped by the skin of his teeth with the help of some big old landslide that will have killed the monster, and destroyed his camera as well as all traces of the arty moon creatures and their suspended animation chambers. All destroyed without a trace, what a shame we will just have to take his word for it. Yeah I've seen it a thousand times, he's a classic case.'

'The lunar rover is heading back with Boomer or the creature and his radio is totally dead, perhaps we should wake the proper captain, he can authorise use of the laser cannon, to blast the rover, you know just in case,' suggested nervous Pete his hand hovering over the intercom emergency line to the real Captain.

'Let me stop you right there Petey my lad, first of all Captain Larry is the real captain on the nightshift and I don't care what the clown that rests his fat arse in my chair in the daytime thinks. They should court martial that fat, sanctimonious, sneering little fuckwit. Second and most importantly I don't need his permission to fire the laser because I stole the control codes and I intend giving old boomer a little scare.'

Lanky Larry, all a giggle and bouncing in his still sodden seat started firing the base's laser cannon causing the lunar rover to swerve all over the place on its way back to the base. 'Take that you dirty little moon man.'

'I'm not sure we should be doing this, Larry,' said Phil, 'I mean Boomer's radio may have got damaged or something and you're getting very close with that laser, you are pretty drunk, you're could kill him or something.'

'Perhaps he has to maintain radio silence in case the creature or its vengeful relatives try and track him back here,' said Pete watching nervously over Larry's shoulder. 'Or it could be some kind of demonic moon monster that Boomer released from that cave and is coming to do to us what it already did to Boomer. Better blast it, to be on the safe side, you know just in case. Go on, Larry, quick blast it straight back to hell.'

'Calm down, Pete, I'm not going to blast Boomer you crazy wombat botherer. At least not until I've heard his story, I bet it will be worthy of one of Larry special awards, this will be his third. I think he finally got rid of the stains from the second one a couple of days ago so he must be due, a nice special stinky one this time me thinks. Oh yes.'

'He has reached the base garage door. Should we send down a meet, greet and terminate squad to welcome him home before I open the doors, Captain Larry?' said Pete.

'No need to worry about that my boys,' said Larry heading for the door. 'I'm going to meet old Boomer boy myself, open those garage doors Pete my lad and leave the rest to your old mate Lar.'

Larry wandered, whistling a merry and annoying tune, into the lunar garage where the rover sat all peaceful and serene. Larry started laughing and laughing thinking it all one big jolly old jape. He shouted for Boomer and started to call him a chicken for not coming out, daring him to reveal some evidence of the moon monster.

Only trouble was cats it was no joking matter as Larry was about find out and as for the monster well he was about to get more evidence for its existence than he bargained for.

'Come out and show us those pictures, what you waiting for Boomer me old muck spreader? Are you sulking because we fired a few little laser blasts at you? That was just a bit of harmless fun, like blokey banter but with large rover rocking explosions. No hard feelings eh? I bet it was just like the roller coasters at lunar Disney. Did you bring back any moon monsters? Hey Boomer buddy, you know you got to come out sooner or later.'

Then the door of the rover popped open real quick and a big bovine beast stumbled out. He was still groggy from the cryo but he looked a menacing cat especially as he was dragging Boomer's body behind him.

You will no doubt have cottoned on to the fact that this was Lord Cadmow and you may have seen photos and think you know what he looked like, well let me tell you cats those still images don't do that scary dude justice. This was one big, mean-looking dude. Like some kind of minotaur, nearly eight foot tall, all bovine muscle, vast sharp horns on which he would regularly impale the heads of his enemies, often while they were still attached to their bodies. His eyes were red and would glow and bulge when he was enraged which to be honest was most of the time. He truly was one naggy cat.

He had sharp and gnarled hoof hands with hard flexible almost claw like fingers, his coat was dominated by a burnt red colour with the odd spiral of white and black mixed in. A brass nose ring marked his rank with was invented by Cadmow himself, that of Bull-lord supreme. It was a cross between a General and despotic overlord. He also wore a bright red cowbell about his neck, a mark of both his house and the Herdist branch of the noble faith of Cowdon to which he belonged. It was one of his far distant herd mothers in a time long back through the great meadow of the ages that founded the noble Herdists. Her bellows surely echoed the heavens at the shameful antics of her descendant.

It was said if an enemy of Cadmow heard his bell's gentle tinkle then he, she or it would hear nothing else save their own death gurgle.

Lord Cadmow snorted furiously at Larry and his bell gave out a gentle little sound. That tinkle of doom made Larry laugh and laugh. We bovines take our faith very seriously, it is unwise to mock our beliefs and to laugh at the bell of a Herdist is blasphemy indeed even to one such as Cadmow whose actions mock the very faith itself.

'Hey Boomer buddy, like the costume, you've got a cute little bell can I ring it buddy?' laughed Larry as Cadmow gave out a mighty bellow. 'Where did you get it? Loser monsters from *Bad Movies Are Us*? Don't think much of the dodgy fake dead body though. You should kill the guy who conned you into buying that outfit and use his body next time; it might look a bit more authentic than that thing. Hell one of those shop window dummies would look more realistic. Hey I bet that's what it is. Let's have a feel, is it a girl doll eh?'

As Larry reached out an excited hand to ring the little bell and molest the dead body of his comrade, Lord Cadmow gripped him firmly by the throat and rammed his squirming form hard against the wall. The Bull-lord brought his face close to Larry's and snorted loudly, the snort steam making Larry cough and splutter.

'Ok, ok,' said Larry chocking, 'I'm sorry I fired lasers at you, gee's it was only a joke. Chill out and get a sense of humour for goodness sake.'

Cadmow tightened his grip and said 'You are of no use to me,' in what might appear to be surprisingly good English, but we space bovines do pick up languages pretty fast to be fair.

'Well then let me go if you don't need me, I am sure a big bull like you has important things to be doing,' said Larry wondering for the first time if this might not be Boomer in a suit after all but a genuine monster in a bit of a bad mood.

'Except, perhaps to give my death hoof a bit of exercise, it's out of practice you see,' said Cadmow as he crushed Larry's throat, which screamed, choked and gurgled. The blood splashed all over Cadmow and the immediate area until Larry's head became severed from his body.

Cadmow picked up Larry's head and popped it on his right horn. Then he turned to the camera, flexed his hoof and smiled saying, 'I'm going to have to get a bit more practice in I think, hope you folks aren't to attached to your necks because I will be ripping them out soon.' That old bad-tempered bull lowered his horns and with a snort charged headlong at the door which separated the garage from the rest of the base. The door disintegrated at Cadmow's violent touch and he just kept on running.

That's what happens when you scrimp on the door budget groovers.

Now those guys in the control room were watching all this via a monitor screen and had just parked their tired and confused brains at ground zero, in main street panic city.

Pete was pacing the control room, stopping every few seconds to stare hypnotically at the main view screen which showed Cadmow's rapid progress through the base. 'I told you we should have blasted it clean away, didn't I say we should blast it but oh no Larry knew best and just got that thing, whatever it is real, pissed and just look were not listening to me got him. He's dead and that thing is coming for the rest of us so it can take our heads as some kind of twisted trophy that he can set out and have little freaky chats with. We need to wake the real Captain and the rest of the day shift, no matter how tired and grumpy they are. They're the only ones who can deal with that freaky bull thing guys, because it's time to face up to the fact that we are all, drunk, tired and have no idea what the hell we are doing.'

Perhaps if they had listened to old panicky Pete at that point old Cadmow could have been stopped in his blood-stained hoof tracks and perhaps as much as half that base's population could have escaped the brutality that he was about to inflict. Instead the drunken ego of one self-important dude drowned out calls for a little common sense.

It was a cocksure cat called Barry who had until a few minutes earlier been asleep under a console clutching a bottle of cheap whiskey as he cuddled up with Doris his very own stroke me silly, fully functional, lust bot, programmed with a thousand and one freaky kinks for every occasion, that pushed himself forward as the new manly hero of the hour.

'That is a load of bullshit, Pete,' shouted Barry as he stood swaying, half full whiskey bottle held aloft like a flaming torch in the centre of the room. 'This thing has attacked the base and killed Larry and Boomer on our watch and it's our responsibility, we can deal with it. Well at least I can deal with it, some of you losers might want to go and curl up in your rooms under pink and frilly security blankets. Any one who wants to do that, go now, we will know that you're pathetic quivering losers but at least you won't get under the feet of the real men, such as myself. We don't want to be tripping over your wimpy, shuddering little bodies as we run headlong towards danger and a serious chance for manly action.'

'Oh Barry don't you want to play eager piggy's again?' oinked Doris suggestively. 'You can snuffle my truffle if you like, you large sweaty horse of a man you.'

'Hold that thought Doris,' said Barry with a wink, 'when I come back from being the big manly hero of the hour you can activate your swooning-in-awe-of-the-big-macho-hero- fresh-from-saving-the-day-program.'

'Gosh how exciting, shall I compliment you on your sexual organs in order to boost your ego and enhance your potency in battle?'

'Ok, Doris, but make it quick, I've a frenzied bull creature to defeat here.'

'Barry,' began Doris her voice strangely solemn and metallic, 'your organs of manhood are not only hugely deformed out of all natural proportions they also excite me to such a degree I fear I may short circuit with joy or my batteries will just pop out before the completion of our frenzied love making.'

'Nice one Doris, now I really need to get this battle started,' said Barry ignoring the various horse impressions that rippled around the room.

'What makes you think you can defeat that thing anyway?' asked Pete.

Barry swung his face next to Pete's, blowing whiskey fumes into his choking lungs. I don't need to think, I leave that sort of thing to sad, loser, nerdy little chess club rejects like you. I know I can defeat that thing, I have experience roping and riding the Holsteins on my uncle's ranch and not only that, a couple of summers back I went to Europe, with my family and watched a genuine-to-goodness bullfight. I took a good look at what that Spanish bloke did and to be honest it looked pretty damn easy. Let's just get out there and kill that bull thing and show those snooty day shifters that the night shift is the best shift and demand a bit of respect. Let's break out the guns quick before that thing gets anywhere near the munitions locker and blast that goddamn critter straight to hell.'

'Better be careful,' said another colleague whose name isn't very important as he won't live very long so we don't need to get emotionally attached to him. 'We only have two guns and that thing seems real mean.'

'We're lucky to have them,' replied Barry striking a macho like pose of defiance. 'Goddamn, no good pacifist, Hippy-skippy European, gun-banning losers. I'll give them all that; let's keep space a peaceful place crap. Thank God for the Gun strokers of America society. If it wasn't for their demonstrations and their armed sieges of the French and German embassies we wouldn't have been allowed any weapons on the moon at all. I am still real pissed that I wasn't allowed to bring my semi-automatic from home though, otherwise that bull thing would be sliced up on the barbecue by now.'

Bombastic and sadly deluded Barry along with his right-hand, unnamed and very doomed sidekick, who was soon to be splattered, headed out to the weapons locker with drunken swaggers as Phil and Pete who had stayed behind, guided them both along the corridor, using a route that avoided the one Cadmow was taking.

Cadmow for his part was systematically going to rooms one at a time throughout the base, ripping out the throats of the occupants before dumping them in the corridors.

As Barry and his companion headed towards the weapons locker, other members of the nightshift who had heard rumours of a dangerous bull beast loose in the base joined them and formed a large angry posse of nearly fifteen souls.

At the weapons locker Barry and unnamed night shifter took the two guns while the rest of posse took up a variety of make shift weapons including chair legs, golf clubs, walking sticks with Stanley knives taped to them and various types of fire extinguisher. Two men carried a large heavy metal anvil which they hoped to either drop on or catapult at the creature. One ingenious creative soul had created a mace using a thick metal chain quickly welded to a model of the Apollo moon Lander which he swung not only round his head but in circles to the front and the side causing the rest of the group to have to duck and suddenly dive out of the way cursing and shouting, often in pain at regular intervals. When any of the group complained about the mace-wielding guy he just became furious shouting, 'There is a dangerous creature in this base and I have the right to defend myself so get the hell out of my way,' so everyone did so.

The posse gathered in a small briefing room with plans of the base and footage of Cadmow's location to make their attack plans. Which they would have to do quickly as the crazy-eyed old bull had already killed nearly half the base's population.

'Right guys and gals,' began Barry acknowledging the angry woman with the crossbow and the row of cutthroat razors around the belt of her blue denims. She flashed him an impatient and irritated smile and kept raising her bow as if she was about to shoot him through the neck, that is when she wasn't gently caressing her razors. 'This is the plan, bad ass creature has stopped in this little computer room here,' he said pointing at the map with a riding crop, 'the room has two different doorways plus a ventilation shaft in the ceiling just above where the critter has parked its no-good bovine ass. We are going to hit it from all three sides at once, in what I call a pincer from a mutant crab whose parents got radiation poisoning which made all their offspring grow an extra third bit to their pincer manoeuvre.'

The posse all cheered, waving their makeshift weapons a little too wildly in the air.

A short time later everyone was in position, the two with the anvil had positioned themselves with their weight primed and ready. They quietly lifted the grill and gazed down at the figure of Cadmow. 'This is for Larry, Boomer and The Gun Strokers of America,' they both shouted dropping the weight on the unsuspecting Cadmow. Unfortunately they both fell through the hole onto the now unconscious Bull-Lord. As they began to get to their feet Barry and the unnamed dude burst through one door and fired wildly while the rest of the angry mob with their chair legs, broken bottles and random pieces of metal taken from the airlock doors, burst in and began their equally frenzied attack, 'for the honour of the night shift,' they yelled just before they were caught up in a hail of bullets. Before she died the crossbow girl managed to get off an arrow which took out the unnamed guy. The two guys who had dropped the anvil managed to get hit with both bullets and makeshift weapons.

Barry stood looking at the large pile of dead bodies. He frantically tried to reload. Where are you hiding you freaky mooing critter, because I plan on blasting you clean away,' he said as an unseen hoof reached up from beneath the pile of dead bodies and found Barry's throat.

After the great scattering of freaked out crew cats from the control room only Phil and Pete remained at their posts. They tried not to look at the image of Cadmow as he ran down the corridor, gun in one hoof and crossbow in the other with both Larry and Barry's heads sitting firmly on his blood-stained horns. Clouds of steam poured from his powerful and angry nostrils fogging up one security camera after another.

'Are you sure that door's secure,' said Pete, his tone more than a little hysterical.

'Yeah we're in full lockdown,' replied Phil no less calm. 'Although I don't know how long it will hold against that thing. You know they really skimped on the internal door budget in the place, most of them are just cheap plywood they say all the money went on the Captain's private golf-course. Any joy contacting Earth control yet?'

Pete jabbed desperately at the radio. 'Damn, I can't break through the interference. Let's make a run for it, get off this rock, warn Earth and let the marines kill that bloody bull thing.'

'Hang on there, Pete,' said Phil, 'shouldn't we see if any of the others made it back, perhaps some of the day shift are still alive. After all we have only got one shuttle; if we abandon them with that thing then we'd be committing homicidal murder.'

'Look at this,' said Pete changing the display to show the various corridors and rooms of the base all lined with dead bodies, 'everyone else is dead and if we don't get down to that launch bay now then so are we. That thing is heading this way and I don't think it's going to settle for a fireside chat and a cup of milky cocoa to resolve whatever deep seated personal issues it seems to have. Let the marines listen to its problems eh.'

'Fair enough, let's go,' said Phil.

As the two men reached the door two disembodied human heads smashed their way through the adjacent wall rapidly followed by wildly snorting Cadmow. The two men leapt and danced in terrified alarm, trying to escape but Cadmow quickly cornered them.

Cadmow smiled a sadistic grin and let out a growling moo of self satisfaction. 'I hope you two weren't trying to get away just now because I haven't finished my game of killing all the humans. I believe you two are the last humans alive on this base and I do like to finish my games. Show me your necks gentlemen because unfortunately they are still attached to your bodies and you know that just isn't the way I want them.'

'Listen man, I mean cow er bull whatever,' rambled Pete. 'Killing us would like be a really bad move. We've radioed Earth for back up; they'll be landing thousands of crack troops any minute, if you just take us hostage instead of killing us they may hold back from splattering your brains all over the walls if you follow my meaning. Not only that but we are both close and personal friends with the great and powerful scary arse Earth leader who will get really pissed off if we die. They wouldn't be that bothered about all the others you have killed out there but harming us in any way would piss off our extremely vengeful leaders, us being such close personal friends and all.'

'Yeah that's right,' said Phil, 'you'd get the chair for sure if you just short changed us in the local shop.'

'Is that so?' said Cadmow looking at them both up and down as they nodded frantically their nervous sweat showering Cadmow with a fear-induced rain. 'Interesting, as it happens I have just been reading about your planet's various political leaders. You are from the nation state known as America I understand. A powerful state that recently chose a new leader.'

The two humans nodded and Cadmow poked a bony hoof at Pete's chest. 'You human are wearing a campaign t-shirt for the rival candidate to the actual winner, the losing candidate. Your chosen candidate spent the selection process wearing an aggressive trained ferret upon his head which was trained to attack not only his opponent who was quite severely bitten I understand but any one who asked a difficult question. In fact it would savage anyone who did not start their question, please enlighten us oh great and wise one. He had just the one policy I understand which was to build a wall around the moon to keep any aliens out. As an alien myself I could take a great offence at that. Now my little friend I would hardly think the lady who was selected is going to get especially upset if I kill someone who backed her opponent. What do you think eh?'

'I voted for the one who won, she was the blond one right?' said Phil sounding a little unsure.

'She was the only female candidate, you pathetic little human. You may have voted for her but the fact that you cannot even remember her name and that you're wandering around in clothes covered in mustard, ketchup and other stains of dubious lineage suggests you are not her close friend and your sudden and brutal death would be of little consequence to her.'

'Ok, ok,' said Pete as the two started edging back. 'Why don't we just surrender, you know we could be your prisoners. You could boss us around, tie us up and shine lights at us while you ask us for information and attempt to bend us to your all-powerful will.'

Cadmow shook his head and advanced hoof outstretched a large evil grin on his face and a wicked twinkle glinting merrily in his evil eyes. 'I really don't think so, taking prisoners always sounds like fun in theory but with all the moaning and trying to escape it's normally much more trouble than its worth. I think it would be easier all round if I just killed you both.'

'But,' began Pete before looking down in horror as his neck was ripped away and his body fell to the ground. After taking a second to throw Pete's head over his shoulder he advanced on Phil.

Cadmow's right caught hoof caught fast in a discarded crisp tube as his left slipped wildly on a slimy piece of congealed cheese. His stumbling gave Phil the chance dodge the bull lord's determined grasp.

'Now come on dude, let's be reasonable,' began Phil trying to maintain as much distance as possible between the demented killer bull and his all too delicate and tender neck. 'We're all grown ups here, we don't have to resort to this kind of primitive knee jerk reaction stuff. I could get you things, I am a rich man, I could make you the richest bovine that ever lived, you could have a fleet of yachts and acres of lush meadow. I can make you famous, you'd be the great dancing cow, er bull, kids would love you. What about action movies, yeah I can see it now, the Cow-minator the killer robot-cow on a mission from the future. You'd have it all the rock-star lifestyle, fields full of hot horny cows and all the hay you can eat.'

Cadmow looked doubtful and shook his head still advancing, but now with more care as many sticky and slimy hazards stood in his path. Not to mention the danger of getting potato chips lodged painfully in his hooves. Let me tell groove cats you get one of those hard chips in your hoof, you know about that is for sure. 'Tempting, human but I don't think so,' said Cadmow his hoof flexing in such a way that made Phil begin to perspire profusely and his bowels threaten to make whatever fate was to befall him extremely undignified.

'Hang on, let's just sit and discuss this in civilised manner, like mature intelligent beings,' said Phil retreating rapidly as his brain desperately tried to find a set of words that would extend his existence at least a short while longer. 'Over a nice cup of tea and hey we could have choccy biccy's too,' rambled Phil as he mindlessly thrust a packet of chocolate digestives under Cadmow's snorting nose while moving his own delicate neck out of bull's crazed grasp.

'Biscuits, you say?' said Cadmow stopping suddenly to consider the packet and its contents while his thick bovine tongue licked his lips.

'Oh yes, chocolate biscuits, dark chocolate naturally, very nice with a cup of tea. You can dunk them if you like. Tell you what I'll put the kettle on,' said Phil dashing off to put the kettle on as Cadmow munched his biscuit.

'I must admit to having a bit of a weakness for biscuits, you see,' said Cadmow an almost jaunty grin appearing on his previously snarling face. 'Umm these are very tasty human.'

'That's great, er mister, Cadmow, have the pack,'

'Why thank you human, it's Lord Cadmow, to you providing you wish to keep living of course, which I assume you do?'

'Yes I am very keen to keep living, my lord Cadmow.'

'I suspected you would be, human. Please do not call me, my lord Cadmow, just Lord Cadmow would be acceptable anything else sounds weird and troubling to my delicate and easily irritated ears. Tell me human can you get more of these biscuits for me?'

'Yes, many, many more, as many as you like,' said Phil nervously as Cadmow moved in close and gave him an alarmingly thorough lick across the face in that way we bovines do to express appreciation in another's actions, although strangely most humans don't feel more appreciated when we do it and certainly Phil did not after this particular tongue bath from Cadmow.

It was less than an hour later that Phil sat at one of the base's computer terminals facing the bemused face of a mission control operator on Earth in front of him and the smiling face of Cadmow to one side and just out of view, gun in hoof, reclining in the commander's chair with foot hooves resting leisurely on a console as he happily munched through his third pack of biscuits.

'Now that's a hell of a lot of biscuits you folks are asking for,' said the woman at mission control wrinkling her brow and giving Phil a long hard stare. 'And you say this is some sort of an emergency? A biscuit-related emergency, is that right sir? An actual base emergency that requires a vast quantity of biscuits...?'

'Chocolate digestive biscuits, plain chocolate they have to be plain chocolate and a high-quality brand, no cheap stuff, you understand,' interrupted Phil as he watched a nodding Cadmow through the corner of his eye.

'Naturally sir, plain chocolate digestives, a true mark of quality, I really could not imagine supplying a refined gentleman such as yourself with anything less. Now if you wouldn't mind getting the base commander for me, as I have an important request for him, you see I need him to take you and your worthless no doubt accomplice Larry out on to the lunar surface and abandon your worthless hides and see how much pizza you can both eat without a space suit.'

'The captain's busy at the moment, playing golf on the surface. If you leave a message I can get him to give you a call perhaps.'

'Tell the commander that a moronic member of the base's nightshift by the name of freaky Phil is guilty of the unauthorised use of the moon base's external communication system for the purpose of making juvenile practical jokes.'

'Can we still have the biscuits?' asked Phil.

'No, you cannot have any biscuits,' said the mission control woman. 'If I hear from you, Larry or any of the other idiots on the night shift again I will personally bring a crate of biscuits to the moon myself and insert each pack extremely slowly into orifices you people didn't even know you had, do you understand?'

'Er what's an orifice?'

Cadmow leaned into shot snarling at the woman from mission control while making sure his weapon was still pointed at the human's delicate facial parts. 'Send the biscuits or this human dies, do you understand?' said Cadmow snorting a powerful jet of nasal steam.

The woman from mission control rolled her eyes, 'Larry, is that you? For God's sake don't you idiots ever quit with the stupid jokes? You need to bloody well grow up and start taking life seriously buddy otherwise...hang on is that a replica gun, you shouldn't have those on the moon. It better not be a real one, it's damn dangerous if it is, they should never have allowed them even locked away, I don't give a damn what the Gun Strokers of America think.'

Cadmow removed Larry's head from his horns and dangled it by the hair in front of the screen. 'Larry is dead and this one will be too if you don't send a large quantity of biscuits, understand human?'

'What the hell are you? Okay keep calm you seem to be some of bull creature with a taste for biscuits, is that right?'

'I am Lord Cadmow, I wish biscuits and then I want your world to surrender to me and make me your supreme lord. Or I kill this human.'

The mission control woman began to laugh. 'Hang on fella let's not get carried away, we might be able to sort you out with a few packets of biscuits for the life of that useless idiot you've got there but if you wanted control of Earth we'd kind of expect freaky Phil to make some kind of noble sacrifice, for the sake of the human race.'

Cadmow looked Phil up and down attempting to appraise his worth. 'I see your point human, I will accept the biscuits for the moment but please inform your leaders I claim their world in the name of the glorious bovine race. Does the fact I control this base count for anything?'

'Well we can just attack the moon-base with our human forces and as I said we would expect Phil to make a noble sacrifice, perhaps if you had prisoners of a higher value it would improve your negotiating position. Do you have any such prisoners? The captain or other members of the senior staff, if I could talk to one or more of them it might help improve your case.'

'Ah, no human, they are not presently available, as this worthless piece of human vermin was saying the senior staff are conducting a primitive Earth tournament on the lunar surface and cannot be disturbed until a victor is announced, perhaps later.'

'That does not sound very likely, Mr Cadmow...'

'Lord Cadmow,' said Cadmow.

'As you say, Lord Cadmow, it sounds more likely that you have ever so slightly killed the senior staff in some kind of spontaneous, frantic murder spree. If true that has significantly reduced your bargaining power.'

'I told you it was a good idea to take prisoners,' said Phil, 'if you had listened to me...'

'When you started begging to be taken prisoner I had already killed everyone of value so it was a bit late wasn't it. Perhaps if you had put an announcement over the tannoy earlier I may have left a few important humans alive but you did not bother did you human? Of course if you were a valuable prisoner yourself rather than a worthless piece of human flotsam then we would not be having this conversation.'

'Excuse me, if I could just interrupt,' began the woman from mission control. 'I am going to terminate communications now. I will be sending you your biscuits but I suggest you consume them quickly as I will be informing our various Earth leaders that a violent individual of apparent bovine decent with a distinctly sweet tooth has taken over the moon-base, killed everyone of any importance and is making insane demands of the governments of Earth. I have no doubt the said governments will begin a massive attack to recapture the base with immediate effect and either shoot you down like a rabid dog straight away or put you on an elaborate televised show trial and have you shot later. In those circumstances you will be interrogated, rather roughly but on the plus side you may have chance to go on television to tell your story which if thought interesting might become the basis for a major motion picture. I can get the biscuits to you in three days and our forces will probably land a day later, so you can use that time to put your affairs in order and clean up any unsightly stains you may have created during your demented killing frenzy, now good evening to you both.'

With that the mission control woman's image disappeared.

'My god they are coming for you man,' said Phil.

'Indeed they are human,' said Cadmow in a surprisingly calm tone, 'I do hope they don't forget to send the biscuits, I would be very disappointed if that was the case. In the meantime I must prepare my defences and ration the biscuits. Go to the stores human and get me all the packs you can find, after that you can clean this floor and pick out the many tiny pieces of food and packaging that are currently lodged extremely painfully in my lower hooves.'

Chapter 2 From Custard Creams to Daisybells

Now I don't know about you folks but if I am stressed a good night's sleep really chills me out but as you can see that was not the case for that old sour cat Cadmow. That cat had been sleeping in his moon-box for nearly three thousand years and was still as bad tempered as ever.

I had more than a few dealings with old Cadmow back in the old days and if I had known what was going down lunar side I may have been able to give the human, powers that be some tips on how to deal with him and nip his crazy antics in the bud. Unfortunately I was hanging out with my all time favourite bovine and lovable old fella Vince on a crazy Hawaiian surfing holiday, it was great except for the going through security part, for some reason those straight-laced security cats always want to examine my horns, perhaps they think I am some sort of endangered rhino or something, I don't know if you have the same problem, it can be very annoying but me and Vince don't let it ruin our holl's.'

Now as you may have guessed Cadmow was not the only bad-tempered bovine buried in lunar Snooze-Ville and those other equally angry moo happy maniacs were about to be woken by the ever-cantankerous Cadmow.

That old doom-child-of-delegation, Lord Cadmow sent Phil into the creepy cave system to risk life and limb reviving those other mooing maniacs. By some miracle old freaky Phil managed to dodge the grasping death hooves of amongst others; Cadmow's right hand bovine that mad moody maniac General Moolock, and Cadmow's personal senior sycophant Norhlick long tongue, the only two other bovines permitted by the slightly paranoid Cadmow into the base's command centre.

As the hours moved on and the bovines constructed their defences only one thing plagued the mind of the bovine lord, the pending arrival of crunchy, crumbly biscuit goodness.

'Good news Lord Cadmow,' said Phil, pushing a dubiously stained silver trolley loaded with tea things into the middle of the command centre.

The ever-sneering General Moolock leapt in front of Phil and his squeaking trolley, carefully inspecting both for signs of treachery.

That moody Moolock cat stood almost as tall as the Bull lord himself. He was an imposing figure in any room, with a solid wall of obsidian fur covering half his body matched by an equally solid coat of white cream to compliment it on the other side. He was wrapped in a simple black robe, the only splash of colour was the gold and red insignia that marked his rank proudly sitting on his powerful upper chest. His huge horns were painted black with two golden bands denoting once again his rank. The infamous sneer that dominated his face stayed in place even when the rest of his countenance was consumed with mirth. At the general's throat hung a small triangular jade pendent, a mark of his faith as a member of the Bull clan, a small and in the past much persecuted sect of the bovine religion.

'What is it now human have you perhaps at long last mastered the mysterious art of tea making? Since my waking the only good tea I have tasted has been made by my own fair hooves. We only agreed to your continued survival because Cadmow said you would serve us refreshments, but I for one human am not feeling very refreshed,' said the thirsty bull general.

'It's better than that, the shuttle with the biscuits has arrived and I have the first packets for you to try,' said Phil throwing a packet at the hungry bull lord before pouring the general a cup of tea that he desperately hoped would be suitably refreshing.

Cadmow caught the packet with a gleeful bellow before excitedly ripping open the wrapper.' Excellent,' exclaimed the Bull lord, 'I will sample them immediately.'

'I would advise against it my lord,' Moolock said, sipping his tea with a big old contented slurp that made Phil breath a great sigh of relief, 'they are probably poisoned, test them on the human maggot if you have no more important tasks you need it to perform.'

'Yes Moolock, you are right of course,' said Cadmow, a large wild-eyed grin spread across his face as he approached the rapidly-retreating Phil, pack thrust aggressively into the human's face. 'Here human have a nice tasty biscuit, for all your hard work. Don't worry they're probably not poisoned.'

'You know I'm not really in a biscuit sort of mood at the moment.'

'I see human, then perhaps you are in the mood for having crunchy neck times, it has been a few days and my killing hoof must be getting a bit rusty,' said Cadmow flexing his hoof with a gleeful flourish.

'I know what you could do,' said Phil, 'get general Moolock to contact Earth and give them one of his cold, penetrating stares and simply threaten if the biscuits are poisoned they will have to deal with him. That should get the truth out of them.'

'Just eat the biscuit human,' said Cadmow ramming the biscuit in to Phil's still chattering mouth.

Phil chewed and swallowed as Cadmow's hoof gently stroked his throat. The human's distress was not in anyway calmed by the bull's demented grin and his habit of rubbing Phil's cheek with the edge of his horns.

'Oh I don't think they are poisoned,' said Phil, 'in fact they are very good I think I'll have another.'

'Not so fast human,' said Cadmow snatching the biscuit from Phil's fingers. 'You wouldn't want to ruin your supper now would you?' With that Cadmow rammed four chocolate digestives into his mouth.

'Truly the food of the gods,' spluttered the Bull lord offering the pack to Moolock. 'Would you not say so Moolock?'

'Only a fat and lazy god Cadmow,' replied Moolock, leaping back to avoid the violent spluttering of biscuit crumbs and waving away the offered pack with disinterest.

His colleague, Norhlick rushed forward kneeling quickly before the Bull lord, gazing devotedly up at him as he took yet another biscuit. 'You should not insult the chosen food of our great lord, Moolock. Show him respect for did he not wake us from our icy prison?'

Let me describe that Norhlick cat my little psychedelic showstoppers. He had the kind of cheese wide grin that would put a super-sickly used car sales-cat to shame, never reached his eyes though groovers. Around that cat's neck hung a small purple bell with a scattering of sparkling gold and silver stars which denoted his membership of the meadow clan, a branch of the bovine religion most often associated with wanderers and mystics according to traditional stereotypes. This is also the clan that yours truly was born into, although I rarely wear my bell these days. I do take it out from time to time and contemplate the mellow-yellow meadow-mother as I meditate my cares away.

Moolock shook his head and turned away from the display of embarrassing sycophancy.

'I fail to see why I should show any particular reverence for an unhealthy snack food, Norhlick no matter who is foolish enough to gorge on them,' replied the ever sneering general as Norhlick kissed Cadmow's hoof. 'As for our rescue I was under the impression that was conducted by an incompetent band of halfwit humans. Indeed that human still bears the scars were I tried to rip out its worthless throat. It is lucky to still be alive, by the way, nicely dodged human.'

'Thanks, Moolock old mate, I am honoured to receive a compliment from a moody snarling maniac such as yourself,' said Phil doing a double thumbs up and winking at Moolock.

'Do not push your luck human, I do not plan on complimenting you again and I most certainly don't plan on becoming your mate, try that sort of thing and the loss of your throat will be the least of your problems.'

Norhlick was still upon his knees cradling the biscuit gently in his hooves while his gaze of wonder flicked between Cadmow and the glorious digestive. 'I will put this precious object in a place of reverence near me so it can reflect the wonderful nature of you my lord.'

It was rumoured groovers that Norlick had his hooves specially sculptured in a shape that best suited the scratching of any body parts belonging to the object of his devotion. He certainly tried to dye his fur to best match the colour and pattern of the leader that he was most devoted too at that time. Sadly this would often go wrong leaving him with purple and green streaks in his fur. Cadmow believed that this odd colouring was something to do with the bohemian practices of Norlick's religious order. The bull lord resisted the temptation to inquire about his lieutenant's curious fur colour choices as he wished to avoid any of the religious or philosophical diatribes that our clan have a reputation for offering, often unsolicited and long winded.

'Give it a rest Norhlick; you have cleaned Lord Cadmow's rear now. Get off your knees and let's get on with our conquest of feeble humans,' shouted Moolock in disgust.

'My lord may I advise you to kill this insolent wretch, let his death inspire true fear and loyalty among all your followers,' said Norhlick as Cadmow indicated for him to rise. 'Lord Cadmow all praise to you, once again you have proved to be the wisest, greatest, most wondrous leader of them all.'

Moolock glanced at the human whose shoulders shrugged in embarrassment. 'Human, are there any sycophantic vomit pots near by?' asked Moolock rolling his eyes and gnashing his hooves in irritation.

'Unfortunately not,' replied Phil, 'I'm starting to feel rather nauseous myself. He does lay it on a bit thick.'

'You know what they say human, those who can do, and those who cannot, creep to the boss.'

'Tell me about it. My dozy cousin Jeff used to try and give his boss on the building site a blowjob every morning even though neither of them was gay or anything. He didn't last very long. I also knew a guy who...'

'Silence earth creature, before I am compelled to reach down your throat and remove your internal organs in strict alphabetical order. I do not wish to hear anymore of your freakish tales, is that understood?' bellowed Moolock in disgusted rage.

'Suit yourself ducky, but I wouldn't talk about freaky tales if I were you.'

Moolock swished his tail and snorted a thick cloud of grassy steam from his nostrils in irritation but otherwise stayed silent.

Cadmow who had been listening to the conversation with some amusement, burst into fully fledged mooing laughter. 'Good biscuits, loyal if occasionally insolent allies, our freedom and a comedy human to boot, what a glorious day. It makes a bovine glad to be alive. I feel so happy I am inclined to give the human race a substantial biscuit ration when I enslave them.'

'How wonderfully magnanimous of you my lord, the humans will be so lucky to live beneath your mighty iron hoof,' said Norhlick.

A sudden frantic battering noise could be heard from all around.

'Is it raining?' said Phil, 'sounds like quite a storm, I am surprised the ground is so dry around here if it rains like that.'

'Rain of a kind, human,' said Moolock, 'your fellow humans are raining down their puny weapons upon us. Bombs and missiles of many kinds are tickling our new advanced shielding. They sound most enthusiastic for the return of this rather unimpressive base.'

'Just look at those crazy colours,' said Phil gazing at the view-screen as the shield sparkled red and then blue absorbing the barrage of human designed weapons. 'It's just like the fourth of July but on the moon. Do they celebrate the fourth of July on the moon? I am sure they must have thanksgiving. Should I sing a patriotic American freedom song?'

'Certainly not human, now please be silent,' said Moolock gnashing his sharpest death hoof so it sparked a rainbow of blue and white static in the air.

'Charming,' muttered Phil turning back with a sigh of pleasure to gaze once again upon the military inspired wall of dust, colour and the rat, tat, tat, rhythm of the barmy bullet beat that could still be heard from above.

'Are they doing any actual damage Moolock?' asked Cadmow.

Moolock consulted the computer terminals for a moment, making adjustments before calmingly responding to the impatient Bull lord.

'A few minor drops in power my lord, nothing substantial. I think the humans have spent too much of their time researching new forms of entertainment rather than the military knowledge necessary to defeat a truly superior foe.'

'Incoming transmission, from an irate earthling demanding our surrender,' continued Moolock after further consultation with the computer.

'Put him on screen Moolock, he can make our day even more amusing,' said Cadmow with a grin as he settled back into the command chair whose pool of stale beer had been replaced with a deep layer of biscuit crumbs.

On the screen appeared the image of a red-faced military officer who seemed to be banging his fist on a wooden desk.

'This is General Cross of the United States military representing the planet Earth. You will surrender your filthy alien hides with immediate affect or we will destroy that base with your no-good butts inside it. A large number of our troops are approaching your position, you will open all access doors and allow our forces to enter the base where you will surrender to them.'

Cadmow leaned back and stared at the ranting human on screen. 'Human, I am Lord Cadmow; you will surrender your world to me immediately and recognise me as your glorious bovine overlord, now kneel and beg forgiveness for your impudence.'

'The United States of America on behalf of the planet Earth demand your immediate unconditional surrender or we will terminate you with maximum prejudice and blow your mooing butts straight back to what ever freakish hell world you came from.'

Terminating the communication Moolock turned to Cadmow. 'The human seems to be stubbornly resisting the inevitable my lord. I am repositioning the laser, if you wish me to leave any of the human attackers alive as prisoners or for interrogation, please indicate now before I eliminate them.'

'No need Moolock,' replied Cadmow, his normally booming voice full of sugar crash sleepiness. 'I doubt they could tell us anything of use. 'One comedy human is quite amusing enough, anymore would likely become a liability, you may kill them all.'

'As you wish my Lord, I am vaporising the small but stubborn human force. I am also making sure our scanners can detect any future ships or missiles that approach so we can, as the humans say, blast them and their no-good butts straight to hell.'

'Tell me Moolock, can this laser be modified to destroy the human cities,' asked Cadmow with a destructive gleam in his evil but quite sleepy eyes.

The general shook his head sadly.

'I am afraid not my lord, the human technology is alas far too primitive. The best we could do is create alarming set of images in the sky, above the populated areas perhaps a vast image of yourself demanding their surrender would be suitable.'

'That will have to do Moolock,' said the Bull Lord appearing to settle in for a nice little snooze, 'you and Norhlick can make the arrangements.

'Of course Moolock you may deny yourself the wonders of the biscuit should you wish. There will be no purges of those who deprive themselves, no indeed, just glances of bemused pity from the rest of our great new society,' muttered the Bull lord as he slept.

A few hours later the bombastic Bull lord stood in strictly holographic form over a large American city. Robed in a great white power cloak, bright shining arrows marking the colours of the various religious clans merged together forming a mighty power pail dominating the front of the robe. His head was as high as a skyscraper, horns painted with red and gold bands dominated the skyline. Cadmow's clenched hoof was held powerfully aloft as he addressed the ever-growing crowd. 'Abandon your weak and indolent leaders; join my mindless slave army while you still have the choice. Humans give in to your destiny and the natural order of the universe, let the bovine race be your masters without any of this silly resistance business which you all know will only make a lot of unnecessary mess that you'll have to clear up anyway.'

Blue lights flashed in a frenzy, sirens wailed and the sound of press and military helicopters playing chicken all around filled the air as the police tried to clear the vast crowd that had gathered, 'nothing to see here folks, nothing to see at all, go home now,' shouted police but the crowd just pointed at the Bull lord's vast image and suggested the police get their eyes tested.

'Excuse me Mr Cadmow,' said a slim, blonde young woman in a figure hugging but practical orange jumpsuit from a roof top near the bull lord's head.

The woman held out a microphone as Cadmow muttered about being Lord Cadmow. 'I am Josephine Barnstorm, of Ferocious Ferret news, the American people have the right to know, exactly what is in it for them if they become obedient citizens in a bovine dominated dictatorship.'

Cadmow snorted and bellowed, 'aside from getting to keep their heads attached to their bodies I will give the human race a great prize beyond measure, I will give each human a massive biscuit ration beyond their wildest dreams.' Cadmow brandished a large holographic packet of biscuits first at the reporter and then at the crowd. 'Behold your good fortune humans,' continued the Bull lord as the crowd laughed and Moolock muttered in horror from his position behind the real Cadmow.

'Cookies, you're offering us cookies?' said Josephine Barnstorm. 'Is this in truth an advertising stunt for a snack food manufacturer?'

'No of course not human,' snorted Cadmow remembering to pull his stomach in and raise his head in a regal pose as the crowd mobbed him with requests for selfies. As the bull lord stood proudly taking in their frenzy, social media lit up with a million posts and memes about 'Bully Biscuit' which was the world's new name for him.

His pompous posturing was only interrupted by the extended microphone of Josephine Barnstorm giving his holographic form a distracting ripple.

'Lord Cadmow,' shouted the reporter, 'we at the ferret have heard that you are a vegetarian and part of a plot by the deep state to enfeeble the American people by forcing them to become vegetarians while totally destroying our beef industry, what do you say?'

'I am a herbivore human, to eat meat would cause me physical harm,' replied Cadmow turning back to the crowd with a jaunty pose before tossing holographic biscuits that exploded into funky coloured crumbs as they hit the cheering crowd.

'A herbivore?' continued Josephine Barnstorm, 'isn't that a radical, some might say militant form of vegetarianism? Do you see yourself as a saviour figure trying to save us from ourselves, by any means necessary including destroying our meat industry? What do you say Mr Cadmow to those farmers whose livelihoods you plan to destroy?'

Cadmow stared at the human a moment, 'I say do as you're told and get extra biscuits otherwise you will be exterminated as an example to others.' With that Cadmow gave a big chocolate coloured toothy grin straight at the camera.

Norhlick quickly grabbed a piece of tissue, after dampening it with his own saliva he began wiping clean Cadmow's biscuit stained muzzle.

'There you are my lord, good as new,' he said appearing briefly as hologram himself to much speculation from the crowd many assuming this to be Cadmow's overprotective mother.

As Cadmow pushed Norhlick firmly aside and posed coolly flipping holographic biscuits in the air, General Moolock rolled his eyes and muttered loudly. 'For Cowdon's sake stop talking about biscuits.'

As the posing continued military jets flew loudly over the hologram of the Bull lord. As he waved his mighty hoof at them they fired a series of missiles which passed naturally through him causing a large amount of damage to buildings all around.

The crowd, now covered in rubble, some sporting serious injuries from the large amount of fallen masonry suddenly became angry and upset the hologram of Cadmow took a deep and rather theatrical bow before promptly disappearing.

'Well, Moolock, I think that went wonderfully,' Cadmow said beating his great tail with a gleeful some might say jaunty swish.

'No my lord I must sadly burst your bubble,' replied the General checking once again the social media feeds from Earth. 'Most humans think you are either selling biscuits or promoting a comedy show about a talking bull with a weight problem. A few think you are part of their government's supposed conspiracy to either force them to eat more or less unhealthy snack foods.'

'Are you certain Moolock, they seemed quite taken with my mighty hologram?' inquired the deflated Bull lord.

'They found you most entertaining my lord,' said Moolock. 'Many said they would give your comedy show a watch while requests for clothing bearing your image and humorous catch phrase are as the humans say trending quite highly.'

'I have a humorous catch phrase Moolock? I said nothing that was intended as amusing.'

'You have two in fact my lord, eat my biscuits humans, and the more popular, meat would physically harm me,' said Moolock to the baffled Bull lord who slumped dejected in the command chair pumping one comforting sugar filled confection into his mouth after another.

'What is wrong with these creatures Moolock? How can we enslave them if they are too stupid to fear a glorious Bull lord raging at them in their very midst?'

'Fear not my Lord,' said Moolock activating the holographic projector. 'I have been working on a plan with Norhlick here to cause terror and destruction across the world in your glorious name.'

'Indeed Moolock, and this plan of yours will be more effective than giving my human slave army an extra packet of jammie dodgers each week?' asked the amazed Cadmow between loud sad crunches.

Moolock grinned and nodded as the hologram began to take shape. 'Behold my Lord the glorious instrument of your great victory, more persuasive than even the fabled custard cream. I call her, demon hoof, for her mighty hooves will rain down terror, destruction and much dizziness on the lowly humans until they accept you as their mighty overlord.'

'By the glorious arid teat of Cowdon the ever un-milked, what, what a marvellous beast, or is it a machine?' gasped Cadmow examining the vision of destruction that snorted, bucked and butted before him.

She was at that man, a freaky holo-fantasy of a deadly enhanced cyber-cow. That old moody maniac Moolock had taken and wickedly twisted a happy harmless farmyard bovine who would have spent the day happily gambolling in the clover and chewing the cud, because cows chill they don't kill is the normal bovine order of the day but there was nothing normal about this old doom cow. She wore metallic armour, steel hooves and red laser eyes that shot deadly and powerful blasts. Her advanced shielding made her virtually unstoppable but even if you did take her out she was designed to act as part of a vast herd of destruction.

'I want herds upon herds of them Moolock,' exclaimed Cadmow rubbing his hooves in so much excitement that sparks leapt wildly into the air. 'They will cause terror and destruction, appearing and reappearing at various points throughout the planet. The population will be begging their impotent leaders to surrender within weeks, get the plans out to our generals and we can identify suitable targets for maximum impact,' said Cadmow a vast grin upon his face as he attempted to pet and tickle the bucking and snorting holographic cyber-cow.

'We must make the destruction swift and decisive, no lingering, no toying with the humans. I suspect despite the fools like the ones on this base, humans have a resourceful streak and that plus the frantic desperation that will have overcome them may make them more dangerous than a cornered and angry weasel-badger,' warned Moolock proudly inspecting the beast from every angle.

'Fear not Moolock, we will strike swift and true. There will be no delay in the destruction of the human's so-called civilisations,' replied Cadmow. 'Although I am not happy with the name, instead of Demon hoof I will call her Daisybell.'

'Daisybell my Lord, surely not?' exclaimed Moolock his sneering lips twitching in horror.

'Doomsday Daisybell, after my aunt Daisybell she was a formidable bovine. I believe you met her once did you not?'

'Yes I believe I did my lord,' replied Moolock. 'She spent the entire time hitting me with her cane while getting my name repeatedly wrong. I was Moocock, Moofrock, Moodysock and Muckyslock if I remember correctly.'

'She always spoke very highly of you, how is that fine General Mardylocks, she would ask? I always assumed she meant you. Ah a fine cow she was and these beasts shall bear her name in noble tribute, I think she would approve. I have made my decision,' said Cadmow as Moolock looked unimpressed.

'I don't get it,' said Phil poking the angry holo-cow with his elbow watching it ripple as confused looks crossed his face like an great ocean of tidal bafflement.

'You don't have to get it human, just make the tea and follow our orders, that will be quite sufficient,' said Moolock trying to move Phil along with dismissive movement of his hoof.

'The thing is,' said Phil oblivious to Moolock's glare, probably because the bull general's glare was much like all his other expressions. 'Why would anyone by afraid of these Demon-Daisy-hooves or whatever you call them, if they are just holograms people will figure that out pretty fast and probably just laugh at them or something. Are you hoping the military will think they are real and bomb all the cities for you, trying to destroy them? It would be really funny if that happened.'

'Human,' said Moolock resting a hoof on Phil's shoulder, 'you are reassuringly stupid, I feel certain that if you lunged at one of us with a weapon you would end up injuring only yourself.'

'I still don't get it though I mean if the Daisy...'

'Then let me explain it to you human. This hologram is merely an example of the Daisybells we plan to build. The real ones will be as solid as you and me. They will be solid, they will be deadly and the human race will be crushed by their furiously stampeding death hooves. Does that move your feeble brain a little further towards a state of understanding?'

'I guess,' said Phil with a shrug as he raised his arm and scratched his head as Moolock suddenly turned his head away with a disgusted bellow.

'That is another thing human,' snorted Moolock glaring at the vast damp patches that swamped Phil's armpits. 'I understand that we inspire much fear and I daresay terror in you but the foul odours your body is producing in your understandable distress have now reached a fever pitch of rank, foulness. My hoof yearns to either rip out your stinking throat or to rip away my own poor suffering nose. Go now and clean yourself thoroughly, also please change that t-shirt it is more stain than pattern. Take your time human, by the smell of things it will take a while to get you fresh and clean.'

Phil headed on his way to explore the fabled mysteries of soap and water and the bovines went back to their wicked work.

Now my little graceful goslings that old General Mardysocks was busy having the other bovine Generals construct the first of those bad-tempered Doomsday Daisybells. The bovines sent probes down to the Earth surface to release other cohorts of Cadmow from secret hidden chambers. These Earthside bovines constructed secret bases for the storage, construction and deployment of the Daisybells.

If that was not enough bad news for human society these minor moo lords built a series of transdementional transportation devices allowing themselves and their herds of destruction to travel instantly from one location to another.

In other words things were about to get hung over in a lions den heavy for the haplessly happening human race.

One other thing groove cats, old Lord sour cat Cadmow was married to fellow bovine by the name of Mowlore. At this point he had no idea if she had been frozen in time like himself, or where her icebox might be located if she had survived in frozen form. He hoped to see her again but was advised by those around him not to get his hopes up.

A week later, the image on the screen in the moon base command centre showed somewhere in the wilds of the deep south of the United States of America, courtesy of one of Moolock's probes.

Those freaky probes, my little poptastic opossums were roughly the size and shape of Cadmow's cantankerous cranium. All in jet black except for the gold and red bands on the horns, denoting rank and clan of the bothersome bull lord. Little rotors emerged from all across the great heads upon entering the atmosphere. The horns themselves were used to scan for the faint signals emitting from the bovine life support units and project an interactive hologram of either Moolock or Cadmow. The probes also sported long, highly dextrous pink tongue-like appendages that could be deployed from the mouth area to manipulate all manner of objects, such as the buttons on a bovine suspended animation unit.

'My lord good news, the chamber of Mowlore is in sight, I will open her chamber and you will be able to speak to her directly.'

Upon contact with the probe a section of rock opened and a rather haughty looking bovine stepped out.

Don't get me wrong all you enthusiastically-empowered, radically-righteous, fantastically-feminist, earth-mothers out there I fully support all strong independent woman. I am a proud bovine member of the sisterhood myself. The thing is glorious groove sisters, Mowlore took haughty arrogance to a whole new level. The bovine race never had a caste system and Mowlore felt that was a big failing for our species and felt certain she belonged to a small select group who were far superior to everyone else. A high-class aristocratic bovine covered in a thick coat of golden fur, often worn with streaks of silver and red, colours of high fashion. Her horn's colour tended to change with the fashion of the season, sometimes silver, sometimes green or even blue. As she emerged from her icebox they were a simple brown with black bands to match her black bell of nobility.

Mowlore's glorious silver power robes fluttered in the breeze as she took the probe firmly in her hooves, she studied it closely. 'What manner of toy is this?' she said, suddenly startled as an image of a beaming Cadmow appeared before her.

'My love it is good to look upon you once again,' said Cadmow positively glowing with happiness. This is so unnatural a look for the old sour puss that it is quite a disturbing thing to witness.

Now it could have been that the influence of Mowlore might have had a calming influence on that old sour puss but as we are about to see, it's true what the old poets say, the course of true love never did run smooth.

'Cadmow, why are you sending me such toys? Are you growing sentimental in your old age? Is this some hint about wanting to start a family perhaps?'

Cadmow looked slightly alarmed by Mowlore's talk of starting a family but the smile and flush of the cheeks soon returned. 'I am having to modify human technology I am afraid, it is rather basic isn't it. None of ours survives unfortunately.'

'How quaint it is,' said Mowlore studying the probe still further. 'Human you say, how sweet. They have at least moved on from those silly pyramids. I take it we are still on the human infested planet but free which I suppose is at least something. Who do we have to thank for our release? Was the weakness of our leaders overwhelmed with foolish compassion the key or perhaps the genius of my husband, the noble lord Cadmow?'

'Neither my love it was in fact a group of halfwit humans, blundering around and pocking their noses into things they could not possibly understand that secured our release.'

'I always told you that those simple creatures with their, curiosity and instincts for general blundering would be of use to us one day,' said Mowlore to a distinctly raised eyebrow from Cadmow.

'Indeed my love, I do not wish to contradict you, but I seem to remember you calling them worthless dirty parasites that it would be best to eliminate. Not that it matters my darling, soon we will conquer them and they will be the instrument of our final conquest of the home world where we will bring them the iron hoofed rule that our species needs so desperately. Come my love be my empress, let us rule the universe together.'

Mowlore laughed and shook her head. 'I have heard this tale before my love. What makes you think your wild schemes will come to anything this time?'

'Come my fragrant cowslip blossom, join me and see the plans for yourself. We have control of the earthling's lunar base. If you head north about three miles we have assembled our first inter-dimensional transporter which will whisk you to my side,' said Cadmow. 'The probe will guide you to the transport terminal and then via the mechanism into my firm but gently mooing arms.'

'I will do as you ask, Cadmow, and when I get to your lunar lair I will be inspecting those plans of yours very carefully after all being frozen in time does little for my disposition,' said Mowlore setting of after the probe.

'As you wish my love, but hurry, my hooves long to stroke your hairy tail and have it whip me like a long and luscious love snake,' mooed an excited Cadmow

'My lord that is way too much information,' mooed an alarmed Moolock in the background.

'Indeed it is my love,' said Mowlore, 'although I do have a pot of extra shiny tail wax for later. Perhaps you could apply it in your own special way.'

Swishing her tail in a carefree and yet focused manner Mowlore headed on her way and Cadmow fainted out of excitement. Moolock, Norhlick and Phil took Cadmow to his quarters in order to recover. They tried to ignore the bull lord's fevered muttering about slippery, shiny, hairy tails that uttered excitably from the bull's delirious mooing lips.

Now beautiful flower kits, it may have seemed like Mowlore was walking through an empty wilderness but that was not the case. Three stereotypical drunken yokels (we are talking bad movie casting central man) were wandering about loaded down with their big shot guns, lots of cans of strong beer called, get real drunk real quick, and let me tell you cats they certainly did what it said on those cans. These three were all real desperate for something to shoot.

Let me describe these three gun-loving good old boys for you groovers. The leader of the little clan was a dark-haired cat by the name of, Billy Bob, a dude of average height and build he sported a goatee that had gone a little feral and was in desperate need of a trim, preferably with some kind of heavy-duty gardening implement. His battered bright red baseball cap bore the emblem of the, Gun Strokers of America. You know the one with the fluttering U.S flag, the startled deer viewed down the barrel of big old shotgun that's being lovingly caressed by a giant hand.

Billy Bob wore a classic red and black check shirt on the day in question and on his back was an army style, green and black backpack full to the brim with beer, bullets and sugar rich chocolate bars.

Next along the row of merry hunter cats was a big, beefy, red headed dude with the bushiest beard you ever did see. This stoic cat went by the name of Jim Jam Jimmy, he constantly scanned the terrain for animals his comrades could shoot often while they chatted. On his head sat a straw hat and an American flag bandana, while a pipe dangled precariously from his lips much to the fascination of all he met who assumed it was about to fall to the ground which bizarrely groovers it never did.

Clad in not much more than pair of blue denim dungarees and a specially adapted ammunition vest that carried bullets, beer and arrows for the crossbow that was strapped to his back, Jim Jam Jimmy staggered drunkenly along the path his gun swaying merrily with the breeze.

The third member of the trio was a thin sleazy dude by the name of Cletus. This dirty old boy sported a light brown cowboy hat upon his luxurious blond and well-maintained mullet. On the day in question he had a pair of rather impractical white cowboy boots with fancy tassels that his friends constantly threatened to cut off or set fire too. His moderately fashionable jeans were held firmly in place by a wagon train patterned brown leather belt topped off with a fancy silver belt buckle featuring a green spiky cactus with a red and black snake slithering merrily between the spikes.

His white t-shirt had a picture of a rather saucy looking cartoon deer with huge antlers and the slogan; I like big bucks and I cannot lie, written in big red letters.

He wore a big old camouflage jacket with lots of pockets which his comrades were afraid to put their hands near in case there was something unsavoury inside, which there often was groove cats.

He had a green and yellow rucksack filled as you would expect with bullets, beer and other exotic items. As a finishing touch he wore around his neck a pair of small but powerful binoculars for studying nature in all its wonder or so he claimed.

'If I don't find something to shoot real soon, I'm going to have to blast Cletus,' said Billy Bob, pointing his gun drunkenly at his comrade.

Cletus pushed the shotgun to one side with a long laugh and a frothy shower of beer-soaked spittle. 'If you shoot me, my Marylou will fill you full of lead quicker than a rattlesnake in a barrel of apple and molasses, she's real good with a gun.'

Billy Bob laughed and fired his gun in the air, hollering as he did so. 'When she gets a look at the size of my gun she'll jump right into my bed before you've stopped twitching.'

'What's that coming through those bushes over there?' said Jim Jam Jimmy swinging his gun round to point at the rustling under growth.

'Some kind of freaky critter,' slurred Billy Bob, 'let's get over there and kill it, my trigger fingers feeling real itchy.'

With their guns all pointed at the bushes, the probe followed by the proud, striding figure of Mowlore came at them suddenly out of the under growth.

'What the hell is it boy?' said Cletus trying to steady his shooting arm.

'Looks like some kind of freaky alien cow critter to me,' replied Billy Bob.

'I reckons it's a mutant from the local military base, some experiment that turned on its creators and broke out feeling all ornery and vengeful like. It's probably got a hankering for human blood and we are looking real tasty right now,' said Jim Jam Jimmy trying to focus on the actual target rather than the three other versions of Mowlore his shine pickled brain had conjured up.

'You got that right,' said Billy Bob swaying as he hypnotically stared at the moving probe. 'It looks like some cloned, mutant, genetically engineered freak from a lab built on a nuclear test site, where they exploded nukes on some old Indian burial ground on a prom night while enacting a wicked un-American violation of old glory no doubt.'

'Well I say it ain't natural and looks positively satanic,' said Cletus as they all muttered in agreement. 'Let's blast that thing back to whatever pit of hell it came from.'

With many shouts and cheers the yokels fired their weapons, taking Mowlore completely by surprise. Mowlore lay dead with the yokels standing over her muttering to themselves about barbecues and the best way to cook and prepare such a freaky looking creature.

The probe kept banging into them as they poked and prodded at the stricken bovine.

'Get away from me you pesky varmint,' said Billy Bob trying desperately to swat the probe.

Suddenly a hologram of Moolock appeared in front of the alarmed yokels. 'Get away from Mowlore you pieces of stinking vermin or your deaths which are already guaranteed will be slower and more painful than any of you can possibly imagine.'

The yokels began to fire at the hologram of Moolock in alarmed terror, the bullets passing through the bull general's image causing it to flicker and ripple widely. Then Billy Bob began to laugh, 'hey cease fire boys, it ain't real it's just one of them newfangled holograms. All it can do is create a lot of noise. Isn't that right boy,' he said wiggling his fingers through the image of Moolocks face.

'Now listen good boy,' said Billy Bob bringing his face close to Moolocks. 'We found this here critter, we are all real hungry and not in the mood for sharing except with some of the more attractive local ladies, of which you ain't one boy, so get on your way now, if you know what's good for you.'

'Hold on there a spell,' said Cletus, 'he looks like the same kind of critter, perhaps he's the kinky sort and wants to have a last kiss and cuddle with the body, you know as an intimate goodbye, quite understandable if they were romantically involved and all.'

'And your point is what Cletus?' said Billy Bob.

'Well it wouldn't spoil the flavour of the meat none I reckon if we let that critter say an intimate farewell and we film it, sell it to one of them specialist channels. They pay good money for that kind of thing, you know?' said Cletus to alarmed looks from his fellow yokels.

'Yeah, we know Cletus,' replied Billy Bob with disgust, 'because you keep telling us how you subscribe to most of them weird shit channels. You freak of nature, you know that is why no one ever comes around to any of your movie nights.'

'Well a man needs his hobbies Billy Bob.'

'I got plenty of hobbies, I likes fishing, shooting, drinking and chasing a little tail down the local bar and you know something that provides me with all the entertainment I need. I certainly don't need any of the weird arse shit you seem to need. You should see one of them fancy big city psychiatrists and get what ever sickness you have out of your head,' said Billy Bob.

'I for one, am not eating anything that has been kissed, cuddled or interfered with in any way by that ugly thing,' said Jim Jam Jimmy. 'Let's pick this freaky but tasty-looking creature up and get it home. I've a mind to whip up a batch of my famous super special barbecue freaky meat sauce. I've made special in the past for freaky looking critters I can't identify but look like they might be real tasty with the right sauce.'

After knocking the probe against a tree until the raging image of Moolock disappeared and the probe itself lay sparking on the floor, the three yokels picked up the body of Mowlore and dragged her away, laughing and arguing about the best way to cook her.

Chapter 3: Literally herds of the things

Things were getting bad-trip-headache-in-a-heatwave heavy groove cats of space and time with his great love being the main course at a barbecue that old bitter kitty Cadmow was none to well-disposed to the human race. He hunted for the three yokels; their crimes he felt were the responsibility of the whole human race and was determined to torture the species, slowly. By the time he deployed the Doomsday Daisybells, Cadmow had chosen to ignore the council of General Moolock and instead, take a very long time conquering the humans, playing with them until his desire for vengeance was finally sated. Phil as you can imagine kept out of the way, protected in part by Moolock who was determined not to make his own tea.

A couple of weeks later when the first batch of Doomsday Daisybells had been completed somewhere in the wrong side of town late at night an innocent looking school girl skipped through the streets and down a dank, dirty and dangerous alley. 'Oh gosh, what a dank and dirty alley,' scolded the girl as she inspected the dirt covered walls shaking her head at the rubbish strewn across the floor. 'Such a lot of rubbish, much of it quite unsanitary, a sweet innocent girl like me could easily trip and do herself a most unladylike disservice.'

From those dark and creepy shadows leapt a vicious young thug, with a cruel and menacing grin not to mention an ever so sharp big old knife.

Hey man don't think I am being judgemental about the guy in the alley, I am just quoting the police report, maybe he had issues, you know growing up in a poor neighbourhood and all that, I don't know. What seems fairly clear is that the dude's intentions towards the girl in the alley were not in any way friendly, if you catch my drift groovers.

'Hello, little girly out late, aren't we?' asked the scary alley dude as he waved the knife close to the girls face in a way that he hoped was suitable menacing. 'Now let me guess, soft liberal parents I bet, no discipline just letting you run wild. They say kids today have got more money than sense, so let's see how true it is. Hand it over and I'll look after it for you or I could just cut off all those pretty red curls of yours.'

As the dude lunged forward the girl ducked quickly out of his way just smiling and cocking her head from side to side as if she was happily listening to a cool piece of music and certainly not taking the situation as seriously as one might expect. 'That's not very friendly, Mr scary man,' said the girl still apparently not recognising the seriousness of her situation.

Now the dude might have thought to himself that there was something slightly odd going on and made a tactical retreat but he just reached out and kept on heading towards the girl hoping to get whatever he could from her.

'Are you some sort of robber?' asked the girl her distracted attention flicking from the blade to the man as she popped some gum in her mouth and started to chew.

'That's right, but I prefer the term mugger as it happens. I am a specialist see, a robber covers a multitude of sins from bank heists to school kids stealing cans of juice,' explained the young man getting increasingly alarmed at the girl's failure to react to the knife jabbing at her face. Was it drugs he wondered or something far, far, worse?

The girl stroked the sharp blade allowing its edge to pierce her skin. She looked at the blood running down her finger with a smile and a slight grimace, 'Oh that is sharp,' said the girl before putting her finger in her mouth. 'Tell me then mugger-boy, have you done a lot of robbing tonight? Got lots of stuff from your victims perhaps?'

The girl blew a big pink bubble with her gum as she listened to the young man answer her question.

'Yeah, it has been a good night as it happens, but what's that got to do with you? Hand over the goods or I'll cut you, real bad. In fact I'll gut you like a fish, yeah that's what I'll do.'

The girl popped her bubble suddenly startling the knife man and flashing him a defiant smile. She dodged another impotent knife lunge, 'Sounds well messy, you'll get covered in my blood. Get a big police hunt after you and then the men in prison would do the most terrible, terrible things to you. All because you gutted little old me, kind of sweet really. Almost enough to restore ones faith in human nature.'

The man started to feel nervous, something wasn't right here, this girl was too damn cool. 'Hey you're not Australian or anything are, you?'

'What, why would I be Australian, sport?' teased the girl trying for her best Australian accent which made her sound more like a cockney flower seller slurping down jellied eels than an antipodean surfer girl chilling at a beach-based barbecue.'

'I've watched that film with the Australian guy coming to America and being mugged but instead of handing over his stuff he just laughed at the guy's knife and whipped out a bigger one. If you're a secret crocodile wrestler hanging out in dark alleys so you can show off your giant bush knife and put the frighteners on innocent members of the alley dwelling mugger community then speak up, so I know what I am up against.'

The girl shook her head, 'Do I sound Australian to you?'

'That doesn't mean anything; you could be an actor or something. Loads of foreign actors put on American accents. You could be the deep method sort, preparing for the role of a girl who fights monsters in dark alleys. You fight muggers like me and mine to get into the right frame of mind for the role.'

'I'm not any of those things, just an innocent girl skipping along a dark and dingy alley late at night,' the girl said, as she failed to suppress a deep and gaping yawn.

'Am I boring you or something little girl,' the scary dude snapped, feeling more than a little insulted.

The girl continued to yawn, and yawn. 'A bit,' she managed before continuing with her glorious yawn of the ages.

'I'll show you boring,' snarled the man as he began to lunge forward, his arms grasping in insulted fury.

His progress stopped as a wistful lament filled the alley, a recording of bagpipe music which made the dude swear and turn his head as a pair of gnarled hands slipped a garrotte over his head and proceeded to choke the very life from him. He was a big brute so put up quite a struggle but that garrotte just pulled all the tighter until that young man slipped to the floor with a gurgle and a bang.

The young thug fell at the feet of a fierce looking elderly lady who held the garrotte tightly in her hands. The elderly lady looked down at the prone body with a strange and sinister smile as if she rather enjoyed this particular kill and killing in general.

The girl stood chewing her gum giving the elderly lady a curious look. She seemed mildly surprised by the turn of events but not as disturbed by them as one might expect.

'Hello my dear,' said the elderly lady in a distinctly thick Scottish accent as she looked the girl up and down appraisingly. 'Now what in the world would a nice young lady such as yourself be doing in these vile, scum-covered streets at this godforsaken hour?'

'What's it to you granny?' asked the girl ignoring the warning flash of menace in the elderly lady's eyes.

'My name young woman is Mrs McDoon and I am certainly not your granny,' said Mrs McDoon flashing the girl a pinched and dangerous smile. 'That's no way to address your elders especially when one has just saved your life, is it now?'

'Yeah right,' replied the girl sounding unrepentant, 'I was just about to knee the bastard in the balls and nab that leather jacket. I could do with a new one.'

'Were you indeed?' said Mrs McDoon. 'It sounded to me as if you were about to form a debating society with him.'

'That was just a bit of alley banter, just something to pass the time, it didn't mean nothing. Double dibs on the jacket though, don't think about nicking it or anything.'

'I wouldn't dream of it my dear', said Mrs McDoon looking down at the man's feet. 'It's too big for me, I had my eye on the boots myself, the wee laddie has surprisingly small feet for such a burly fellow.'

The girl considered the boots, 'they look cheap, fall apart in less than a month hardly worth nicking I reckon.'

'On second thoughts I think you're right,' said Mrs McDoon. 'All style but no substance, by the looks of it.'

The girl nodded. 'You're right about his feet, they are tiny, you know what they say about men with little feet don't you?'

'Aye lassie,' the old woman said with a knowing look, 'less likely to step on your toes in the local dancehall I would have thought.'

'Yeah, something like that,' laughed the girl 'so where did you learn all that strangling stuff then? You sound like you're from the Midwest somewhere, like Kansas, yeah?'

'Well my dear,' said Mrs McDoon her smile becoming slightly more twisted and evil. 'When you grow up in the roughest part of Glasgow you learn how to survive in the dark streets and be strong. You learn to take the big ones from behind if you want to stay alive.'

'Glasgow?' said the girl sounding a little confused, 'where is that, Montana?'

'No sweet child,' said Mrs McDoon giving the girl a look that could have seemed almost maternal in the poor light of the alleyway. 'Glasgow is a great city in the finest country that ever the good lord, in his wisdom, set forth upon the Earth. Scotland the brave, Scotland the true, maker of the hardest of men who bravely let the wind blow free beneath their noble kilts no matter the weather be fair or foul like a savage beastie,' she continued raising her head nobly as a proud tear rolled down her cheek and a patriotic Scottish song wafted through the alley.

The girl for her part was starting to look a little bored with this encounter which was yet to furnish her with the new leather jacket that she desired. 'Oh yeah Scotland, I've heard of that, it's the bit of England where blokes all wear skirts and have pet haggises. I've tried the whiskey as well it's alright but not as good as bourbon.'

Mrs McDoon played with her garrotte in a menacing fashion as she cast the girl a vicious glare. She spoke with a dangerous edge to her voice that suggested she was barely able to contain her hate filled rage. 'What Scotland part of England, never! Scotland is a proud and noble place better than England could ever be. We were free once until the hated act of union, when England cheated us out of our great land. But now we have a parliament of our own again and soon that blessed land of hill and loch, of tartan smock. That noble land of fried mars bars and of frugal jocks, that great land, that Scotland shall once more be free,'

'Whatever,' said the girl wondering if the old lady normally bored her victims to death? 'If this Scotland place is so great, what are you doing here?'

'Doing what all Scottish people in America are doing, seeking for the wee beastie Nessie.'

'Isn't that in a lake in Scotland or something?'

'That's loch my dear not lake. It's the lowly English that have the lakes, try to remember that sweet child.'

'Yeah right lake, loch whatever you want to call it,' said the girl.

'Well now my dear,' continued Mrs McDoon trying to ignore the increasingly bored look on the girl's face. 'Years ago lots of meddling scientists came to Loch Ness with all manner of fancy equipment to hunt down the poor creature. Well Nessie got spooked by all these people poking and prodding at the wee lassie's home and she swam off to the great lakes of America. When those scientists went away at long last, we Scots went to America with the aim of finding her and letting her know it was safe to go back home to Scotland where she belonged.'

'You're along way from the great lakes, granny, this is California, the lakes are up north, near Canada somewhere.'

'That's the thing my dear we found wee Nessie a few years ago and she ate my husband, Mr McDoon, may god find gainful employment for his soul, as a snack for her journey back across the Atlantic. That's when I came down to California for what was meant to be a short holiday. While I was here I watched that film, Taxi Driver, with that actor Robert Denero. I agreed with his character about the dirt and scum on the filthy city streets and I found myself wanting to clean them too, I wanted to eradicate all the scum and vermin like this piece of filth at our feet. What I really wanted was to go home and clean up Glasgow but I'm not going back until Scotland is free once more. I've spent the years since cleaning the streets of San Francisco and Los Angeles. They call me the cleaning lady around these parts you know!'

'Right that's great, whatever it is you're on about' said the girl 'Let's just strip this guy and split the loot. Remember dibs on the jacket though, okay?'

Mrs McDoon gave the girl a look that mixed pity, contempt and raw malice in equal proportions as she fingered her garrotte. 'I blame all those television shows with teenagers running around at all hours of the night, having adventures and killing monsters. You're confused; it's not like that in the real world. A girl like you should be tucked up in bed, alone, at this evil hour.'

'Yeah well it's not going to happen,' said the girl moving towards the man's body. 'Let's just split the loot and go.'

Before Mrs McDoon could reply to the girl a loud thundering noise erupted from the main road. Crashing past the alley came a furious stampede of more than one hundred snorting Doomsday Daisybells creating a wild wall of dust and destruction.

Watching from the end of the alley the two women looked on as the snorting herd smashed their way down the street. Out of this mist of destruction came the red eyes and butting silver horns of doom. Silver hooves smeared red trampled and kicked all before them. The air swirled with dust, street lights and cars by the hundred, like some freaky carnado the traffic whirled round in the air and over the backs of the bellowing bad-tempered herd.

Across the road from the alley a group of the Daisybells stopped briefly to attack a building with their horns and laser eyes. The building collapsed within a few minutes. As the women watched from the alley one of the deadly bovines turned around to face them, its red eyes locking for a moment on those of Mrs McDoon, the beast began to snort and lower its mighty head, sparks flying from its front right foot as it pawed the ground apparently getting ready to charge the alley.

It was a truly heavy scene my little bad trip mantra mewers.

At that moment a squad of military helicopters appeared in the sky and opened fire at the cows who fired back in fury as a section of their herd was destroyed. After a short but intense battle the military helicopters retreated across the city with a herd of angry stampeding cyber-cows following them in hot pursuit.

With the immediate danger passed the alley dwellers breathed a sigh of relief.

'What the hell was that?' said the girl. 'Mad cow disease or what?'

Mrs McDoon looked down the ruin of a road rather wistfully as the last of the Daisybells disappeared into the distance. 'A new power is at loose in the world my girl, now if someone could only harness that power then they could truly clean up these and all the other streets, perhaps the whole world.'

'Whatever you say, granny, but I'm getting out of here before the cows from hell get bored chasing helicopters and come back for us,' said the girl reaching down to grab the man's coat.

As the girl reached down she felt the firm hand of Mrs McDoon grab her arm.

'I don't think so my dear!'

The girl pulled and pulled to get away from the menacing grip of Mrs McDoon, but it was futile. All her fighting did nothing to stop the grasp of the powerful Scottish lady.

Just as all seemed lost for the girl a microphone was thrust between them.

'And here we have two miraculous survivors of this truly horrendous attack, tell the viewers what you both saw from your vantage point in this alley,' said Josephine Barnstorm looking solemnly at the camera while directing an assistant to cover the pair with more dust and grime so they looked appropriately dishevelled.

'I saw nothing, I ain't no grass,' snapped the girl.

'Oh I see,' said the reporter, 'blinded by the wicked Moon-cows and their laser fire. Struck down in the prime of life, this poor girl's plight a clear example of the mooing evil that lurks on our streets. This sweet innocent will never see a freaky dancing fox or angry pawing cat video ever again. Although considering the kinds of unsolicited videos young men like to send out these days to unsuspecting young women, maybe it's a blessing in disguise.'

The reporter pointed at the young man who lay at their feet. 'What happened to this poor young man? A brave young victim of the cruel Daisybells, who died trying to defend you both perhaps? It would make a good story if that was the case, a noble-hero-for-our-time type thing, shall we just go with that, yes?'

'Aye if that suits you lassie, it's all the same to us, isn't it my dear,' said Mrs McDoon tucking away the garrotte and making mental note not to draw any attention to the bright red marks about the young man's neck.

'Wonderful, I mean what a terrible waste of human life. This brave hero must be remembered.' Josephine Barnstorm, now in a green jumpsuit, directed the camera toward the body and gave the signal to cue in the sad violin music.

'What was his name?'

'Oh I have no idea, lassie, we just bumped into the laddie for the first time in this here alley tonight as myself and the girl were out for an evening constitutional. Perhaps you could go with James, that's a good solid name.'

The reporter grinned excitedly and pointed at Mrs McDoon, 'That sounds great, noble Jimmy, an all-American hero gives his life defending two women walking in the alley late at night, for some reason, from the hooves of Holstein hate.'

'I know one thing about him,' said the girl. 'He promised me that jacket.'

'Right, well, don't be saying that on camera if you don't mind. I am trying to do a piece about a noble hero standing proudly against the forces of evil, I don't want it to turn into a documentary about the weird shit people do in dark alleys late at night.'

'I hope you're not implying anything unseemly was going on between us and young Jimmy here, I'll have you know I'm a respectable, clean living married woman and this girl is a nice respectable innocent girl from a stable household ... I imagine.'

'I thought you knew her, oh never mind. I don't want to know. It is a bit obvious though, thoughtful but a bit gold diggery granddaughter spices up grandmother's old age with sexy, dangerous alley fantasy gigolo hoping to trigger a heart attack and early inheritance, the payments are in the jacket pocket I bet.'

'You got us,' said the girl, 'the guy took his payment before he could do his business, I demand a refund and compensation, that jacket should cover it.'

'Don't be dragging me into your sordid stories, if he had tried any of that funny business with me, he'd have met the business end of my broom in a tender spot,' said Mrs McDoon as the girl stripped of the man's jacket and disappeared back down the alley.

'I'll be slipping away into the night then lassie,' said Mrs McDoon after a moment watching Josephine Barnstorm speak emotionally about the life and noble death of brave and mostly made up Jimmy.

And slip away is exactly what she did my oh so leveller loving lyrical Lilith's, probably like some kind of Brigadoon inspired boggart, into that dark and dangerous night if you can imagine such a thing.

Chapter 4: Professor Winkle's lonely hearts club lab

Those doom-bringing Daisybells shook the world in the weeks following that first attack. Flitting from city to city in each and every nation, clouds of destruction would appear and from them came a deluge of despair, devastation and manic mooing misery that went by the dreaded name of Daisybell. To grind that bitter salt in the open wound of humanity, many of the attacks came with an acidic side dish in the form of that vengeful bull lord himself once again in holographic form, no longer tempting the human race with sweet chocolate covered, crumbly biscuit treats but instead offering them only the clenched banging hoof of self-destructive unfulfilling rage.

Cadmow hoped those attacks, fuelled by grief, despair and rage, would in some way reduce his pain, and ease his bullish burden if you will. As the wise gurus teach, turning our pain on others is no magic balm but more often a muck spreader of misery. Hate is a contagious disease groove, cats, and can only be treated with peace, love and mellow merriments.

His last hope was those three drunken yokels who had shot down his love and served her at that drunken barbecue. He felt deep in his tortured soul that hunting them down was the answer, but so far they had slipped through his newly-sharpened, ever-grasping hooves.

As the attacks continued, humans, in their terror took to the streets demanding action from their various governments and a wave of anti-bovine hate engulfed the world.

Despite all the destruction, fear and general mayhem engulfing the human race one human was seeking opportunities amongst the rubble. That human was Mrs McDoon.

Now picture the scene groove cats, as that strong and dangerous Scots woman stood in her living room studying a barrage of bovine related news sporting claims about those furious cyber Friesians that ranged from them being a botched military experiment that somehow butted and snorted its way out of the lab to the visions of a preacher who claimed to have seen the number six, six, six branded on their backs and this plus similarities between the words satanic and bovanic proving to his freaky mind that they were clearly Satan's pet cows and a clear sign of Armageddon being upon the world. The preacher in question, ignoring the presenter's attempts to explain that there was no such word as bovanic. Saying simply that it was a word invented by Satan and she was just making excuses for the devil which he presumed she worshipped. 'For did you not do a commercial for goats milk sinful sister? We all know that goats are the dark one's favourite familiar don't we now.'

Not being one for slobbing out in front of the one-eyed goggle monster, Mrs McDoon kept herself busy as she took it all in. Her nimble fingers busily attaching all manner of deadly looking cleaning equipment to her outfit including a broom with blades worn on a holster at her back like a sword. Ready no doubt for a trip to another dark and dangerous alley on the rough and ready side of town.

Hey grooved out moon kits I don't mean to sound judgemental about these neighbourhoods that Mrs McDoon roamed, I am sure they were full of poor but decent folk who had watched their community go down hill through lack of investment and a heaping helping of corruption and exploitation by big fat greed wranglers high on hog and low on principles.

As Mrs McDoon finished getting ready there was a knock at the door and a young woman of a similar age to the girl in the alley walked in. This woman was a full-on cyber-chick, covered in electronics from head to foot, fully jacked in to the net with a cyber encounter mask covering half her face.

'Hi there Mrs McDoon, you wanted to see me?' said the techno groove child as she watched several green and yellow augmented reality goblins leap around the apartment, some were hyperactive advertising goblins trying to interest her in dating sites featuring men with well-trimmed facial hair who were tough but sensitive and liked puppies, rock climbing, milkshake smoothies and a very specific brand of sportswear. The rest of the goblins, red ones this time, were her own anti-viral goblins who proceeded to chase the advertising ones around the room with only limited effect, causing the girl to sigh and realise she should really get round to up-dating her anti-goblin software otherwise she would be walking down the street with her view totally obscured with goblins fighting each other over what brand of diet chips they thought she should be eating. This on reflection considering the carnage on the street would be an improvement. One of the things that had alarmed her was an anti-cow spray being advertised called moo-away, which according to the makers made an odour that killer cows did not like and would run away from.

'Yes my dear thank you for stopping by,' said Mrs McDoon, oblivious to the ring of chanting goblins that danced around her, initially trying to promote sedate elderly lady things until they downloaded her profile and began singing about knives, rare varieties of Scotch from small island distilleries and books on the tactics of William Wallace. 'I am in need of some information. I was wondering if these killer cows that have been such a menace of late have indeed escaped from a military lab, where do you suppose that might be?'

'There is really only one place,' said the jacked in Jennifer trying to ignore the dancing goblin at her feet whistling an annoyingly catchy jingle for a popular brand of ice cream beer. 'The ultra secret cyber animal intelligence weapons lab over at Fort Griffin way out in the desert. They say the head scientist there, a genius guy called Professor Winkle who the military forced to work for them by declaring him legally dead and erasing all records of him. They say he has never been allowed to leave and now has gone totally mad. Even if they didn't create those cows when they catch one that is the place it will be studied,'

'You seem to know an awful lot about this supposedly secret base,' said Mrs McDoon.

One of the cyber woman's own goblins began to leap about in front of her with a placard brandished determinedly in its green and slimy hands. 'Oh it looks like they are advertising for a cleaner over at the base, in case you are interested.'

'Why, aren't you a little mine of information, my dear,' said Mrs McDoon.

'The government always puts their most secret stuff on the net so that when the paranoia freaks and alien spotters start spouting it, no one will believe a word, it's the oldest trick in the book, plausible gullibility,' said the girl downloading a long-awaited anti-virus update that manifested itself as a large shaggy troll in a super sharp orange suit who proceeded to smash at the goblins with a large club and then went and stood in the corner with its arms folded. The girl stared at it for a moment wondering why the programmer had given it dark glasses. Was it a reference to trolls traditionally in folklore not liking sunlight or was it that the programmer thought the troll would look cool with shades, if it was the latter she had news for him, the troll did not look in any way cool, he just looked a bit of a poser, and not in anyway dignified.

'Thank you, my dear, you have been most helpful.'

Mrs McDoon, with her broom at the ready, headed out into the wild scorching desert wastes in a search of the power behind the Doomsday Daisybells. Being a hardy Scottish woman the hardships of the baking wilderness were taken in her stride. As she continued across the many miles of scorched yellow sand, remains of failed travellers littered the route but the grinning white skulls raised barely an eyebrow and then only when her foot went into the mouth of some long-dead soul causing Mrs McDoon to trip and mutter about being able to tell there was a lack of satisfactory cleaning staff at the base and that when she was running the cleaning rota the desert who soon be sorted. 'Leaving old bones around for any unsuspecting traveller to do themselves a mischief on, it's a health and safety nightmare, to say nothing of the hygiene implications.'

A few more days of walking through the baking heat and a lot of general tutting about the upkeep of the desert later brought Mrs McDoon to the gates of the base and the two well-armed, serious-looking guards who stood pointing their guns at her and eying her with the deepest of suspicion.

'Halt there m'am', said one of the guards, 'this is a restricted area and they let us shoot folks who get any closer than you are right now.'

Mrs McDoon stopped and smiled at the guards but they did not smile back, if anything their looks of suspicion deepened to ones of borderline paranoia. 'Oh hello sonny,' she said deciding a more serious expression was called for which she flashed, and this seemed to relax the guards ever so slightly. 'I'm Mrs McDoon. I have come for the cleaning job at the base. In Professor Winkle's lab to be exact.'

'There is no military base here ma'am,' began the guard, 'and we don't have anyone by the name of Winkle working here either, never had and never will, in fact the guy doesn't even exist so he could not possibly be working at any base should such a base exist which it most certainly does not.'

'Oh I see,' said Mrs McDoon looking over the guards shoulder at the very large military base that could clearly be seen in the distance.

The other guard cleared his throat, 'but we do have a cleaning job and we are expecting you. If you care to show us some ID I will let you in and you will be escorted to your interview.'

'Why thank you, young man,' said Mrs McDoon showing her papers before being escorted onto the base.

Mrs McDoon headed deep into the base and her meeting with the mysterious Professor Winkle, now this crazy Winkle cat was a wild-haired, scruffy-dressed crazy scientist with a poor level of personal hygiene and a glint in his eye that was part friendly sparkle, part wild stare.

'Good day, Mrs McDoon,' said the professor gripping her hand and shaking it far more firmly and for far longer than would normally be appropriate. 'I am Professor Winkle and it is very wonderful to meet you. You have no idea how hard it is to get cleaning staff way out here in the desert.'

'I thought you didn't exist,' said Mrs McDoon finally releasing her hand from the Professors steely grip.

'Officially I do not but then neither does this base, I believe if you look at us on Google Earth you just get a stern-looking yellow smiley face with the words, you ain't seen nothing you understand,' chuckled the Professor, 'I have told them it is a double negative but they don't listen to me, get back to work Winkle you crazy loon is all they say. Now if you follow me I will show you where you will be working, my lab is getting such a mess. I hope you can make a start today.'

'Don't you want to interview me first?' asked a startled Mrs McDoon.

'Heavens no,' said the Professor rushing off along the corridor with Mrs McDoon close behind. 'I have been advertising for a new cleaner for the past two years and you are the first one to actually find the base. If you can get here you've got the job is my motto. Many would be applicants have been lost in the desert never to see civilisation again. We have a very fat vulture population here about. The most obese scavengers in the world, I'll be bound.'

Within an hour that crazy Scot was brushing the floor and happily reading a top secret file, clearly marked with bright red capital letters, as she did so with an initially oblivious Professor

Winkle just happy to have a reasonably clean lab and a bit of company from a lady of his own age.

It was a lonely life that crazy old professor lived and no mistake my little test tube teasers. Even though that big old base was full to the brim with military personnel and funky science wranglers, nobody stopped by to just chew the fat or chill out a spell unless it was work- related.

Professor Winkle hoped in his heart to kindle some romance with Mrs McDoon. When he found out she had been widowed some four years, living he imagined a quiet and uneventful life, his heart filled with the joy of a spring lamb or an overly sentimental teenager.

He felt without a doubt that this firm-minded Scottish lady who had swept her way into his life, must be as lonely as him and be grateful for all the love and warm cuddles he was about to shower her with.

'Hot chocolate, Mrs McDoon,' said the lonely lovelorn old Professor clearly relishing that simple human contact, as he handed her the steaming mug of creamy chocolate goodness.

'Why thank you Professor,' she said putting down her broom but continuing to read the clearly labelled top secret file. 'I don't mind if I do, cleanings such thirsty work isn't it.'

'Oh I imagine so Mrs McDoon,' said the Professor. 'My, my, that is a most impressive blade you have on the end of that fine broom of yours.'

'Yes it is very handy, for litter and dealing with stubborn stains. When you get to my age bending down is always a risky business and this mighty blade has been quite a boon.'

'I don't mean to be overly critical on your first day, good lady,' said the Professor eyeing the top-secret file grasped tightly in the Scots woman's hand. 'That file could be considered inappropriate reading material especially as your security clearance is not in any way secret.'

'Oh laddie I quite understand your concern, really I do,' said Mrs McDoon, her eyes never lifting from the file's forbidden content. 'I absolutely must read all these documents in order understand what exactly I am cleaning in this here lab. So I don't damage any of the delicate and no doubt expensive equipment when I am cleaning it. Being an intelligent man I am sure you appreciate how important that is professor.'

'Well I understand your concerns dear lady,' said the Professor, 'but I'm still not entirely comfortable with you reading those files, perhaps if you were just careful in all your cleaning, treat each test tube and microscope as if they were precious jewels. Or look upon them as I do like wayward but nonetheless lovable children.'

'Oh professor, can you not humour the strange ways of a kind-hearted and yet eccentric old woman,' said Mrs McDoon finally looking up at the professor.

'Well I'm really not sure,' muttered the man beginning to weaken as Mrs McDoon's steely fingers brushed a scattering of multicoloured crumbs from the Professor's once white coat.

'I've only read a couple of these mighty files Professor,' continued Mrs McDoon knocking clouds of long settled dust from the man's clothes, 'I can already tell you are a man of superior intellect, even I would wager among the very wisest men and no doubt women of science, who mock you out of their own ignorance and jealousy no doubt.'

'There is some truth in what you say dear lady.'

'I thought so laddie, I thought so, now I have always had a fascination with science and if you would indulge me once again I would be fascinated to hear all about your work here. You might want to start with these dangerous and yet strangely fascinating creatures known in the media as, Doomsday Daisybells, or by some as, Moon-Cows.'

Chapter 5. Make milk not war, man.

While that old sour puss was on the rampage filling the world with a fear of all things bovine the old Hol-meister, (that is me in case you had forgotten) was in a bit of an oblivious little party bubble due to my holiday in Hawaii with my funky old fella Vince. A fellow cool bovine of the bullish gender in case you cats had forgotten that as well. Anyway old Cadmow had ignored the Hawaiian islands as they seemed too small for him to bother with. The villa we own over in the island is a bit secluded with our interests being focused on partying, surfing and tin-barrel racing rather than following all the usual negative Nellies that normally inhabit the news channels.

Perhaps you're all sitting there thinking to yourself who is the bovine, I don't know the cat and her life partner so why should I care about them going on their holidays and not catching a single news bulletin.

Let me quickly bring all you curious cats up to speed on my good self and my groovy cud chewing chap Vince, here is a bit of background on the pair of us.

We had both been frozen in ice boxes since the last time old sour cat tried to go on a reign of conquest, that time against the cow people initially on the bovine home world, it was a war fought upon a number of worlds our cow people were studying at the time. The final battle happened on Earth at one of those since lost and sunken cities, not Atlantis, one of the other ones. Anyway old Cadmow was defeated and got put on trial and for some reason myself and my then just good bud Vince are associated with that old belligerent bovine in the minds of our leaders, some slight confusion indeed.

Anyway one miscarriage of justice led to another and we both got locked in ice boxes just like the old lunar sour cat. Our boxes were hidden in the wilderness of a place that would one day become southern California.

We had both stayed at maximum cool until the groovy human year 1967. Our boxes were inside a small cave that was next to where outdoor hippy rave was going. Not one of the big historical ones but one of those cool little ones, for the hippest of the hip and the coolest of the cool.

A freaked out, romantically inclined hippy couple went hand in hand into the cave for a little alone time if you catch my loved-up drift groove cats. This funky pair filled that little cave with all manner of freaky mellow smoke from the joints they were chilling on.

One of those loved up mellow groove cats leaned back on a section of the rock that was really my chamber and they accidently activated the door which opened and I staggered out hoof outstretched, breathing in all those funky fumes as the beat of the tuneful groove from outside world worked its way into my waking brain.

The funked-out fella jumped back in shock saying,'wow it's freaky man, it's a cow.'

'Yeah it's cool man,' said his laid-back lady, 'don't you know cows chill, they don't kill.' With that she took my outstretched hoof in her hand and made a peace sign with it. 'Welcome groovy bovine sister,' she said swaying with her fella as they made their own peace gestures. 'We come in peace and joy oh mooing grassy sister, say you share our philosophy.'

Their groove moved me in a way that was profound and transcendental so I mooed in a trippy funk, 'Peace, man,' as I staggered fully out of the chamber breathing in the spicy psychedelic air, one of those fragrant flower folks passed me a big fat reefy spliffasaurus and I breathed in long and deep. Those cats told me later that my eyes became a crazy rainbow of colours that swirled like freaky spinning whirlpools although it should be said that both of those freak bombs were higher than mad march moon kites, but then again that cave did seem all bright and swirly to me.

Now the girl if I remember was called Lemon Drop, and the dude called himself, Drizzle Beard, a name he kept until 1987 when he reverted to the name on his birth certificate which was Nigel Snowdrop.

As I am trying to get my bearings with all the sweet smoke and pretty lights while Lemon Drop and Drizzle Beard just stood gazing upon my bovineness.

'Wow man, you look just like a cow,' said Drizzle Beard.

'Yeah far out,' said Lemon Drop reaching out to touch my horns. 'You from a farming family, man?'

'Don't get us wrong man,' said Drizzle Beard, 'we aren't like you know all shallow, judging people by the way they look or anything.'

'No way, we totally dig you looking like a cow. Because cows are all cool and chilled, all tranquil and peaceful man,' said Lemon Drop.

'Yeah, that's right because cows don't like you know, send other cows to kill in Vietnam or build a bomb that can like wipe out the whole world. That would never happen because moo cows are far to mellow to do anyone any harm,' said Drizzle Beard. 'You're better than all us humans man, we so dig you.'

'We love you mellow mooing sister, make milk not war,' sighed lemon Drop swaying to the good vibrations that swirled about our hearts.

'Thanks my name is Holly,' I said my brain still a whirl of freakiness, 'I'm a real cow, not a human who looks like a cow.

'Heavy, a talking cow,' said the freaky pair leading me out of the cave and handing me another freaky fungus spliff. 'Good to meet you Holly, now that is one cool name. Here have another joint for later, come and share your bovine wisdom with the rest of us.'

'Groovy,' I said as those two drum circle dreamers led me out into the sunlight and a wave of cool music that assaulted my ears like nothing I had experienced before.

'Do you, like find milk offensive man,' said Lemon Drop.

'Is chewing the cud like a form of transcendental meditation?' asked Drizzle Beard as we walked into a large crowd of friendly and curious hippies. 'Does grass make you mellow and trip out to other dimensions and far out levels of consciousness? Teach us your ways we have so much to learn.'

With a skip in my step and funky vibe in my being I went and partied with those groovy hippy cats and in the months and years that followed I learnt all about freaky fashions, groovy music and politics, not forgetting how to get high as a silver sailing lunar moon kite.

I am embarrassed to say I was having such a good time and was living in such daze craze whirlpool adventure that I forgot all about my old pal Vince. Until that is the summer of 1972.

I told my freaky hippy friends all about old Vince and we decided to do something funky for his introduction to the modern human society that was 70s California.

We decided to wake him at a big old local disco, a baptism of funky music. That dancehall of delights, that disco of daring and dubious dreams was packed to the raving-rafters with my most mellow and groove loving hippy crew. I stood at the side with Vince's icebox and my other good buddy Drizzle Beard, who was looking at me kind of strangely.

'Hey groovy cud chewing sister, you really are a cow aren't you?' said Drizzle Beard staring dreamlike at my horns all painted with chains of swirling daisies as they poked above my mellow yellow peace bandanna.

'Hey Drizzle man, I've known you for like forever and you've only just noticed I'm a cow?' I said swaying my bare udders gently to the beat.

Unlike human females we bovines don't tend to cover our udders and so all our clothes have to be adjusted with a big old hole at the front to give us female bovines udder most freedom if you'll pardon the pun groovers. Additionally both the males and females need a hole at the rear for our tails. There is nothing like swishing your tail to the rhythm in a happening venue let me tell you cats true.

'It's just that, I know you've always looked like a cow but I always wondered if it might be a trip thing from all the years of freaky fungus. But I've been off the stuff for the last six months and everything else has gone back to normal and despite that you're still a cow, which I so dig. I just hope your friend here is as cool as you when we defrost the cat,' mused the Drizzle diva.

'Don't worry,' I said, 'he'll be as chilled as that ice age they say is coming, especially when we deck him out in all these seriously cool threads I've brought along for him, he always was a fashion victim in the old days.

I had picked out a purple velvet jacket, a funky frilly flower-filled shirt and tight satin pants in a lovely shade of maroon for Vince. With some additional accessories and a little orange chest spray that cat would look the queen bee's knees. Although the moustache he would grow later really did not suit him and made him look like a pimp reject from a Blaxploitation movie.

My own mellow style that night was a full-length satin dress in a lava lamp explosion of swirling shades of red, lime greens and orange. It was a full-on mind whirl optical illusion. If you stared at that dress too long it would reveal a welcome message to my old pal Vince. Let me tell you that bovine boy did a fair bit of staring at me that night, in a way he never had in the old days.

I cracked the seal on the ice box and within a couple of minutes the baffled head of Vince popped out, still half asleep looking around before glancing at me rather uncertainly.

'Hey Vince buddy, how's it hanging, you all rested up and ready to party?' I said waving at the old Vincemeister.

'Holly is that you? Where are we?' replied Vince.

'This is Earth Vince man and it's gone really cool. I woke you up so we could enjoy it together,' I said passing him the cool threads and a shiny red pair of roller boots. 'Here put these on and come out and party.'

A few minutes later Vince came out dressed in all the cool seventies gear and the roller boots on as well. Then I pushed the cat straight into the middle of the dance floor shouting, 'Go on man, get down and party we'll be right behind you.'

'Hey Holly man,' said Drizzle Beard, 'you know this isn't roller disco, don't you man?'

'Yeah I know, Drizzle dude,' I said heading out onto the dance floor. 'I just wanted to get one up on the old Vince-meister.'

'Hey Vince man, I think you invented a new dance dude.'

Reunited, again at last, me and my old buddy Vince just like the old days just with fewer volcanoes and less risk of serious space sickness.

On a world where the grass was green, which was freaky and took some getting used to but in the end we both agreed it just added to the quirky charm of Earth.

After getting reacquainted and me bringing the cat up to speed with the world we both decided to tune in and drop out for a few freaky years of travel around the world, including a spiritual trip to India, we found the people ever so friendly, made us feel kinda special. Shame that all the cows we met there had a serious attitude problem like they thought they were too good to speak to us or something man, un cool cats man.

We wandered back, first to South America, buying two high-spirited alpacas in Chile before leading those two frisky, wool-bound prima donnas, north until we were back in sunny southern California. Before turning them into a herd and selling rainbow tartan patterned wool to all the freaky folks around the world. Bear in mind this was the mid nineteen seventies so there was plenty of freaky folks wanting loud woolly jumpers around back then. That is how we made our fortune while keeping it real and allowing plenty of time to party.

We became super rich, super funky bovines over the following decades, retiring many years before they built that freaky old moon base. All our time was spent being socialites mixing with all the rich and famous party animals. We even made a low budget movie called, cop cows at large in the city, we were paired with a young wannabe actor who played an eccentric undercover cop who insisted on taking a small herd of unofficial police cows into deep cover with dangerous drug dealers, in sleazy vice dens and riding with violent, murderous biker gangs. The cop character was constantly getting tied up and threatened with machetes while coming up with the most ludicrous excuses for having a herd of cows with him. Very often the criminals would conclude his behaviour was so crazy that he could not possibly be an undercover cop despite them finding a variety of cop-related items on him.

It will come as no surprise that one was a straight to video, when people still had videos, and finally died the death at the bottom of some charity shop bargain bin.

During all the moon cow mania we had spent a long Hawaiian vacation unaware of old Cadmow's worldwide rampage, occasionally we did hear the word 'cows' on the radio but we thought it was just another video of us surfing being put on the net and people were just arguing over its authenticity.

We came back to California the long way via Alaska, getting a little polar bear wrestling in before following the wilderness wolf trail down the coast all the way to our home in San Francisco.

We had not told any of our friends when we would be returning and had planned to surprise them during our first night out at one of our favourite social venues, a little groovy club called, the Astro-cat groove club, a cool little place were all our friends hang out.

Upon seeing all the destruction in San Francisco and the suspicious, even hostile looks we were suddenly getting, it was clear that humanity had gone from being cool with cows to a dark and nervous place that made us feel rather unwelcome.

'What do we do man?' I said to Vince. 'Should we even go to the club if humanity is being terrorised by a bad- tempered herd of barmy bovines, I mean our presence could freak them out even more.'

'I think we have to go Holly,' said Vince, 'all they have seen is bad cows who want to kill, that's all many of them know now. We have to tell them the other side of the tale. Perhaps if people see us being all funky and friendly they might realise that all cows aren't evil and be able to chill out a bit.'

'Yeah, I think you're right man. Good job we bought lots of souvenirs for everyone. I told you it was a good idea to lug all those surf boards down through Canada.'

'I thought the surf boards were to fend off polar bear and walrus attacks,' said Vince.

'Yeah that as well Vince man, they are multipurpose, you know, like those freaky Swiss navy surf boards.'

Flip forward my little fiery-bottomed-free-basers there we were my little power-ballad prima donnas, a couple of days later, loaded with presents, hanging in the nightclub queue sharing gossip with our many freaky friends and amiable acquaintances. All the folks we knew were happy and cool especially when we handed out our goody bags.

Those folks unfamiliar with our peaceful nature and grooved-out ways kept shooting us nervous and sometimes quite hostile looks but we kept making peace signs and saying a whole load of friendly and fruity Aloha's in order to soothe the local humans tattered nerves and perhaps restore a little of their faith in the natural goodness of bovines. Although our cries of, cows chill we don't kill, rang rather hollow given the ruins nearby. We had to stop that particular mantra when a number of distressed humans showed us pictures of loved ones trampled to death by the demented Daisybells.

A few places back down the line was a very angry-looking man wearing a large grey coat and muttering loudly about chopping us up and serving us to all the victims of the most recent cow attacks. We didn't get all that concerned at the time as he seemed to want to chop lots of humans up as well, especially those that were looking at the odd gun and knife-shaped bulges in his huge coat.

We were getting close to the front of the queue and assumed the door staff who were naturally close personal friends would quickly deal with the crazy muttering guy who seemed to have pulled out a large meat cleaver which he was loudly sharpening.

'Why don't you come here you juicy, yummy, meaty moo cows? I'll put your no-good hides to real good and tasty use. Oh yes indeed, I'll even supply the mustard. What do you say moo cows?' taunted the angry guy who had gone from angry vicious mutters to loud and extremely audible threats to our being, accompanied by the sound of a metal blade slicing the air as well as the clothing of the very distressed people who shared that part of the queue with him.

Ignoring as best we could all the slashing sounds behind us we breathed a sigh of relief and stepped to the front position in the queue and beheld the always amiable faces of Sebastian and Andre our door persons for the evening.

'Sorry folks, not tonight,' said Andre putting out his hand to stop us entering before pointing to the street.

'Hey Andre what's going on man?' I said, 'it's us Holly and Vince this party parlour's coolest and most spend happy customers.'

'Yeah and we come bearing gifts to tantalise your very soul as well,' said Vince holding up our expertly-wrapped and rather expensive presents that we had carefully selected for the door staff at the club. You've got to keep those door wranglers happy.

'Yeah, well thanks and it's good to see you both. The thing is it's, no cow night, tonight,' said Sebastian, pointing to an advertising hoarding that declared the Astro cat club a cow-free zone and that night in particular was designated a no cow night when revellers could apparently do all their desired revelling without the danger of being harassed by snorting killer bovines or indeed any peaceful dancing ones for that matter.

'No cow night?' I said, 'but surely that just applies to killer cows. We just get down to the funky beat and spend lots of money here.'

'Sorry, I understand you cows are cool but the management have said strictly no cows. No exceptions, and I'm afraid that includes you two,' said Sebastian looking suitably embarrassed.

'Yeah,' said Andre, 'we'd like to let you both in, we know you're cool. It's just folks around here and I guess just about everywhere else have got spooked with all these weird attacks lately.'

'Well that's kind of understandable,' I said, 'but we don't want to hurt anyone. Perhaps if people see us just chilling out all cool and being funky in a friendly style they might realise that all cows aren't evil and be able to chill out a bit.'

'Hey Holly, Vince is that you guys?'

It was a group of our close personal friends just inside the club, beckoning us to come in and boogie the night away.

Those fruity forbidden stairs to the verdant Valhalla of good vibration never shined so sweet as that moment they were denied to us, oh man ain't that the ever-mooing truth.

'Are you two coming in? We need some cats with funky moves, everyone in here is afraid to look even a bit freaky in case some troll-prod wannabe film maker makes them the star of a dance shame documentary. We all know you two have no inhibitions when it comes to disco-punk,' yelled our funkiest of fine fun-loving friends, Jane, who ran down the stairs and gave us big hugs.'

'Sorry Jane,' I said, 'but we are being turned away, we're out of fashion at the moment.'

'Oh no,' said Jane shooting daggers at our normally accommodating door staff. 'Is this about the whole dress code, shoe policy again? Because as I've said like a million times, cows have natural shoes, they are called hooves so they don't need shiny plastic covers. If you stop them coming in due to their hooves, that is discrimination and like an actual hate crime. You can go to actual prison for your hate crimes, is that what you both want?' said Jane getting up a full head of self- righteous steam.

'It's not our hooves,' I said interrupting Jane before she drew blood. 'It's our horns, our tails, our hairy brown hides; in fact it's our whole bovine being.'

'Apparently it's no cow night,' said Vince pointing at the poster, 'and we are bovine non-grata at the moment.'

'Is that right, you're including these two cool cows in your anti-killer-cow night?' said Jane, storming over to the poster.

'Well a cow is a cow,' said Andre, 'not everyone knows these guys, some people might freak out and panic. Especially if they mistake their funky moves for the wild and crazed motions of a short-circuiting killer cow running amok, I mean these guys do have a form when it comes to dance moves that provoke funkophobia in some delicate souls who don't understand the experimental nature of their unique dance steps.'

'Bullshit,' said Jane taking out a bright red lipstick and scrawling the word, killer, on the poster. 'See, now it says, no killer cow night! These guys aren't killer cows, so they can come in right!?'

'You can't just deface a poster and just expect to...'

'Come on let them in,' shouted a chorus of voices from the club entrance.

'We can't just let you in.'

Suddenly a vast mob of friendly faces swarmed out of the club, took our arms and whisked us past the door staff, who stood open-mouthed, powerless to stop us.

'Ok, but try and keep a low profile,' said Andre.

'If that's at all possible,' shouted Sebastian, 'try to avoid the dance floor or at least keep to the shadows.'

As we were carried upstairs to began our night of partying, the queue outside moved forward. It was not long before the angry man with the big coat stood in front of Andre and Sebastian, an impatient snarl on his face and a big old machete cradled lovingly in his arms.

'I hope you boys aren't going to keep old slasher hanging about. I'm eager to get in there and impress all those ladies with my big weapon. They must be desperate to meet a real man with all the nancy boys you two have let in tonight,' said the angry knife dude flashing the scariest snarl you ever did see. He was trying for a smile but it wasn't really in that cruel cat's nature.

Andre shook his head and folded his arms hoping the man would take the hint. 'I am sorry sir you cannot come in with that dangerous weapon. It's menacing and people could get hurt especially if you wave it round the way you have been'

'What this old thing, menacing? I'm not going to cause trouble with it, just show it of to the ladies, women love big men with big knives. You boys should get blades yourselves; the women might start taking you fancy door boys seriously if you started wielding a decent bit of steel now,' growled old slasher as he gazed lovingly at his constantly moving blade.

In a show of security solidarity with his colleague, Sebastian stepped forward and held out his hands for the blade. 'We have a very strict knife policy I am afraid sir.'

'Well if you boys say so,' said that raging hate monger handing over his machete with a twisted sneer. 'Although I was under the impression you had a strict policy about cows as well.'

'We are also going to have to see inside your coat sir,' said Sebastian.

'You want to look inside my coat, do you boy? Now tell me what does a pair of fancy, Nancy, back-rub-dancing, silky door boys want to look at under my coat?'

'Just checking for any concealed weapons sir,' said Andre pulling open the angry spite cat's coat.

Andre and Sebastian began to slowly remove guns, knives and other deadly weapons from inside the man's coat. He glared at them as a huge pile of weapons grew at his feet.

'Listen here you two baby oil, beach-bum, candyfloss, sugar-rash boys, I need every one of those guns to protect myself and feel safe on the streets. You are violating my constitutional rights. You're trying to make me weak and turn me into some sort of loser. I'm no loser, do you two little gold top, creamy bait, boys understand what I am saying underneath all your oh so special pirate curls? I am no loser, losers like you pair for instance get shot, while winners like me do the shooting, you two gooseberry fools starting to catch my cold steel, driftwood yet?'

Sebastian pulled out a long list from the man's pocket and showed it to his colleague.

'I didn't see you searching those damn cows. This is discrimination; I am going to speak to my congressman first thing in the morning.'

'This is a very interesting list sir,' began Sebastian. 'Let's see; Russell Bailey manager of the Astro-cat club is a flash snooty fucker who waters down the drinks he needs to die fast with a bullet to the head. D.J. Spandex Twirl, tuneless tone-deaf freak, won't turn the music down when I'm talking to my ladies so should die slow with a knife at his throat. D.J. Lucy Jones is the devils sickly man-hating tart, she never wants to stroke my blades someone should string her up from a glitter ball. Very interesting list indeed sir. There are at least ten similar entries all relating to Astro-cat club staff and various forms of homicide.'

'Hey that list is my private personal property,' growled the slash happy chap trying to snatch back the list, 'and none of your goddamn business. Besides I am simply expressing a personal opinion, that's freedom of speech; do you two sponge-finger, backroom-bakery boys understand that? After all this is still a free country isn't it? Or are you two bottles of light fruity beer trying to rip up my constitutional rights? I'll need every one of those guns and all of my knives back too. That's a dangerous club; you've got cows walking around in there.'

'Sorry sir,' said Sebastian, 'You're going to have to leave, we have strict rules about admitting persons who are heavily armed especially when they express an interest in killing most of the club's staff.'

That snarling, red-faced slash pot shook his knives in the faces of Andre and Sebastian. 'Now I understand that you boys being less than full men might be threatened by a force of raw masculinity such as myself. I can understand why you pair of week-old celery sticks would want to get rid of the competition, I can forgive that. The things I really cannot forgive though is your attempt to take away my freedom weapons, trample on my freedom of speech and worst of all is the way you two no good cow kissers consort with the enemy of the human species. The sooner this place burns down the better, I hope a fiery herd of burning bovines wipes this place out tonight.'

After laughing in mock hysteria at the impassive door crew the knife-wielding dude stalked away haughtily into the deep dark, dangerous night.

'Have a nice, peaceful evening sir,' said Sebastian to the man's raised middle finger as it slowly disappeared.

'Yeah come back as soon as you're no longer a nut loop squirrel dodger buddy,' muttered Andre.

We had all settled in for a groove-tastic night of fun and frivolity but little did us cool cats know that the fates and a certain knife loving dude, the cat most in need of anger management leaving aside the whole angry lunar caldron of cantankerousness Cadmow naturally, was about to make a pact with that twenty-four hour rolling devil known as fake news. Hear that groovy beat? Swing out and get down a while, but you better make the most of it because some bad cats got hold of the rug and is about to sweep you all off your dancing feet, and not in a good way.

Later that night in another part of town one angry knife-loving cat was prowling his apartment, steam positively billowing out of his ears as he raged at the rolling news from the network that serves all those permanently enraged and self-righteous cats that lean on the over-stimulated right wing of life.

What story has piqued the ire of the blade botherer? You may well ask. Well wonder no longer. It is a rather upbeat tale in fact about the very nightspot all us groove cats were rocking the night away at.

On the big old screen in blade boys living room a bouncy over-excited reporter stood outside the club with the founder of our feast of funk, club manager Russell

Bailey.

'There you have it folks, if you want a fun night away from the danger and worry of killer bovines go to club Astro, it's guaranteed cow-free zone every Thursday, Friday and Saturday night,' said the reporter grinning wildly for all she was worth.

'That's right, club Astro wants to do everything we can for our community and our country in this time of need, why not take a break from the chaos and let your hair down tonight at Club Astro. Bring those dancing shoes and your wallets because we're not a goddamn charity, we have overheads you people don't understand. Shit this isn't live is it? Can we cut that last bit Josie,' he said with a wink.

'No problem Russell babes,' she replied staring at the camera, 'this is Josephine Barnstorm for Ferocious Ferret news signing off.'

'Thanks honey,' continued Russell unaware he could still be heard by the tele-visual masses. 'Been a bit of a stressful week all round the stupid customers have been complaining about me watering down the drinks again and I think my wife is starting to suspect my affair with your sister Suzy, I don't know what tipped her off.'

'Give me the news desk,' snarled the old cold steel conjurer into his phone that strained in the grip of his furious fists. 'Yeah I got a big old news story for you, scoop of the century newsboy, do you want a story about a two-faced, cow-kissing, anti-American traitor by the name of one Russell Bailey who pretends to run an anti cow night but is in fact runs a killer-cow collaborator club? Yeah I thought you would boy, I thought you would.'

And so it begins as the geek cats say, as slanderous accusations about Club Astro and its colourful cat of a manager fly across the airways. Resulting in the inevitable second interview now showing on the blade bothers television. The un-cool cat had now swapped his blades for a pair of sawn-off shot guns which he fired excitedly at the ceiling much to the distress of his neighbours in the floor above.

Josephine Barnstorm stood once again outside Club Astro, a much more serious expression on her face. 'As rumours spread that club Astro the supposed bastion of safety from killer cows is in reality a front for a network of human cow collaborators providing juicy human flesh to their mooing moon masters, I am back outside Club Astro with it's manager Russell Bailey. Mr Bailey what is your response to these claims? Do you really allow killer bovines to not only enter your club but trample our flag beneath their murderous hooves of hate, hooves, which no doubt only hours before would have been trampling out the lives of innocent loyal Americans?'

That old dog Bailey tried for a steely look but his ashen face didn't make it very convincing, the murmur of a quietly growing baying mob rolling in on the wind just out of camera shot couldn't have been helping to enhance that mood much either.

'I respond very simply by saying, this is the most insane load of old bullshit I have ever heard. No cow has ever or will ever enter my club. I love my customers; they are like family to me. I am loyal to humanity and loyal to America too. As for our glorious flag, I love that flag more that a huge basket full of babies, puppies, kittens and those cute little furry seal pups and no cow is getting anywhere near it so help me freedom,' he said saluting and looking nobly as possible while sweating profusely into the camera.

As club manager Bailey saluted the viewers a certain gun- toting angry man blasted his television with all four barrels, whoops of rage, triumph and howls of pain exploded from him as he was blasted back across the room. He seemed shocked by both the amount of glass now sticking out of his face and the volume of black smoke whirling around by the ceiling. 'Got the sucker,' he moaned triumphantly as his pain was finally drowned out by a screaming fire alarm and gun shots from the flat above.

Back outside the club Josephine Barnstorm continued her interrogation. 'Well Mr Bailey, if things are as patriotic inside your totally non-cow club as you claim you will be happy to let my camera crew inside and show the viewers at home for themselves?'

'Why of course, the great American people are very welcome to take a sneak peak inside our wonderful club, I hope it will whet their appetites and many of them will choose to pay us a visit, not all at once though we don't have that kind of capacity, well at least not yet but maybe in a few years when we franchise out the club Astro brand,' he said flashing a cheesy yet slightly nervous grin at camera.

'Well come then, let's go inside,' said Josephine heading to the club entrance with the film crew and Manager Bailey in hot pursuit. 'Hey Josie what the hell is this all about,' said Bailey catching up and trying to grab Josephine's arm before being pushed away.

'Can you keep your hands to yourself please Mr Bailey,' she said heading through the door.

'I thought we were friends Josie, why are you doing this. Pushing this stupid cow collaboration story, you could harm my business and ruin my reputation, is that what you want?'

'What I want Russell,' she said storming up the steps, 'is for you to stop messing my sister about. You're clearly never going to leave your wife, and I have been talking to Jenny the new runner at the network, she said you were like some kind of giant randy squid last night trying put you pervy tentacles all over her.'

'Oh for heavens sake Josie I was just showing Jenny around town, I was being welcoming, she must have got the wrong end of the stick. She's a small-town country girl; you know how innocent and naïve they are.'

Ignoring the pleas of Club Astros manager, Josephine Barnstorm and her film crew burst onto the main dance floor. Right in front of the live news camera was my main bull Vince doing the funky freak-out across half the dance floor, frantic arcs of static shooting out from his hoof and horn studs making for a freaky electric rainbow of colourful sparks swirling about him and the nearby frantic funkinestas that tripped that far out scene.

'Oh my god, it's a killer moon cow right here on no cow night, not only that but it appears to be shorting out, any comments Mr Bailey,' said Josephine thrusting the microphone in to man's alarmed face.

'It's not what it looks like...' stammered Bailey, as the camera swung round to me.

'Look another one,' shouted a camera wrangler, 'it's violating the flag code and kidnapping that incapacitated human female.'

Well man I am in the limelight as I swing around a drunken human friend on my shoulders doing the whole dizzy disco dance which I tried to patent in 2004. The human in question was wrapped in the stars and stripes which fell off the ceiling an hour earlier and I decided to turn into a special patriot's edition of the dizzy disco.

'Mr Bailey you seem to have a very strange idea of a no cow night, do you have anything to say to the American people about your act of treason?'

'Listen it's all a big misunderstanding, those cows aren't killer cows, that's just Holly and Vince. They are meant to be on holiday in Hawaii I didn't think they were back for another week. The door staff shouldn't have let them in tonight, although they are good customers, they spend plenty of money and don't cause trouble really.'

'I take it you know these cows personally then,' said Josephine.

'Yes I've known them both for many years; Holly over there was a bridesmaid at my wedding.'

As the lights came up and music stopped Josephine Barnstorm addressed the nation. 'And there we have it good citizens Russell Bailey manager of club Astro who claimed he was a bastion of liberty against the modern scourge of killer bovines is in reality secret long term friend of these deadly bovines and even gives them sanctuary in his club. Take a long hard look at the face of a traitor and his diabolical den of killer bovines and the humans some of whom will be brainwashed victims of a killer cow cult but many this reporter suspects are willing collaborators and cow worshipping traitors. People of the world as you look on this wicked place take heart as it won't be here much longer, I am told an enraged baying mob armed with flaming torches is heading in this direction rapidly as we speak. I think we should all say a quick prayer of thanks to this self-righteous mob of vigilantes, taking the law into their own hands for the good of our nation.'

'Hey lady where do you get off spreading your poison to all those sofa-surfing, fake-news junkies?' it was Jane, spinning Josephine around and getting in her face with a ferocity that made everyone take a step back and just get out of their way.

'And you are?' replied Josephine only flinching for a second, she was one tough cookie I'll say that for her dude cats, I've seen Jane take big old angry biker dudes down with one of her in your face interventions.

'I am a close personal friend of those two-peace loving bovines over there, they are cool cows, you haven't even spoken to them and you're already judging them. Whatever happened to innocent until proven guilty?' said Jane trying to up the ante against the stony face of Josephine Barnstorm.

'I am happy to let the American people be the judges, and there is an angry mob of loyal citizens on their way, perhaps you should make your traitorous pleas for clemency and the rights of murderous moo cows to them or just run away like a cowardly cow lover into the cover of night with the rest of the criminal underworld.'

Jane shoved the reporter out of the way and addressed the nation directly. 'Don't listen to these lies, those cows are good, they aren't anything to do with the killer moon cows. They are peace loving cool cows; it's not fair to persecute them for the crimes of other bovines. It's not fair and it's like a hate crime, don't let ignorance lull you into committing a crime against peaceful bovinity that you'll all live to regret.'

'We need to get out of here fast,' it was Andre and Sebastian rushing into the room, a look of urgent terror on their faces. 'There's a mob right behind us, get to the back fire exit, they've got gasoline grenades with your faces on.'

'Retreat and regroup at our pad in two hours dudes, remember there is no shame in a well-organised tactical retreat,' I shouted as we headed out the back way. Andre and Sebastian had to drag Jane, who was still shouting at the camera, until we were outside and then we scattered running like the devil himself was poking a red-hot pitchfork at our furry arses, which wasn't that far from the truth.

Back in the club Josephine Barnstorm addressed the camera again as the howling mob arrived. 'There we have it folks the true depth of these cows depravity is shown as a brainwashed young human woman who otherwise would have had her whole life before her is tricked into defending them before being whisked away to whatever chaotic cattle shed of doom these foul beasts call home. I think it would be appropriate for the nation to take a moment of silent reflection and pray for sweet young Jane, another victim of those murderous manic moon cows.'

'I am a victim of what now?' it was Jane back at our pad a couple of hours later watching the news report on the events at Club Astro. 'I'm going to phone up that studio and tell them...'

'No you're not Jane,' I said taking the phone out of her hand. 'They will track us here and we've spent too long getting this place right just to let an enraged mob trash our beautiful designer moo-pad and no doubt upset the neighbours.'

The television continued to show images of our club and roving reporter Josephine Barnstorm. This time the shots were from outside showing the club fully ablaze with triumphant and angry crowds celebrating with barbecues and beer. The angry guy from the queue could be seen clearly, still bleeding and firing his guns in the air as he did a little dance which took him closer and closer to the flames, periodically setting his clothes and hair alight making his movements more frantic than funkadelic in his attempts to put out the fires about his person but carry on with his hate-filled happy groove.

'After our special report on Club Astro and its secret den of killer cow collaborators giving aid, comfort and a regular oil change to our enemy, it seems a mob of truly patriotic Americans have set the traitor's den ablaze. Most fire departments have said they are just going to let it burn. The one fire truck that did turn up was quickly set on fire by a group of true-blue Americans. Club Manager and head traitor Russell Bailey after initially claiming to be close personal friends with the cavorting bovines changed his tune and said the film showed a fancy dress party at the club with a farming theme before running away, probably to some cow-loving country like India, instead of facing the people like an innocent individual would do.'

Back at our pad everyone was looking pretty glum. 'This is hailstones-on-a-nudist-beach heavy man, said Vince. 'Our favourite party place up in flames and all the humans in the country and probably the world hating our furry mooing hides.'

'Yeah man this town is lynch mob central, heavy with the anger of humanity from every corner were do we go man, what do we do,' I began only to be interrupted by Jane angrily clearing her throat.

'Excuse me,' she said looking mighty fierce, 'this human doesn't hate you two; I have your backs the way I always have. The same goes for everyone here, isn't that right?'

We heard a glorious and unanimous wave of 'yes' from all of our beautiful human friends, if you'd have seen it, well it was enough to bring tears to the eyes and it did man it truly did.

'The news is bullshit, man; no one believes that stuff anyway. We got to fight the power. Like you guys did back in the sixties,' continued Jane punching the air in a way that made me both terribly proud and more than a little afraid for my delicate light fittings.

'She is right,' I said glancing nervously at our new lava funk chandelier as Jane stormed about the living room gesticulating rudely at the television. 'We've got to fight the power and stick it to the man.'

'We've got to fight two enemies man, those pesky moon botherers and the insidious fake news agenda, how in the name of all things loonlicious are we going to square that hallucinogenic hexagon man?'

An air of serious concerned consideration lay across the room for a long cold moment until I had a glorious brain tsunami. 'Eureka, cats I think I've got it.'

'You got an idea Holls?' said both Vince and Jane together.

'Not just an idea but a plan to put the cherry on the fairy cake. It's so crazily groovetastic it might just work. Huddle round and let me lay out the scene for you and tell me if you dig it too.'

Chapter 6 Never look your gift cow in the mouth

Well my tripped out tricky Richards, picture this hot hail heavy scene if you can. Three huge bell jars, right out of mad scientist monthly magazine classified section, each with its very own terrified human inside appeared to hang horn height above a busy street in a large city. Those terrified humans screamed out in the appropriate level of general terror as a deadly dust cloud of Doomsday Daisybells smashed straight towards them. The screams continued as the herd passed through the human holograms and lasted until the jars appeared at another town or city scheduled for attack. This happened again and again as Lord Cadmow, still in his lunar lair laughed a hearty bitter laugh at the terrified screams of those good old country boys who if you all remember ever so slightly shot and not to put to fine a point on it ate the good Lady Mowlore which angered the already snorting bull lord to a frenzy as she was the love of his life.

The real jars containing the rapidly sobering yokels sat at the side of the moon-base control room. Each jar was three-quarters filled with blue and yellow liquid that swirled and bubbled. This strange brew sparked with pretty silver streaks that delivered all manner of painful electric shocks to the bewildered men every time the vengeful bovine activated a remote-control device that hung about his neck.

The three country boys looked around at the interior of the control room in bemused terror, giving out the odd yelp of pain as Cadmow pumped the pain button and laughed in manic but slightly pitifully hollow way.

'What in the name of all the high falluting hellhounds of hayseed dixie was that all about boy? I dreamed a crazed herd of rabid robot Holsteins had broken loose and were on the rampage in some big city,' said Cletus.

'I reckons them steaks we had at that big old barbecue the other night were a bit dodgy coming from a talking cow and all,' nodded Billy bob like a genuine southern wisdom bringer.

'Well that's as maybe,' said Jim Jam Jimmy casting Cadmow a hard stare, 'but I'm thinking someone slipped a handful of them new cyber pill things into our beer and now we are trapped in that new fangled holo-web thing that's all the rage amongst the young folks just now.'

'Holo-web?' said Cletus, 'ain't that the one like the old internet but you can touch and feel things on it? Hell doggy I've been meaning to have me a go of that.'

'Yeah, I bet you have Cletus, I bet you have,' said Billy Bob rolling his eyes. 'I don't think you want to be touching and feeling that thing over there though.'

Cadmow stalked slowly towards the distressed humans and began staring at them closely through the glass.

'Now you gone and attracted the critter's attention with all your darn fool gwarking you stupid swamp rat Billy Bob, I was going to ignore it until it went away,' said Cletus as he frantically tried to shoo away the snorting figure of Cadmow. 'Why don't you skit freaky critter get out of here, go on now, skedaddle away with you, ain't nothing for you round here boy.'

Cadmow tapped on the glass of the nearest jar.

'Oh verminous human maggots, tell me are you comfortable in your jars,' sang the sadistic Cadmow grinning manically at each human in turn.

'Hell no,' replied Jim Jam Jimmy. 'It's real cramped in here why don't you let us out a spell fella.'

The other two yokels cried out in agreement while Cadmow smiled and nodded before pressing the pain button causing the jars to light up and each man to do a little dance. Like the devils demented disco minus the out of tune violin music.

'Tell me human pieces of filth, have you felt much terror and agonising pain in recent days?' snorted Cadmow rubbing his mighty horns against the jars. The scraping sound made by the horns was almost as painful upon the ears as the electric shocks had been on the rest of the body.

'Sure have boy,' said Cletus, 'all kinds of electric shocks all over the place, I think something must have shorted out somewhere, you needs yourself an electrician boy. Now my cousin Frank who lives over Bringle county way he is pretty good with electrics, sort out your fault no trouble, give you a good price to if you need this place rewiring, which I'm guessing it does judging from all the shocks and all.'

'Yeah old boy, I'm getting cramp something awful in my legs, real nasty it is,' said Billy Bob. 'Now if you could get me a bit of top-grade horse liniment I reckon that would do it, sort it out real fine, if the vet gets awkward with you tell him it's for a pony that's been in the family a long time and you're real attached to the critter. You, could let us out for a walk about boy, that would probably help even more, but get the horse liniment anyway it's always handy to have a bit in the house.'

Cadmow stalked around the room considering the three men with an air of confused satisfaction playing dangerously about his lips.

'Good humans, pain, terror, muscle cramps, difficulty accessing horse liniment, whatever that is, it is all excellent if you are in torment over it,' said Cadmow a devilish glint in his eye as he moved back to the computer console.

'Don't forget top grade liniment fella, none of the cheap stuff now, boy.'

'Do you recognise this image, humans?' said Cadmow bringing up an image of Mowlore on a large wall display.

'Hey isn't that the critter we ate at the big roast the other night?' said Jim Jam Jimmy.

'Yeah, sure is, big thing it was, plenty of meat for the whole jamboree,' yelled Billy Bob smacking his lips. 'The steaks were a bit tough though, whatever it was it was no spring chicken. If we could just find ourselves a younger one, now I bet it would be real tender and umm tasty.'

Cadmow banged the control panel with his hoof in fury, the steam from his flaring nostrils swirling around the room like some lost and lonely cloud.

'This bovine goddess, envy of the high creamy one herself, was the love of my life you barbaric pieces of maggot filth, stole her away and put her beautiful flesh into your rotten stinking mouths,' mooed that bitter old bull lord in a mix of rage and distraught bitterness.

'Now I know you're upset there fella, but that's no reason to get all personal and nasty like,' said Billy Bob. 'I mean you have your own special odour that is kind of earthy and rural but we weren't going mention it because we didn't want to get all personal like.'

'Say, you were dating that thing boy?' said Jim Jam Jimmy. 'Well they do say love is blind but even Cletus, dates better looking woman than her and most of them are barnyard critters.'

As Billy Bob and Jim Jam Jimmy spluttered with laughter, Cletus gave an equally emphatic splutter of indignation at the slight to his good and wholesome character.

'Now fella's as I keep on telling you I happen to date a lot of women from the animal costumed pleasure community, those ladies like to engage in romantic relationships while wearing animal costumes,' began Cletus. 'The animal persona helps them throw off the repressive and rigid orthodoxies of human sexuality and embrace the full variety of their natural animalistic passions.'

'Is that right Cletus?' said Billy Bob.

'Damn right it's right,' said Cletus, 'and I'll tell you another thing, under those costumes they are all hot and full of wanton womanly goodness, and that's a fact.'

'If they are so fine looking like you say,' said Billy Bob, 'why do they keep their critter masks on all the time? I heard they stay on even when they are in the throws of passion so to speak.'

'As I've told you two before, those ladies simply like to stay in character before, during and after the act of love so they can truly experience the wild pleasures the natural world has to offer,' said Cletus.

'Now tell me what character are you acting out Cletus? The part of the dirty old farmer with wandering hands? Not much acting required there I suppose,' said Billy Bob as the two yokels that weren't called Cletus squelched and squealed with near terminal amusement.

Those squeals of joy suddenly flipped over to screams of equally emphatic agony as streaks of silver and neon blue electricity shot through the fluid in the jars and made the three good old boys do another freaky little dance.

Some jealous and judgemental jive cats have suggested the yokels electric shock bogey routine resembled the soulful soft shoe shimmies performed by myself and my grassy groove child and all loving life partner Vincent down the local disco on a Saturday night.

'Back to matters at hoof I think human vermin,' demanded Cadmow.

'You go ahead fella, say whatever is on your mind, get it all out, express that inner turmoil good buddy, don't let us get in the way,' said Cletus.

'As I was saying, human vermin you have caused me pain beyond your feeble understanding so I am tormenting your world with wave after wave of chaos and destruction, using the unstoppable power of my glorious herd of Doomsday Daisybells,' gloated Cadmow as he showed images of terrified humans running from the destruction. 'Your world is being ripped apart and your kind, are running for their lives. Tell me human maggots how does all this chaos make you feel?'

'Well the thing is good boy,' began Billy Bob considering the images carefully. 'We are all country folk see and all the chaos, destruction and so forth you have shown us at least so far has been happening to snooty city types, so we only have a limited amount of sympathy. Considering how those big city slickers look down their snooty noses at us good, decent, hardworking sons of the soil, then maybe, just maybe those folks are just getting a bit of well-deserved payback, and sometimes that's a bitch ain't it just old son.'

The other two yokels nodded and muttered in agreement.

'I see human maggots, that is rather unfortunate,' said Cadmow sounding a little disappointed.

'And that's another thing boy,' said Jim Jam Jimmy. 'You're meant to be all twisted with bitter rage and furious hate towards us, for shooting and eating your good lady ain't that so.?'

'You understand the situation correctly filthy human maggots,' said Cadmow as the yokels shook their heads.

'That's the thing, you're all mad and all but the worst insults you can manage are maggot, filth or vermin, I mean last week Cletus spilled my beer and I called him a damn sight worse than a filthy piece of maggot vermin. My question to you is why you holding back son, get that rage out boy and for heavens sake use a few decent terms of abuse otherwise we aren't going to think you're all that bothered about the loss of your good woman and were perhaps thinking of breaking up anyway.'

'I can assure you human magg...' began Cadmow as the yokels folded their arms and treated Cadmow to a hard stare.

'Let it out proper boy, now go on let rip and turn the air violet if you feel the need,' said Cletus.

Cadmow began to open his mouth.

'Unless you want to let us fix you up with a new lover,' said Billy Bob. 'I mean a strong powerful bullish fella like yourself could have the pick of the herd, in fact I reckons you could have a whole field full, how about it boy a herd of young, pretty and umm frisky lady bovines all to yourself. Yes sir, there is some good loving to be had if you're ready that is.'

'It is too soon,' said Cadmow, it would be disrespectful to Mowlores memory. I should wait and torment the Earth creatures some more.'

'You need to get back in the game fella,' said Cletus. 'It doesn't have to be anything serious, just a little passion to distract you from the pain. Think of it as part of the mourning process.'

'I don't really know if it's time...' said Cadmow.

'It sounds like an excellent idea my lord,' said Moolock as he strolled into the room.

'Hell look its old hollo breeches,' said Billy Bob. 'How's it going fella?'

'I am well human, and no longer a hologram,' grinned Moolock flexing his hoof fist and tapping it menacing on Billy Bob's jar to make a jaunty but disturbing tune on the glass.

'Well it's real nice to make your more substantial acquaintance, I didn't catch your name fella,' said Billy Bob.

'Moolock, human but I am commonly known as neck cruncher.'

'Well it's mighty nice to meet you Mr Moolock, or do prefer Mr Cruncher, anyway I hope there ain't any hard feeling about last time we met and all. We thought the good lady Mowlore was a dangerous creature menacing our livestock, on account of us not having many talking bovines that walk upright in our local area, if you understand now fella,' continued Billy Bob nervously.

Cadmow bellowed a mighty yet disturbing laugh. 'Humans Moolock was just having a little joke with you; he was not really called neck cruncher.'

'Well now that's a relief,' said Cletus.

'No humans he was known as neck ripper by his enemies, isn't that right Moolock?' said Cadmow.

'Yes indeed my lord, but only briefly,' confirmed Moolock swishing his tail in a rather evil manner.

'Ain't you two a pair of right comedians,' said Jim Jam Jimmy.

'Yes humans and you should be grateful for our good humour,' said Moolock. 'We could be in a more serious frame of mind and be inflicting the appropriate punishment for your crimes and listening as your screams ring merrily through this base and around the moon. One of your mindless entertainments maintains that, in space no one can hear you scream, well they would certainly hear you three, all the way back to merry old mother Earth.'

'Ok, ok fella we see your point,' said Billy Bob.

'Now humans, back to matters at hoof,' said Moolock drawing up close to the jars in a most conspiratorially manner. 'Can you three truly find Lord Cadmow some female companionship to ease the mourning process? A gentle horn to numb the pain and a tender hoof to see him through these days that strain heavy on his heart, and if we are being honest cause him to make some very poor strategic decisions.'

'Absolutely no problem at all fella,' replied Cletus with a big grin and a lecherous glint in his eyes. 'I am personally acquainted with a number of highly attractive bovines that I am sure will please Lord Cadmow no end, he'll be quite literally over the moon, you know like the critter in the nursery rhyme.'

'Nursery rhyme, human? I am not familiar with this poetic form human, is it a form of epic poetry perhaps? Please explain,' said Moolock.

'Never mind fella, it's a more obscure type it's not important.'

'There you are my Lord this human can introduce you to some attractive bovines,' said Moolock. 'Why not let them take your mind of your grief and need to toy with these humans instead of snatching a quick victory.'

'I am not sure, Moolock, I am enjoying tormenting these creatures, they cannot beat us after all and breaking their spirit slowly will make them easier to control when we snatch final victory. There really is no rush; every moment of torment for these creatures is a glorious monument to the memory of my beloved Mowlore.'

'With all due respect Cadmow you are being a short-sighted fool,' said Moolock. 'Your delay in striking a decisive blow puts our victory in jeopardy. These humans are a creative and imaginative lot. They are dangerous, desperate creatures, delay too long and they will find a way to defeat us. Is this not right humans?'

The yokels nodded enthusiastically from their jars.

'For sure you only have to look to the movies for the truth of it,' said Billy Bob. 'Look at spy movies, alien invasion movies and even horror movies, the villain has the hero almost beaten but instead of pulling their finger out and finishing the fella off, they hang back with some silly countdown or long-winded killing contraption or they take a spell to spill all their secrets. The good guys always use the time wasted by the villain to turn things around and come up smelling of roses.'

Cadmow gave his General a dismissive shake of the head.

'I am sure all manner of ludicrous things happen in the human's mindless entertainment fantasies Moolock, these feeble-minded fictions are hardly evidence of the inevitability of some surprise human victory.'

'I got some A4 glossy photos of twenty real fine-looking local cows in my jacket, wherever you folks have stashed it, show it to the big fella, they may stir his blood a little,' said Cletus with glint in his eye.

'Excellent idea human, I will get them,' said Moolock hurrying away.

'Cletus, why do you have glossy pictures of cows about your person?' Billy Bob asked.

'It's just my new hobby Billy Bob, I am getting myself into photography,' said Cletus. 'Exploring my artistic side, it's good for the soul so they say.'

'Tell me Cletus,' began Jim Jam Jimmy, 'This new interest in photography wouldn't have anything to do with that granddaughter of Ma Bendle being back from university for the summer with those two friends would it?'

'I don't know what you're implicating Jim Jam, but whatever it is, it sounds like slander and it's a good job for you I don't hold with lawyers otherwise I would be discussing that slur on my good and upstanding character in a court of law. Probably sue for a whole wheelbarrow full of money, if you had any to start with.'

'I'd be careful with that Cletus,' said Billy Bob, 'Ma Bendle is very protective over her granddaughter and her cows for that matter.'

'You know something fella,' began Jim Jam Jimmy, 'I've always thought Ma Bendle's cows were a mite peculiar. They look at you kinda funny, I hope you ain't planning to introduce any of them creepy critters to old bull boy over there.'

As the yokels discussed the curious nature of Ma Bendle's cattle Moolock returned and proceeded to show a series of photographs to a suddenly wide-eyed Cadmow.

'Feast your eyes boy, feast your eyes, oh yes that's the good stuff right there so it is,' said Cletus giving a loud whistle as the other two yokels muttered about him being a weird freak of nature.

Cadmow turned the photos at various angles as he gazed upon the images. His mouth hung slack with desire as steam vented furiously from his nostrils. 'Moolock arrange for a large hay bed to be set up in the recreational area and then have these delightful females, brought up from the planet below as my personal guests of honour.'

'Indeed my lord, consider it done,' said Moolock with a grin as the yokels shouted and whistled their approval.

'Wait Moolock, the conquest of the Earth and the enslavement of the verminous humans,' said Cadmow looking doubtful.

'Leave it to me, my lord, I will crush the lowly human slime beneath my hoof of ultimate doom,' said Moolock as Cadmow raised an eyebrow and gave a bemused snort.

'I think you would be wise to both ease off the caffeine and stop researching those mindless human entertainments Moolock, we want to bring them to their knees with terror and destruction not with laughter as they mock our clown-like rambling,'

Well my deliriously delinquent dancehall dragonflies while Phil had been advised to keep out of the bitter bull lord's way, Moolock had monitored him closely for signs of treachery.

So closely had the General monitored Phil that he had become slowly drawn in to an obsessive interest in various forms of popular entertainment.

The bull general had secretly spent many happy hours absorbed by box sets of Star Trek, the Lucy show and the Magic Roundabout, the cow in the latter had apparently reminded him of his mother.

That cat was becoming a serious television junkie. He was just a few steps away from writing fan fiction scripts and submitting them for judgement by the fan community.

'But my lord researching their culture is a necessary tool that will help us gain the knowledge we need to control them much easier. Besides I only have five or six more box sets to finish all the shows I am following, if I don't watch then I will never know how they end,' said Moolock

'We don't need knowledge of their primitive cultures at all Moolock, any culture they have will cease to exist upon our smashing of their civilisation and it will be replaced by our superior culture which they will learn to serve, quickly if they know what is good for them.'

'That Phil is a bad influence upon you Moolock, maybe you should monitor him and his entertainment addictions a little less closely.'

Chapter 7. The sound of cowbells in the morning.

Well man with that old crater botherer Cadmow being distracted by his midlife crisis and twitching loins old Moolock took the opportunity to intensify his campaign against the already weary human race.

In the office of President Belinda .L. Walstan formally Senator Walstan of Texas (the beef head state) and now the first female president of the United states of America, whose election tagline had been, why not try a sane president for change, a disturbing piece of film was being shown to the group of senior advisers and head of the military, General Cross.

The footage showed the entrance to a highly fortified military installation near a major city in the sunny but ever so slightly battle-weary state of California. Standing outside the gates of the base, wearing a cowboy hat and a western style gun belt, was the base commander. He stood proudly looking out to the horizon, a gun raised in one hand and a white-hot branding iron in the other.

'For heaven's sake sir, come in, this is madness,' pleaded his second in command Major Browne, as she tried to guide the man back inside.

'No way in hell soldier. I am sick of hiding away; I am sick of retreat, retreat, retreat. If we fall back any further we'll fall of the goddamn world. Attack, we've got to attack it's the only way.'

'Sir we can't attack, we've got nothing to attack with, look there are cows on the horizon sir and they look like the killing kind, come in before they see you. They're serving warm apple cobbler with three flavours of ice cream in the mess tonight, you wouldn't want to miss that would you sir?'

'I'm not hungry Major,' replied the commander gazing into the distance as the Daisybells began to snort and stamp at the earth.

'It's western night sir, we're showing a John Wayne double bill, you like them sir, come on you can keep your gun belt and cowboy hat on sir and I promise no one will laugh this time,' said Major Browne watching the Daisybells as they lowered their heads in a pre charge mode.

'We need to show those animals what we're made of, Major, I won't skulk away any more, I'm going to attack them head on. I am going to brand those cows, and brand them good with the mark of freedom. I fashioned the brand myself, Major, do you like it?'

'It's a lovely brand, Sir, so very shiny but this is crazy talk, you'll be killed sir, come back in while you still have time.'

'No Major, I figure the stalking horse of death canters through all our paddocks sooner or later. At least this way I choose when he comes to my apple tree of life instead of a herd of farmyard freaks. I'm going to brand those mooing sons of bitches good, if it's the last thing I do, damn it all.'

With that the two soldiers saluted each other and glanced at the Daisybells. They wished each other good luck. The commander ran towards the killer bovines, his head held high and glowing branding iron pushed firmly forward.

The Daisybells kicked up huge quantities of dust. As the Major looked on still saluting, the dust and the glare of the setting sun obscured the fate of the base commander. As the herd of doom raced away one of the cows appeared to bear the raw hot mark of newly branded flesh. The Major thought she could hear a wild yee-har on the hot desert wind. 'You got em sir, you got em good, real good,' she whispered before slipping back into the relative safety of the base.

As the film stopped the President cast a concerned look at General Cross. 'General, tell me this incident is a one of freak occurrence?'

The General looked grave and ashen faced as he shook his head. 'I am afraid not Madam President, incidents like the one we just witnessed are happening everyday. Stable reliable commanding officers suddenly going off the rails, engaging the Daisybells one on one, we have had some dressed as bullfighters, pantomime cows with bombs attached to their udders, others going out wearing nothing but boots and a hat their lassos whirling in the breeze, that is not a film you want to see.'

'Have you selected a replacement for the commander, General,' asked the President?

'We've decided to go with Colonel Twirl, Madam President.'

'Twirl, General, are you sure? Isn't he meant to be rather...' began the President raising both eyebrows.

'Bat shit crazy, yes Madam President he is.'

'I was going to say eccentric, unconventional and unstable General. Haven't we got anyone more reliable and less as you put bat shit crazy? I heard he camouflaged a helicopter with giant inflatable cow to confuse the enemy, is that really the best strategy we've got left?'

'Madam President, at the start of this crazy moon cow madness we had all the sane, competent and stable officers you could hope for, and you know what, every last one of those upstanding commanders ended up running around in nothing but boots and a cowboy hat trying to rope, brand or milk a Doomsday Daisybell while loudly expressing their appreciation for the sound of cowbells in the morning. I think perhaps we need someone who is a little less conventional and a little more bat shit crazy. Yes it is true about the helicopter, but he had that a long time before those damn moon cows showed up. He was a UFO freak back then, he used the Moo-copter as he calls it to try and lure aliens. He wanted to capture a saucer so we could reverse engineer it. He drove the conspiracy theorists crazy, in fact if I remember rightly that's why we promoted him in the first place. It crashed every single conspiracy website in the country, even those we had set up to keep the new world order botherers busy.'

'I'll leave it in your capable hands General; hopefully an injection of eccentricity will help us turn a corner in this war. We certainly need something, up until recently they seemed to be just toying with us but now they seem to have turned up the heat, I get the distinct impression they are just about to go in for the kill. I hope you are going tell me I am wrong General.'

'I wish I could Madam President,' said the General, 'But I am afraid the joint chiefs concur with you. These murderous moon cows aren't playing games anymore.'

'If it's really that bad, General, maybe it's time to use the nuclear option again,' said the President. 'I know it's extreme but if we have no other options, better nuked than slaves to evil mooing moon cows.'

'That's another thing Madam President; the moon cows have nabbed our nukes.'

'What all of them even the black ops stuff you Generals think I don't know about?'

'Every single one, it's not just us. Our agents are reporting missing nukes in almost every country that held them.'

'Almost, General, is the exception India by any chance?'

Now my little milky moon moppets you need to realise these were desperate, paranoid times. Folks lash out in all directions when they are threatened, in those dark days scapegoats and the shadows of moon cow collaborators were spotted at every turn. A lot of negative vibes were being directed at the good people of India partly due to their historic respect for the bovine species and also because they were brown-skinned humans from far away. Crazy preachers had claimed they had a pact with the devil to bring chaos to the Christian world using herds of demonic bovines. Right wing political commentators called them traitors, often demanding they be nuked.

There had even been anti-India marches by all kinds of hate groups all over the world. Many folks claimed Cadmow had gone easy on India in exchange for their collaboration. Well I have not seen any evidence of that, groove cats, in any of my investigations. Sad to say the stigma of these claims hang over India even until today. It's a heavy and uncool situation. I don't know about the nuke thing, certainly no country in the world actually came out and openly said they had lost their nukes, no one announced it on the news or anything.

Some conspiracy cats say these days the whole stolen nuke thing was cooked up by military around the world as an excuse to invade India. They have a lot of cool stuff other countries want, just ask the British, India made their stiff upper lips go all a quiver with colonial excitement back in the day.

'It is indeed, Madam President,' continued General Cross, 'their apparent continued respect for cows seems to mean the moon cows have left them with a full arsenal of nuclear weapons. The Chinese are massing troops on the border and the Russian forces are already attacking northern India, even the British have attack ships on the way. We have forces on the way ourselves, permission to invade India Madam President, with maximum prejudice.'

'Permission granted General, we need those nukes, we are the leaders of the free world and we should have full custody of any nuclear weapons they have, if they are both members of and even more importantly loyal to the free world and our battle with the bovines they will hand them over without a fight, either way we are getting those nukes, is that clear General.'

Um yes I know what you're thinking, was this woman really the sane choice? Well groove cats all I can say is, you should have seen her opponent Congressman Samuel glory banner patriot Millington the seventh was a real piece of work. Remember he deployed a vicious attack ferret during all press conferences and debates that would latch on to anyone who disagreed with the gentleman and usually cause life changing injuries. His main polices had been building a wall around the moon to keep aliens out and looking for coal and oil on the moon which he assured any detractors that the good lord would have put there for America to find. He also had a strange grudge against the science fiction community who he felt could not be trusted due to their apparent love of aliens. 'When the aliens come whose side will those sci-fi crazy space cadets with their fancy knowledge of computers really be on? Will it be ours or those Martian invaders?' That was just for starters groove cats.

'Clear as a Canadian mountain stream, Madam President, we'll nab those nukes and blast those moon cows straight to hell, where they belong,' said the General.

'Thank you, General, you have my full confidence. And now I have an appointment with another dangerous enemy baying for my blood, it's the two pm press conference.'

A short time later the President stood in front of an army of press shouting questions but above the melee of voices one rang louder and clearer than all the others. 'Josephine Barnstorm ferocious ferret news, Madam President is the rumour that you have been negotiating the surrender of the human race with these murderous moon cows correct?' said Ms Barnstorm while elbowing a couple of eager reporters subtly but effectively out of the way.

'No Ms Barnstorm, as I have said before there are no plans to surrender, we will fight until the moon cows are beaten,' said the President trying to attract questions from a different quarter, but Josephine Barnstorm was having none of it.

'Madam President, considering the increasing amount of killer cow attacks, your promised victory over the moon cow menace seems to be nowhere in sight. Do you think in hindsight ignoring the proposed plan by senator Millington in the Presidential election to build a great space wall around the moon to keep alien invaders such as these killers moon cows out, was a mistake?'

'Let me make it very clear, we have a plan to achieve complete and total victory. As for the weasel-loving senator Millington his big headline policy idea of building wall around the moon was simply insane and would have done nothing to deal with the current situation. The American people were fed up with one lunatic president after another, promising crazy, unworkable dreams and only delivering inflated egos, massive half-baked and half-finished monuments to folly and delusion. I am glad to say the glorious American people finally saw through all the flimflam and choose sanity. And it's that sanity the world needs at this time of crisis.'

Josephine Barnstorm carried on despite the President's attempt to make eye contact with any other member of the press core. 'Yes Madam President, in your campaign you did make a big issue of the idea that you were the sane choice, what was your slogan again? Let's make America sane again, wasn't it? Perhaps we would have been better of with a bit of eccentricity and some creative victory- based solutions considering how badly the war is going. Your opponent has said you should be shackling domestic cows to buildings and vehicles as a sort of bovine shield, after all the relatively small amount of attacks in rural cattle-raising areas, which suggests the mooing maniac Cadmow is reluctant to attack his own. Your opponent also has put forward a plan to congress for every cow and alien-loving science fiction geek to undergo loyalty checks in order to make sure they are not planning to go over to the moon cow side if they are promised extra hay and an extended lifespan. These checks would naturally need to be extended to those who refuse to eat the flesh of cattle such as vegetarians and especially vegans who won't even milk a cow lest they cause a murderous daisybell distress with their cold hands.'

The President rolled her eyes. 'Ms Barnstorm the gentleman whose lunatic ideas you are so keen to promote wears a savage attack ferret upon his head at all times which he has trained to attack anyone in his vicinity who dares to either criticise him or ask a question he doesn't like. I still have the scars Ms Barnstorm. Do you know what the man did when I made a formal complaint about his attack ferret latching on to my throat? The delightful man you are so keen to promote sued me for violating his constitutional rights, trampling on his freedom of speech and damaging the fur of the vile animal with my arterial blood. So no in answer to your question, no I will not taking any policy advice from that individual. It's going to be sanity all the way and that is how we will triumph in the present crisis like we have triumphed in so many before.'

'That is very interesting, Madam President, but one has got to ask if you are so committed to sanity as the way forward why have you just put a man who has spent most of his military career riding around in a giant, cow-shaped helicopter trying to find flying saucers in order to lure little green men, in charge of a strategically important military base. I think the American people would be intrigued to know how that promotion fits in with your policy of making only sane policy decisions especially in the light of the fact that the man you have been so keen to denigrate actually agrees with your decision to promote Colonel cow-copter Twirl.'

'I take it your network supports the decision as well, Ms Barnstorm,' said the President. 'It's wonderful to have your support, now does anyone else have any questions?'

Chapter 8 : Golden Horns

Back on that high-in-the-sky-bad-trip-marsh-mallow moon station things were getting freakier and freakier my funky little tentacle teasers. Yeah ain't that the ever cud munching truth.

A small herd of ordinary but I am told very physically attractive Earth cows waited in line to entertain Cadmow who seemed to be going through some sort of midlife crisis judging from his silk, ill-fitting kimono, dragon sandals, funky red and gold satin boxer shorts and an excessive greasiness caused by way too much tail and horn wax smothered generously across his entire body.

Now take in that freaky picture, breathe in its musky incense blooms deep, oh so very deep my little knickerbocker Glorianas.

That sticky, silky, saucy bull lord sauntered round the control room, eying the queue of apparently eager bovines. Caressing his right horn in a way he hoped signified youthful virility and beckoned one of the bovines towards him.

'It's Buttercup isn't it?' said Cadmow as she moved forward battering her eyelids and mooing softly.

'Why don't we go and smooze a while, in my private room, the hay is fresh and oh so fluffy,' mooed that misogynistic bull lord winking as he knocked the ash from his pipe.

As Cadmow led Buttercup through a nearby door, that shameless sycophant Norhlick leapt between the Bull lord and his new lady friend.

'May I be of any assistance my lord?'

Cadmow snorted with frustrated irritation. 'Yes, Norhlick, you may get us some refreshments and a pot of fresh extra greasy tail wax', Mooed Cadmow snorting in an excited manner.

'Of course my lord, and the other ladies do you want them to wait in the pleasure cave?'

'No Norhlick I don't think so,' said Cadmow glancing over at the queue of cows. 'Give them all half a bale of hay and return them to

Earth, with my thanks. I have found my lady and she is all the cow this bull needs.'

With that Cadmow took his lady into a nearby room slamming the door in Norhlicks face.

As Norlick led the rejected bovines out the yokels began to chat.

'Hell, that critter is almost as creepy as you, Cletus,' said Billy Bob, 'I think you might have led that fella astray.'

'Well at least he is away from trying to electrocute our butts every two minutes,' said Jim Jam Jimmy, 'although I am glad he hasn't taken a shine to any of my cows.'

'Don't you be disrespecting old golden horns over there, that fella is our ticket to fame and fortune I reckon,' said Cletus.

'What are you talking about, Cletus,' said Billy Bob, 'you been licking that funny coloured lichen off the trees in Ma Bendles wood again?'

'Listen fellas, it makes sense I mean when America beats these crazy cow critters, we will be hailed great American war heroes. We shot one of the critters, were taken prisoner and suffered all kinds of torture and we resisted giving away any information about Earth's defences, mainly on account of us not knowing anything but that detail is by the by. They'll want to pin big old bovine busting hero medals on our chests have us telling our sweet tale of freedom on every network, they will be lining up to pay us millions for public appearances. Hot models will be fighting each other for the chance to give us sweet, sweet kisses. Umm yes heroism and being filthy rich are the biggest aphrodisiacs you can get, and we three will have pickup trucks heaving with both.'

'I hate to say it but I think you might be on to something there, Cletus,' said Billy Bob. 'We should be able to turn this to our advantage if we play our cards right.'

'Well if it works out the way you two thinks I reckon I will dig out my good old boy banjo and have myself a hit record,' said Jim Jam Jimmy. 'I'll call it; all-American cow killing boy.'

'Who the hell is going to want to hear you sing, Jim Jam?' said Billy Bob. 'Unless they wanted to empty the bar at closing time, then I guess a Jim Jam banjo serenade would clear that place in record time.'

'Ain't that the truth boy,' said Cletus and as he shared a howling burst of laughter with Billy Bob.

'I'll show you fellas,' said Jim Jam Jimmy getting real indignant. 'I will do one of them charity records, and then everyone will have to buy it so they feel better about themselves.'

'Hell, you're not thinking of doing it for one of those crazy liberal socialised charities, is ya? Those loonies would use the money to replace the all-American statue of liberty with some wack a loop French revolutionary symbol or some such thing,' said Billy Bob.

'No way, Billy Bob, I plan to support the good old Gun Strokers of America.'

'I don't think that is an actual charity, is it?'

'Well if it ain't it darn well should be,' said Jim Jam Jimmy. 'Perhaps I will use my influence as a super rich war hero to make it a charity if it isn't already.'

'You want to do it for one of them fluffy critter charities,' said Cletus, 'it would get the young uns pestering the hell out of their folks for it, you'd sell a million, despite not actually being able to sing or play, in fact with the wonders of modern technology they can even make you sound good, although I guess you have to push it to the limit for that kind of acoustic miracle.'

Phil and Norhlick walked through the command centre, loaded down with trays of tea, biscuits and extra silky tail wax heading for the room occupied by Cadmow and Buttercup.

'Hey there, fellas,' shouted Billy Bob, 'if you've got any of those cookies going spare, head them in this direction, we could do with something to chew on, being trapped in these here jars is giving me the munchies something wicked.'

'They are not for the likes of you, human,' snorted Norhlick, 'they are for my glorious lord Cadmow and your vile attempts to distract him with pretty faces will be discovered and you will pay the ultimate price.

Norhlick glared at the three yokels and slipped through the door leaving Phil shrugging his shoulders at the three men in their glass jars.

'What's got his knickers in a twist?' asked Billy Bob.

'He is jealous guys,' said Phil.

'Is that right?' said Cletus. 'What exactly is he jealous of now?'

'He is jealous of all those cows you persuaded Cadmow to bring here. Being a bit of an arse licker he was used to being the centre of attention,' said Phil leaning against the jars. 'Now all old bull boy can talk about is Buttercup, Daisy, little Mooing Mary, Fancy-free or Bluebell and old bitter Norhlick isn't getting any attention.'

'Oh yeah, little Buttercup, she is a bit special ain't she!' said Cletus, to splutters from Phil and the two other yokels.

'Cletus, what the hell is wrong with you,' said Billy Bob. 'Buttercup is a cow for heaven's sake.'

'That don't mean she ain't a pretty little thing boys,' replied Cletus.

'Well anyway, you three have made a bit of a dangerous enemy in that one, watch your back if you know what's good for you,' said Phil casting a bemused look at Cletus.

'Much appreciated, fella,' said Billy Bob. 'Now while we got you here, Phil old buddy, while we are all being friendly like, lets all four of us get our story straight for V.O.T.M.C day, shall we.'

'V.O.T.M.C day, what the hell is that?' said Phil sounding bemused. 'Victory of the moon cows day? Earth ain't lost yet fellas, have a little faith in the human spirit, we'll win you just wait and see.'

'Now there boy, you getting this all wrong,' said Billy Bob wagging a finger at Phil, 'VOTMC is, victory over the moon cows day, we think humanity will win the day as well, but we need to make sure our stories make it clear we are all prisoners of war and heroes. We certainly don't want anyone getting no funny ideas that we did any collaborating with the enemy, because that kind of talk is real dangerous, as it can lead to totally the wrong kind of publicity all together and no fortune at all. It could lead to treason talk and one-way visits to very terminal chairs for us. Are you on message as the city slickers say, Phil?'

'No problem guys, I am on board all the way, after all we lunar war heroes have got to stick together right. I can see it now they'll hail us noble warrior star heroes. We'll be the incarcerated crater crew, the funky freedom four, the quartet of marvellous moon marauders...'

'Okay, nice to hear you're on message but don't get carried away there, fella,' said Billy Bob. 'That kind of rambling freaky, geeky talk could blow our cover if you're not careful.'

'Understood over and out good bud skis,' said Phil with an exaggerated wink and thumbs up, that made the three jar dwellers groan and roll their eyes. 'If anyone's going to blow our cover it will be that Norhlick, he a real sneakasaurous. The good news though is that Moolock on the other hand really likes you three. He thinks you're idiots but useful idiots, so that's something isn't it?'

'Moolock thinks we are idiots? Well of all the ball- busting, cotton picking, raccoon racing cheek,' began Cletus, 'I'll show that arrogant son of bobcat snake charmer who is an idiot when I get out of this glass jar so help me Texas Pete.'

'Hold your horses there Cletus,' said Billy Bob, 'if old moody Moolock thinks we are idiots then he won't see us as a threat to him, and that can only be a good thing from the point of view of our future survival. I am a bit surprised to hear Phil here say the fella likes us though, ain't he still pissed about us killing Mowlore and everything.'

'Well I was chatting to a couple of the cow commanders they woke from suspended animation,' said Phil looking around conspiratorially before leaning against Billy Bob's jar. 'They were saying that Moolock and Mowlore did not see eye to eye when it came to strategy in the big bovine civil war that old Cadmow started back on the bovine home world. A civil war that they lost and which ended up with them being imprisoned in suspended animation and causing us all kinds of trouble, if only the cow rulers believed in the death penalty we wouldn't be in this situation.'

'Is that right,' said Billy Bob, 'I am guessing back in the day old Cadmow went with the guidance of his lady friend over that of his top General and now old Moolock is trying to rectify that situation by grasping the reins of power while his boss is distracted by buttercup, bluebell and this whole midlife crisis the top bull boy is going through right now.'

'I don't know why folks call it a crisis,' said Cletus, 'I see it as a wonderful midlife opportunity.'

'You don't know why they call it a crisis, Cletus, did you see the kimono that critter was barely wearing? Then there was all that greasy tail and hair wax, talk about mutton-beef dressed as veal, boy, that bull looked a positive tragedy and no mistake,' said Billy Bob.

'And what are you four hornless sapiens conspiring about?' said Moolock entering the room with a jaunty grin and wicked glint in his eyes.

'We were just discussing that sneaky Norhlick fella,' said Billy Bob. 'He keeps stomping around shooting us evil looks because he ain't getting enough attention from the big boss now that he has got a few lady friends.'

'Yes Norhlick is much like the spoilt and needy calf in his manner, his family were of the meadow clan so I suppose he was spoilt when young and expects a rewarding lick up on the head for every little moo he utters,' said Moolock heading to the command station.

'Yeah big fella, we kind of figured that bit out ourselves,' said Jim Jam Jimmy. 'The question is, is he dangerous, might he try and kill us of in a fit of jealousy.'

'That is a distinct possibility human,' said Moolock rather casually. 'He will probably do it quick and sneaky from behind, in your sleep so you won't give him nightmares with your gurgling screams of terror and pain.'

'Yeah well what is you going to do about it?' said Billy Bob, 'I mean you wouldn't want any harm to come to us now would you?'

'Human let me assure you, if the snivelling weasel attempts to kill you, I will do nothing at all except, perhaps, insist he clears up any mess made by your bodies as they ooze out their rancid life juices. I refuse to have the strategic execution of this war be disrupted by distracting odours and unfortunate stains,' said Moolock.

'Well that's just charming ain't it, after all we did for you and the boss fella as well,' said Cletus tapping on the inside of his jar as Moolock turned to the communication screen which showed an image of a great battle in progress.

'And stay out,' screamed the enraged voice of Cadmow, as the door to his rooms suddenly opened and Norhlick flew through the air before landing at Moolock's feet.

'But my lord, I was only trying to assist Buttercup in oiling your glorious lower hooves, her technique could do with some improvement, I only wanted to help,' said Norhlick looking pleadingly the door to Cadmow's chamber of pleasures while making extremely rude gestures towards the jar bound trio.

'That is truly, truly tragic, man, truly tragic,' said Billy Bob, to mutters of agreement from the other humans.

A short time later the silky bull lord slithered into the command room, the tight-fitting dragon embossed dressing gown straining against his greasy stomach as he performed a series of stretches that he had been assured by an excitable older human on the internet would keep him young and virile just as the jars of potent bull wax apparently would.

Removing the large cigar from his mouth and blowing the most glorious blue smoke shapes into the air he approached his top General. 'I hope this is important Moolock, I was busy tending to my lady's needs if you catch my drift.'

'My lord, this is something you need to see,' said Moolock as the image of two groovetastic bovines appeared, yeah man it was me and that old disco dancing moo daddy himself Vincent mean martini Moochuckle.

'By Cowdon's rancid udders, where did those two freakish lunatics spring from?' said Cadmow both rude and more than a little blasphemous. 'They should be dead or still frozen in their boxes, who are responsible for waking them? I will have their horns for this.'

'It appears they have been awake for some time, and influenced by deviant human ways, they will have to be dealt with quickly,' said Moolock as both he and Cadmow drew close to the command screen.

'Oh yes Moolock they will be dealt with,' said Cadmow, 'but tell me, what exactly is it they are doing?'

'I believe they call it the funky chicken, my lord.'

'Indeed Moolock, and is this funky chicken usually performed on the battlefield?' asked Cadmow twisting his head to one side.

'Apparently so, it does seem remarkable effective, our Daisybells are struggling to cope against its strange gyrations and unnaturally hypnotic beat.'

Catch you on the flip side fry kits.

Chapter 9: Go to hell Daisybell

Apologies groove cats if the story seems to have jumped ahead a spell. Holly doing the funky chicken on a battlefield? Did a chapter drop in a wormhole or something? So let me rewind and tell you all about it. Stay natural and wild like a true funky nature child.

'Let me get this right,' said Jane, as we all sat round at our pad the night an enraged mob burned down the Astro Cat club, 'you want to build an army of disco dancing, kung fu fighting, rhinestone Elvis cow droids and then set them on the Doomsday Daisybells?'

'Sounds funkadelicly fantastic Holl's,' said my main bombastic bovine Vince giving me a supportive little hug. 'We can train them in the old abandoned dance studio down town.'

'How do we get the parts though?' said Jane, 'I don't want to sound like a negative Nelly but it seems really complicated to build all those robot cow things.'

'Don't worry Jane,' I said, 'we'll have a freaky scavenger hunt in the morning for all the parts we need. There must be loads of broken Daisybell parts all over the place we can use and Vince has that wonder welder kit I bought him two Christmases ago, to put them together. Don't be fooled by our wacked-out hippy auras Jane, we are both from an extremely advanced culture, we've got a few thousand years head start on you groovy little humans, at least from a technological point of view.'

We made a list of all the things we would need and headed off on a crazy search through the town, stopping briefly by the smouldering ruins of our old club to bow our heads and show reflection for all the good times with all the funk cats. A group of the drunken fire starters that had burnt it down and then partied in the ruins were beginning to stir from their angry slumber in the rubble so we headed quickly on our way.

A couple of days later the old abandoned dance studio was full of freaky dancing drones that an old friend of ours called Malinda, a genuine dance teacher and a strict one as well, was whipping into shape. Full-on fanatical choreography, you got to be professional about these things folks, no half measures in our academy of the androids.

'Watch out Jane, better take cover,' I shouted as another batch of drone heads flew across the room.

'You need to sort this detaching head thing out, before someone gets head bounced unconscious,' said Jane, ducking out of the way of one head while grabbing another and tossing it in my direction.'

'We could attach each head to long pieces of elastic,' said Vince, 'then use them as a medium range battering-ram and wacko weapon.'

'They would just get all tangled up Vince,' I said, 'we need to break out some of that super strength glue and get them stuck tight in place.'

'They need to be able to look around them, Holly; restricted vision would just make them less effective.'

'That's easily solved Vince man,' I said, 'just give them eyes that move around the head even lots of eyes like that creature in that old b-movie we watched the other week, thousand eyed terror from planet doom, or something like that.'

'Have you decided a venue for the big debut?' asked Jane as she picked up heads from around her and tossed them in my direction.

'Careful how hard you're throwing those things; you don't know your own strength, Jane. I have got bruises on my bruises crazy sister, save it for the demented Daisybells,' I said spreading out a series of maps on a big table.

'Snaps Ville Holls,' said Jane holding her arms up and displaying a few nasty bruises of her own. 'You didn't build any of them with soft heads.'

'Sorry about that,' I said.

'That's alright, as long it is in a good cause, now in the name of the funky Stella goddess and all of her sparkly space brats, where are we making our debut?' said Jane following me to the map table.

'Oh that's easy,' I said pointing at the map, as the others gathered round.

'Vegas!' giggled Jane, 'oh Holly you cheesy little moo cow, why am I not surprised.'

Two days later we stood out in the sun-blasted Nevada desert, the funky city of Las Vegas in the distance. Most of our merry band was far too hot for much in the way of physical activity. Our vast kung fu, rhinestone Elvis cow droid army was making up for our inactivity by doing a funky dance and merrily singing, viva cow Vegas, as we scanned the horizon for the enemy.

'You really have no shame do you, Holly?' said Jane laughing at our bopping moo bots.

'Neither shame nor pride Jane, just a blind love of the beat and feeling funky,' I said.

'Beside all this retro cool is just about to come back into fashion,' said Vince taking my hoof in his and rubbing his horn against mine. We mooed gently together as a wild dust cloud appeared on the horizon.

'Goodness I hope not,' said Jane, 'I don't think I could pull off rhinestones.'

'Look, Daisybells,' I shouted. 'Attention robo cats, time to teach those groove-less doomsday drones some new beats. It's dance class time, first lesson free, now by Cowdon the ever un-milked, charge!'

Those cats charged like there was no tomorrow, whipping up a groovy disco sandstorm. As they raced into the distance towards the Daisybells, Jane took my other hoof in her hand and whispered with pain-fuelled steel in her voice, 'Go to hell Daisybells.'

We had been brought up to speed by Jane and the others and it seemed we had lost a lot of friends in the moon cow attacks. Jane had lost a lot of people she was real close to. The fact that she still had faith in us despite everything that had gone down was touching. The fight back was very raw and personal to her that was clear so we felt obliged to get it right.

'Did you spot the names she has written on the dance bots?' Vince had said earlier. 'They are all the folks she has lost; some of them are our pals too.'

'This is for all the fallen, friends, family and folks none of us knew,' I said as we watched the battle and we all took a minute to think of those good folks lost beneath the rubble of the world.

As the dust of battle cleared we could see the desert littered with hundreds of fallen Doomsday Daisybells. The ones that remained upright chased their tails and snorted in confused disorientation as our robo Elvis bots danced around them, generating a funky-footed beat.

I guess that's when we must have all danced the Funky Chicken, to be honest I thought it was the Monster Mash, who knows groove cats who knows.

On that sweet and funky note we pulled back our robo moos, raised our flags of rainbow-unicorn peace and headed into town to celebrate. The press copters had been filming the battle so the population knew we had just saved their bacon when we came for the after party they were only to happy to accommodate.

'Let's go party,' I said as we all leapt aboard the robo Elvis bots and grooved right on into town.

As the party swung late into the night, four very large, oddly shaped humans mooed at us and lifted me and Vince up whisking us quickly away. 'Come with us traitors, Lord Cadmow wants to make a painful example of you both,' they said.

We struggled and shouted but our pleas were drowned out by the, oh so groovy beat of our very own party. If our celebrations had been restricted to inviting a few friends round for pizzas and box set fest we might have escaped the kidnappers but we are the cats we are man.

They pulled us down an alley and opened a vortex. Our kidnappers removed their bulky human suits revealing themselves as fully bovine. We were dragged through the vortex which sent us spinning around for a while.

Eventually we landed with a bang on a hard concrete floor in a vast warehouse full of hay and a fresh snorting army of Doomsday Daisybells.

The cow Generals who had taken us prisoner dragged us to face a huge view screen that took up the entire wall.

'Kneel before your lord,' said our captors as the screen flickered into life.

We shielded our eyes from the disturbing sight that flashed before us.

'Too much information, too much information man,' I cried trying to purge my delicate retinas as images of such freakish horror that could never be unseen, no matter how much eyewash and top-of-the-line therapy was applied, flashed before us.

'What are you two lunatics doing?' snorted Cadmow.

'You're blinding us with the depths of your midlife crisis man, we're too young and innocent to be exposed to such things,' said Vince.

'Expose is the right word too, I am scarred for life and I only had a brief flash,' I said feeling the need to speed-dial my guru teacher and my therapist for an afternoon of deep mind cleansing.

'Have you both got the mind fungus?' snapped Cadmow glaring at all before him.

'We might have now dude,' replied Vince.

'And the rest of you, why are you all turning away from the screen, look at your lord and master as he speaks,' snorted Cadmow in a cloud of furious red and black nostril smoke that apparently smelled of cinnamon and freshly baked biscuits as he addressed his loyal generals many of whom had hair standing up in alarm as they tried to avoid directly looking at the horror that lay before us all.

We could see Billy Bob banging on his jar for all he was worth, 'heavens to Bettsy big fella, shore that thing up for goodness sake, we can all see clear through to the promised land from here, and let me tell you it ain't promising anything wholesome and family friendly that's for darn certain.'

Cadmow rewarded Billy Bob with an electro blast before turning to General Moolock.

'Moolock, have these lunatics infected my generals with their madness? If so we will have to liquidate them all, to be on the safe side. Well Moolock what do you say?'

'My lord perhaps it would be for the best to close fully the front of the outfit you are wearing, for the sake of your own modesty and dignity as well as the emotional well being of the rest of us,' said Moolock pulling the kimono fully closed causing the rest of us to gasp in blessed relief finally released from the disturbing visions that had danced about our minds, at least until we all next slept when no doubt they would return as feverish night terrors.

'That's better man, you're really taking that midlife crisis seriously dude, I mean I didn't know they still made that shade of orange chest spray, well done for finding it though,' said Vince letting his eyes wander across to buttercup until I gave him a nudge.

'Don't be getting any funny ideas Vince man,' I said. 'That horn wax would be a nightmare to get out of the upholstery.'

'I wasn't thinking about horn wax,' said Vince more than a little defensively.

'Yeah, I know what you are thinking about and I don't want her on my upholstery either.'

'Silence you two, show respect before the great Lord Cadmow,' said a guard poking us both in the ribs.

'Yeah pretend he ain't wearing that funky dressing gown, or at least pretend the one he has on actually fits,' shouted one of the yokels from behind Cadmow until Norhlick silenced him with a snarl and a painful electro blast.

'How's it hanging man?' I said as Cadmow looked us both up and down like we were insects on his bar of soap only considerably less welcome.

'You're both supposed to be dead along time dead, instead you are not only alive but you are interfering with my plans for the domination of this planet. Your weird appearance and strange speech patterns suggest you have been tainted by the deviant human ways and this has been going on for some time. Explain your continued existence and give me a reason to let you live.'

'Sorry to bring you down with our continued existence man, but we were having such a groovy time hanging with the humans that we kind of forgot to stop breathing, its habit-forming man,' I said doing a funky peace swing while flashing a nervous to the max groove grin.

'If I let you two deviants live will you join with me and help me destroy these Earth maggots that have turned you both into whatever you both are, do you not want vengeance?' said Cadmow.

'We are cool with the humans man; they are good cats in the main. Stop attacking them man, live in peace and understanding with them. Although don't expect them to trust you straight away, after all you have been blasting their cities and that kind of thing can make a body a tad suspicious of a dude. 'You'll have to take it slow and perhaps rebuild a city or two. What do you say man? Are you ready to turn over a new funky peace pail of bovine kindness?' I said before me and my man Vince started into a totally far out rendition of, give peace a chance.

Despite the fantastic musical treat we had provided, not one of those cats lent us the applause it deserved. Philistine's man, that's what those dudes were to a bovine.

We were instead met with blank stares and total silence, despite us topping off our performance with a bow, which in civilised company would be a hint for a little polite applause at the very least.

'I will take that as a no,' said Cadmow with the front of his silk kimono finally under full control.

As Moolock whispered in that crazed cats ear a glimmer of joyous evil appeared in his eyes.

'Now I understand you two enjoy movies,' said Moolock.

'Yeah Moolock man, we try and get to the movies at least twice a week, one blockbuster and one art movie, it's about the balance, yin and yang,' I said.

'We got a full-on home cinema system in our pad as well man, with a little popcorn bot to sate our manic movie munchies on demand,' said Vince. 'It's crunchily, funky- luscious.'

'Well you're in luck because I have a little piece of film for you both to watch,' said Cadmow, 'but I fear you won't enjoy it as much as I did, oh well here you go.'

'I hope it's not one of those solar punk westerns because they really don't work. I mean steam punk westerns, fine but solar punk, I mean what are they thinking?' waffled Vince, he always witters on when he is nervous.

I dug the cat in the ribs and then the lights went down, but there were no popcorn bots, nothing sweet at all, no sir, just sour vibes, bitter all the way down.

The film showed a sleepy Las Vegas morning. Most of the revellers from our party still slept or stumbled about in a desperate search for caffeine. A few of our robo-elvis bots stood on guard but most wandered around aimlessly confused and uncoordinated without either myself or Vince to give them any kind of direction.

Most folks didn't notice the doomsday dust cloud or hear the rumble of hooves in the distance. The crazed death herd choked half the population with the sandstorm it whipped up before smashing down upon the city in a frenzy of death and destruction.

We watched helpless as the city that until a short time before had been a beacon of resistance and a symbol of hope crumpled into chaos and confusion before our tear- stained eyes.

Cadmow laughed as the dust finally settled and the degree of devastation was finally revealed.

'That is not cool man, what good has all that killing done,' I said as my heart and soul drowned in a sickening whirlpool of despair.

'War, what is it good for man?' cliqued Vince a bitter tone of desperation ringing in that heartfelt moo.

'Killing the enemy, imposing my will, would you like me to continue,' said Cadmow.

'No man we'd really like you to stop,' I said.

'It seems you have concern for these humans,' said Cadmow. 'With that misplaced affection in mind I will ignore the urging of my closest advisors and delay your termination a while. Allow you both to watch their suffering and perhaps feel their wrath as they blame all bovines for their weakness. Let you both contemplate your poor life choices.'

As Cadmow flicked a switch poor old Vince let out a sudden moo of pain.

'Awe man that hurts, like some sort of biting ice cream headache,' said Vince clutching his face.

'That my treasonous bovines, is the lowest possible setting,' said Moolock.

'Yes that is right,' said Cadmow flashing his General an irritated look. 'The highest setting is like a molten cattle prod being rammed in one ear and coming out the other side. It is as you might expect certain death.'

'Heavy,' I said feeling a bit of a migraine coming on.

'Yeah,' replied Vince, 'with the sugar plum fairy and a hungry goblin king dancing the fandango on top.'

'With this lovely little device,' said Cadmow petting and stroking the console like a wicked kid whose a new snake had just swallowed it's siblings pet kitten. 'I can detect your brain waves and either inflict pain or death. If you help these humans that is what will happen. I suggest you don't, I am only keeping you both alive in order to enjoy your suffering. When these humans are defeated you will die, unless they rip you apart before hand.'

'You're in for a nasty shock man. The humans are resilient, they will resist and win the day,' I said trying to look that sour cat straight in the eyes while calmly meditating on the full-on terror chill that gripped me like a million angry lobsters.

'You'll never live to see it,' said Cadmow, that crazed old glint dancing in his manic eyes. 'I will return you to that city, were you dared to challenge me. Those humans will see you and in their vengeful craving for blood they will attack you. Yes even those you called friends and allies will scream in fury for your hides.'

'It'll never happen man, our friends are loyal,' said Vince.

Cadmow shook his head and laughed. 'How innocent and naïve you both are. Not only will they attack you but in your last desperate moments you will lash out in rage and hate against them and all of humanity.'

As we protested this statement Cadmow sat back and stared at us while gently caressing the pain switch as if it was his lover's horn.

'Take them away,' said the loon bull, flicking harder at the switch.

As we were led towards a newly opened vortex a wild burning pain lashed at me and Vince which was so intense we stumbled to our knees.

'Don't forget, betray me and your agony will make that pain seem mild in comparison, oh and your deaths will be certain but not quick enough for you. You'll both fall to your knees and beg me to finish you,' said Cadmow as we were both dragged to our feet and flung roughly into the vortex.

'That cat hasn't mellowed much Holls,' said Vince as we span round in the freaky vortex.

'No, man and Moolock ain't learnt how to do the whole smile thing either.'

We landed tail first on a rubble-strewn, dust-swirling street surrounded by the twisted remains of the party and a heap of twisted, burning robo Elvis bots.

We dusted ourselves down and took a sickening stroll through the ruined streets in horrified silence, the destruction striking us both dumb. The devastation was compounded by the deaths of thousands of those who had headed to the city seeking refuge after our initial victory. A dark drizzling cloud of responsibility hung heavy on us that afternoon.

'I wonder if our friends got away?' I said.

'I hope so, Holls, I hope so,' said Vince not sounding very hopeful at all.

Turning a corner we spotted a crowd surrounding a news crew with Josephine Barnstorm speaking furiously into the camera. We hid in the shadows and listened to her and the angry chants of the crowd.

'Citizens of this great city thought they had found refuge, welcome saviours in their hour of need, when what appeared to be a renegade group of killer cows appeared to turn on and defeat an army of moon cows. They claimed to be on the side of humanity, they claimed to want to help. The good trusting people of America took them at their word and sought shelter here, believing they would come to no harm. That precious trust, that noble faith, placed perhaps naively in the word of these bovines was betrayed. It was a sneaky trick, a filthy mooing moon cow trap, revealed when as this city slept after celebrating its apparent good fortune. A hateful herd of deadly moon cows swept through this sleeping city betraying their sacred trust in the worst way possible. Rewarding hope with hate and trust with wanton death and destruction.'

We didn't know it at the time but they were flashing our photos across all conceivable screens be it phone, television, computer or giant electronic billboard with captions that were both unflattering and positively slanderous.

We trended on social media as you may expect dude cats fast becoming the most hated beings on the planet even inspiring an array of podcasts discussing how evil we were and how we should be terminated and the best way to barbecue us. Celebrity chefs across the word concocted stylish new sauces they thought we should be cooked in. Some even requested our hides for their fancy restaurants.

As the raving reporter started speculating about angry mobs hunting us down, we slipped quietly away.

We spent most of that day scuttling from blasted building to burnt out ruin trying to seek some sort of sanctuary from the elements and the angry faces of the humans trying to survive.

We wanted to help but the rocks and hateful words that were hurled our way by every human that caught a glimpse of us kind of put a dampener on our natural caring instincts.

As the day moved to early evening it was clear rumours of our presence spread throughout the city. The amount of corners we turned only to be faced with an angry crowd armed with pieces of pipe and barbecue sauce had increased to the point where no corner of the city was safe.

We ran frantically from place to place as two competing mobs surged from either side towards us. As mobs converged, we found ourselves terrified and cornered. Trying to protect ourselves we lashed out with our hooves and horns not caring who we hurt or how much damage we did.

'Get away you stupid humans,' I heard myself saying with desperate venom in my voice, and I realised we were doing exactly what that sour puss Cadmow had said we would.

As rage over took both us and the mob of desperate humans I am sure I heard Cadmow's cruel laugh tormenting us on the desert wind.

'Daisybells, they're coming this way, run,' shouted one of the mob leaders.

In the distance was a familiar dust cloud with a vaguely bovine aura thundering down the street towards us. What was Cadmow up to I wondered, trying to finish us off perhaps or maybe drive away the mob so he could continue mocking our distress another day.

The mob members had taken refuge in the nearest building and as we struggled to find safety all we met were angry clawing hands trying to drag us into buildings and not in a friendly wanting to rescue us way either.

Suddenly Vince started to drag me toward the Daisybells.

'What are you doing?' I started to say and then I heard it loud and proud.

'Is that, what I think it is?' I said following my bullish beau's lead.

'Yes Holly it is.'

'Thunder dome,' we both said together as the dust cleared.

Then we saw seven glorious robo Elvis ninja bovines riding fast towards our location and for some reason blasting out thunder dome from one of those funky mad max movies, sung at the time by the glorious Tina Turner, one of my all-time personal idols.

Each of the funky moo bots was ridden by one of our friends. The lead one had Jane standing proud in the saddle, lasso in hand, doing a damn fine impression of the diva of the dome herself. She has the hair to carry it off too groove cats.

'You folks looked like you could use some rescuing,' said Jane roping me up into the saddle behind her.

'Much appreciated Jane,' I said, 'but Thunder dome, really?'

'It could have been worse Holls,' said Vince as he was swept up by our crystal, aura- weaving friend wolf thorn (also known as kraken fruit between the autumn and winter equinoxes). 'She could have gone with steamy windows.'

'What can I say,' said Jane riding the bovine Elvis bots around the grasping hands and jabbing bats of the mob and on to freedom. 'I have taste and style and I can carry off a power ballad while riding an Elvis bot through a blasted ruin of a cheesy desert city.'

'That you can, Jane, that you can,' I said as we rode into the desert and towards the sunset, because Jane has class and is seriously obsessed with westerns.

'You know this riding for a sunset thing isn't half as sexy as seems in the movies,' said Jane putting her hand in front of her face. 'The sun is getting in my eyes something awful.'

Chapter 10: Picnic on Parade.

'Is that it, soldier?' asked Major Sarah Browne, staring at the whirling, almost butting object that headed towards them.

'Yes ma'am, that's the moo-copter,' replied the soldier, saluting nervously.

'Does it always have that tail soldier?' asked the Major as a figure from the hovering cow-copter opened the door and made its way along the body of the vehicle. 'What the hell is he doing now?'

'As far as I know the tail is just for special occasions,' said the soldier mesmerised by the figure of Colonel Twirl who was now shimmying down the rope tail that hung from the back of the hovering machine. 'I believe the Colonel is trying to make an entrance ma'am.'

'Yes soldier, but what exactly is he trying to enter, a fancy-dress contest?'

'I couldn't say ma'am, perhaps they are running out of colonels. I am surprised they didn't give the command to you,' said the soldier as Colonel Twirl leapt from halfway down the rope and bounded towards them.

'I'm probably a bit too stable and organised to be considered for promotion in these weird times, but I never said that soldier unless you want to spend the next two weeks clearing the battlefield of pat mines and I don't think anyone wants that.'

'Wouldn't dream of it, ma'am, for the record I think you're probably right.'

'Sir, Colonel, good to meet you sir,' saluted the Major. 'Welcome to our, I mean your base. Looking forward to carrying out your esteemed and totally rational orders.'

Colonel Twirl removed his feather-strewn hat and did a small bow before returning the Major's salute. 'Good to meet you Major. Tell me, private, does she always lay it on this thick?'

'Yes sir, she always creeps to the boss sir, if there was a land of the sycophants Major Browne would be its queen,' said the private as Major Browne poked him in the ribs.

'Remember those pat mines soldier?'

'Sorry, ma'am, I didn't want to lie to the Colonel, him being an officer an all.'

'Colonel let me show to you to your quarters,' said the Major. 'You can get the chopper put down on the helipad round the back, I'll radio the pilot.'

'No need Major, on either count. I won't be needing quarters I'll sleep in the cow-copter, if I need any sleep. The chopper stays in the air ready for action until we beat these damn mooing moon freaks,' said the Colonel marching off towards the parade grounds.

'Don't you want to come in and see the base sir?'

'No time soldier, we are losing this war and we need to turn things around ASAP,' said the Colonel still marching. 'Assemble the troops, Major; I have an inspirational and rousing speech to make. Then we have a plan to carry out, I assume you've read the briefing.'

'Yes sir, it's a daring and brilliantly original plan. I'll assemble the troops,' said the Major speaking into her radio.

'Don't over do it, Major, the plan is sheer demented insanity but it's the best shot we've got.'

A short time later on the parade ground, the Colonel and the Major inspected the troops. The soldiers looked weary, beaten down and dispirited until the Colonel pulled out his tickling stick and proceeded to make each soldier in turn giggle to a frenzy.

'That's it soldier, turn that frown around, winners laugh in the face of danger especially when victory is within sight, which it is today.'

'Are you sure this is wise sir,' cautioned Major Browne, 'tickling the troops could be construed as sexual harassment.'

'I'm not touching them soldier, just wielding a morale-boosting feather duster. It's a little trick I learnt when I was attached to special forces, trying to take down the yeti, very ticklish in the toe department those bigfoot let me tell you.'

'As well as being fictional, sir,' muttered the Major as the Colonel carried his instrument of advanced mirth along the line of troops.

As they moved along the row of soldiers Major Browne spotted one of the troops dressed in a cooking apron and wielding a mean pair of tongs as he flipped burgers on an honest-to-funkiness barbecue while singing the rude version of *food glorious food.*

'What the hell are you doing with that damn barbecue set soldier, this is a parade ground not a mess hall?' demanded the Major squaring up to the burger happy private who just grinned and kept right on flipping, burgers that is.

'Well ma'am I am aiming to cook up a few of them killer cows. I reckon we should get a fair few juicy steaks and burgers from them,' said the private licking his lips, before sliding two burgers into their buns and offering them to the Colonel and the Major, after applying mustard, onions and ketchup naturally.

'Soldier, you're crazy, get those things put away before the Colonel spots you,' shouted the Major.

'Did you want cheese on yours ma'am,' said the oblivious soldier waving cheese slices that he had pulled from his apron pocket in the face of the snarling red-faced officer.

'No soldier, I want you to take that cheese along with those burgers and place them firmly in ...' began the Major before being interrupted by the boomingly dulcet tones of Colonel Twirl.

'What's all this, Major, having a picnic on parade, are we?' said the Colonel sniffing with interest at the burgers but eyeing the cheese squares with deep suspicion.

'Ah Colonel, sorry about this sir. This soldier had the crazy idea of making a meal or two out of these killer cows. I've told him to put away his cooking kit.'

'Nonsense Major, this patriotic soldier has got the right idea. Cook these killer cows and show them who's boss. I want posters with this soldier and his killer cow steaks to go up all over the country; I'm going to get the television people to see this too. You're a true hero and a damn fine patriot soldier. You're going to symbolise the fight back against these Holsteins of hate soldier. Do you hear that, Major?'

'Loud and clear Colonel, I will alter my attitude towards this situation from crazy and undesirable to normal, positive and damn patriotic, with immediate effect sir,' said the Major with a salute to the colonel and a warning glance at the soldier with the cooking kit.

'Good, Major, see that you do,' said the Colonel helping himself to a burger and taking a quick picture, with the tagline, be a winner have a cow for dinner, for the social networks in vogue at that particular time of year.

'He's not even a member of the bloody catering corps,' muttered the Major under her breath.

Now my mellow groove weasels I think it is important to point out that as a bovine myself I no way endorse the eating of the flesh of my fellow bovines or indeed meat in any form. We cows are herbivores dude cats and really don't like it when folks try and munch on our juicy, succulent furry butts. I am simply reporting the facts as they went down at the time.

From that point on posters and adverts went up everywhere featuring the cooking soldier happily barbecuing beneath the American flag while a herd of nervous looking killer cows looked on. In some versions the soldier would fling one of the killer bovines onto the barbecue, as the cow mooed in alarm the soldier would put his thumbs up and say something like, 'umm tasty,' or, 'mmm that's one juicy moon-cow,' or 'eat for freedom.'

'Now soldier, I want you to pass out your patriot burgers so every soldier here gets one. I have an announcement to make,' said the Colonel munching his burger, minus the cheese slice which he still eyed with deep suspicion bordering on paranoia.

'Yes sir,' said the soldier, slinging a large tray of burgers onto his shoulder while saluting excitedly.

'And soldier I don't want to hear about anyone requesting vegetarian burgers or chicken for that matter, it's to be beef, beef, beef every single rib-wrangling time. I will personally court-marshal any soldier who mentions hot dogs, they are the Devil's junk food, my daddy taught me that, he was no liar, and I'll wipe the floor with anyone who says otherwise. Got that soldier?' said the Colonel, grabbing a megaphone.

'Sir, yes sir.'

The soldiers crowded around the Colonel and the Major in a semicircle. The Colonel stood on a moon-painted beach ball so he can see and be seen by all the troops. All eyes locked on the now gently rocking Colonel, all the soldiers expecting him to topple from his precarious perch but despite the constant wobbling he never did.

'That cheese you got there soldier, throw it all on the floor over here, I ain't touching it,' said the Colonel before pulling out his regulation firearm and emptying one clip and then another three clips into the pieces of cheese as they landed on the floor. 'Got you, you darn oily varmint.'

'It was non-dairy,' said the Colonel to the bemused front row of soldiers. 'I hate that hydrogenated, slimy son of snake skin salesman stuff. My daddy used to call it Lucifer's chewing gum, he made us take our own cheese to any burger joint that didn't serve the real dairy deal, a habit I have proudly kept up all my life. I always keep a pack of cheddar super strength with me, for emergencies you understand.'

'I think, we should get to the briefing sir,' whispered the Major.

'Right you are Major,' said the Colonel sweeping the gathered troops with a penetrating stare.

'Troops, my name is Colonel Twirl, I will be your new commanding officer until we have beaten these damn moon-cows. I know that these are doggone tenacious times, but you know I can remember my daddy telling me all about the cold war and fighting those darn commies. Well they were everywhere; they had reds in Russia,

Reds in China, reds in Cuba, reds in Eastern Europe, reds in Central America, reds in Hollywood, reds in the education system, hell darn it all there were even reds under their beds. Now I am sure none of you have found a cow under your beds. They say a critter is at its most dangerous when it's wounded and cornered. Up to now them bad bovine beasts have got us hurt and cornered. I say it's time for us to start getting darn well dangerous. In the coming weeks we will be kicking a whole heaping load of bovine butt, you can quote me on that dang it all to cat down creek,'

The soldiers cheered and saluted before chanting, 'Go, go Colonel Twirl, he'll get those moon cows in a whirl.'

'What's the plan sir, are we going to nuke the moon?' shouted one of the troops.

'Nuke the moon, nuke the moon, nuke the moon,' chanted the troops.

'No soldiers, we will not be nuking the moon,' said the Colonel, 'at least not for the moment.'

'Can we at least nuke Alaska, I swear it's looking at the contiguous states in a funny way, why does it only border Canada, are the American states not good enough for it?' shouted one of the soldiers.

‘Hawaii too,’ shouted another, ‘why is it so far away from us, does it think we smell funny or something? Strutting around the Pacific, all snooty like its volcanoes smell of rose water perfume, nuke it sir, bring it down a peg or two, nuke it real good.’

‘Nuke em, nuke em, nuke em,’ chanted the troops, until the Colonel fired a missile from his helicopter that destroyed a derelict building near the parade ground covering the soldiers with debris.

‘Simmer down troops, listen to the Colonel,’ shouted the Major.

‘Nuking either the moon, or anywhere else is at the President’s discretion, not mine, but we do have a mission, a dangerous and important mission,’ said the Colonel to positive murmurs from the assembled troops. ‘As you may have guessed, no one so far in this war has managed to capture an intact killer moon cow, we are going to change all that. We will be executing operation Milkshake, this weekend, I have got full air force and Special Forces support. We will be taking the fight to the enemy and turn this war around.’

The troops cheered as the Colonel continued. ‘A lot of you folks are going to get killed or at least seriously mangled and twisted under the hooves of doom before this thing is over, but your sacrifice will be remembered, at least for a few years. Now this Saturday we are going to kick a hell of a lot of bovine butt and get ourselves a killer cow or my name’s not Colonel Ebonies Twirl the third and you can quote me on that dang it all to cattywampus county.’

It was the day of the big battle, helicopters hovered in the sky with huge super strong nets hanging across the street in a large city. The moo-copter containing Colonel Twirl sat above the rest commanding operations.

The Major commanded forces on the ground as the air force lured a herd of Doomsday Daisybells along the road towards the nets.

The air support attacked the herd as it approached the nets and Major Browne's forces swamped and distracted the herd as it hit the nets.

Most bovines smashed right on through the nets, taking out troops and air support as they went. Other bovines who found themselves tangled inside the nets managed to open up strange vortexes and vanish through them.

One of the damaged Daisybells hovered near the entrance of a net as Major Browne's forces moved in, as the bovine was driven into the back of the net it lashed out frantically, catching the Major with its hooves throwing her far across the road.

As the Major lay stricken and unconscious on the hard concrete, the net pulled tight around the damaged Daisybell and carried the now stunned beast up high into the air.

'Pilot get that critter over to Fort Griffin, they're waiting for you,' said the Colonel before being interrupted by the radio.

'Colonel, sir it's Major Browne, she's down sir,' said the voice over the radio.

Inside a hospital room Major Browne lay unconscious, a mess of plastic tubes and plaster casts.

Colonel Twirl and a doctor stood by the bedside deep in conversation.

'What are her chances, doc, she looks pretty banged up?' asked the Colonel.

'To be honest, Colonel, they're not good at all. I don't know why she is still alive, with her level of injuries,' said the doctor. 'Quite frankly I doubt she will make it through the night but my team will do all we can.'

'Thank you doc, that's much appreciated,' said the Colonel before turning to the stricken Major.

Colonel Twirl stood at attention while saluting the prone form of Major Browne. 'I don't know if you can hear me soldier, but I just want you to know that you did a damn fine job today, you got us our cow against all the odds and gave us all a chance. You should be damn proud of yourself. I am damn proud of you. I've never met a braver soldier in all of my butt-kicking life. Thank you soldier you're a patriot and a true-blue American hero.'

A long moo-copter tail suddenly dangled in front of a nearby open window. 'See you on the flipside soldier, I've got a date with a manic moon cow in a secret desert locale,' said the Colonel before racing towards the open window. The Colonel dived out of the window and grabbed hold of the moo-copter tail, continuing to salute as he was borne away into the night.

Chapter 11: Holly and Vince go to Washington

'You can't build any more ninja robot Elvis moo-bots?' asked Jane for the third time as we sat around a large table at her uncle's ranch. We could hear the surviving moo-bots through the open window as they, mooed thank you very mooch.

'No Jane, Cadmow would melt our brains with his pain box, if we built anymore,' I said. 'You seem to control them pretty well though. If you're prepared to carry on the fight guerrilla style, with a hit and run groove, I am sure you cats are up to the job and would have our full blessing. When we find a way to block these pesky, molten-ice- cream-headache mind rays, then we'll be straight back in the fight.'

'Of course we'll keep up the fight,' said Jane. 'What about you guys, are you just going to go into hiding, laying low in the face of adversity isn't your style.'

'Hell no, what kind of bovines do you take us for,' said Vince.

Jane shot us a questioning eyebrow raising look.

'Jane we're going to do what we always do in times of trouble,' I said linking arms with Vince. 'We're going to throw a party, maybe we can't fight for the humans but we can at least raise their spirits.'

'We're heading over to Washington to liven up the big demo they've got on this weekend,' we said as we did the cancan around the room.

'No,' said Jane, 'you can't, they've told people not to go to Washington, there will be killer moon cows for sure. If you can't fight them then they could wipe you both out, and as the person who just rescued you I would not be impressed with you getting yourselves killed.'

'Don't worry about us Jane, we'll deal with the Daisybells when they turn up,' said Vince twirling me around the room.

'But you said Cadmow will kill you both if you attack the Daisybells,' said Jane.

'I know Jane,' I said, 'but Cadmow never said we couldn't dance with the Daisybells.'

'Dance with the Daisybells?' said Jane sounding more than a little bemused.

'Yeah we'll teach those bad bovines how to boogie on down,' I said snapping my hooves, to a disco beat that had been playing in my head since a week-long disco marathon I won in nineteen seventy seven. I still have that trophy and I framed the satin pants I wore for that as well, pride of place on our playroom room wall. Right above the super king-sized hay bed, for fun, rest and late night snacking.

'Holly, that's crazy,' said Jane.

'You say that like it's a bad thing Jane,' I said.

'I take it you're both, set on this crazy course of action?' asked Jane.

'We are indeed Jane,' I said.

'Well at least be careful,' we shook our heads at Jane. 'Ok if you can't be careful, at least be effective.'

'Oh Jane honey, we'll be effective, we're playing to our strengths after all. Partying is in our blood, the demonstrators and the Daisybells won't know what's hit them.'

In Washington the night before the big demo, we frantically put the finishing touches to our seventies-themed, funky-disco dancing, moo bots. Satin pants in seven garish colours that in some cases matched the trippy shades of their lowcut silk shirts. Shagpile thick chest wigs with a variety of large gold medallions added a nice touch of class to the look, as did the flashing rainbow, disco shades. You couldn't see in those old disco shades but that made sure you made lots of new, really close friends on the dance floor.

We took them through all the dance grooves as the television blared in the background. Josephine Barnstorm had been interviewing a series of would-be demonstrators ahead of the big Washington rally. For the moment she seemed to have met her match in the form of wide-eyed cult leader the blessed Reverend Fruit Bringer.

'But I'm confused Reverend Fruit Bringer,' began the reporter before being interrupted by the constantly nodding and grinning preacher.

'As are all sinners my dear, the whirl of demented debauchery that is your life, is bound to leave a soul dizzy with confusion. Let me calm you with a joyous chant to the heavens and a cool soothing hand upon your sinful flesh,' leered the reverend as he reached out a healing hand towards Josephine's knee.

'I'll take a rain check on that, Reverend,' she said knocking his grasping hand away with a firm swat from her microphone.

'As you wish my child, remember the door to my private cleansing sanctuary is always open. Now tell me what is the source of your present confusion? How to gorge on cake and still squeeze into a dress fit for a devil? Perhaps it's how to store all your shiny shoes of shame? Do tell my dear.'

'When the moon cows attacked Las Vegas, you described them as the Lord's blessed bovines destroying the city of sin and vice, for which America and the world should give thanks for their holy actions.'

'This is correct sinful, sister, it seems you have not yet been deafened by the sound of doom-filled rap'n'roll that drags so many young souls to fires of hell. I saw righteous burning halos surround those cattle as they brought destruction to that wicked place, and I said hallelujah, halleluiah. Does that resolve your confusion child?'

'No Reverend it doesn't, you see in the weeks before you said on several occasions that they were the work of Satan, you had even spotted six, six, six branded on their backs. Holsteins of hate straight from hell I believe you said.'

The Reverend turned a wide and demented grin to the camera staring at the audience for what seemed like an eternity.

'Reverend, Reverend, are you alright?'

Raising his long gangly arms to the ceiling and gazing blissfully upwards, 'I am beyond the earthly mocking calm of alright, for I am truly bathed in the light of revelation, for the lord hath shone me how after taking control of these bovine beasts of the dark one and using them to destroy the sinful city of vice, he in his glorious wisdom will now use them to wipe from the Earth the sinful city of politics and corruption that makes so many laws offensive to his eye. Washington, doomed city will fall and my congregation will bare witness to the glory.'

'Hey I was listening to that,' said Vince as I turned to television of.

'That's the seventh crazy in a row, and I'm bored listening to them,' I said giving the dance bots a final tweak. 'I think everyone there tomorrow is going to be as brain fried as a fruit bat in the batter mix and not in a fun, cheesy disco diva kind of way either.'

'I liked the old farmer with his dog,' said Vince remembering crazy number three, who had come as a blessed relief from the second one a rabid woman hater who linked killer cows with the supposed undermining of male identity and the raise of the latest feminist wave.

'Was that the one who wanted to round up the Daisybells using his dog Bella and that dangerous looking clack stick,' I asked trying to picture the dude through the blur of crazy attention seekers.

'Yeah I thought he was cool,' said Vince miming the clack stick with a little too much gusto for my comfort.

'His dog bit two of the presenters, it clearly had a taste for human flesh,' I said diving onto the sofa out of the way of Vince's flying hooves still clacking furiously and driving an imaginary herd of Daisybells around the room for all he was worth.

'Holly, I am sure they were just love nips, you know to show affection. Like licking but taking it to the next level.'

'Well, Vince, I just hope you never try and show me that level of affection, or I'll spray you with a full canister of super strength affection mace, in a loving and caring way you understand of course man.'

We made an early start the next day, so we could get the best spot for our dance bots to strut their funky stuff.

The police swooped in to check us out but when we explained our dance bots were rebel bovines dancing against the moon cows, the cops wished us well but asked that we didn't party too late as even politicians need their beauty sleep. Well we couldn't argue with that really.

Our groove bots boogied merrily in the main demonstration area as the various tribes of demonstrators filed into their allocated spots, proudly holding their banners of identity aloft in an act pride and defiance.

'It's been too long since the last one of these we went to man,' I said looking at the ever-growing crowd. 'We used to go to demos like this all the time man, what happened, did we lose our edge, Vince, did we do a soft shoe sell out? Taking it easy instead of sticking it to the man?'

Vince gave me a hug and a reassuring grassy nuzzle. 'No groovy sister we just got distracted by life, don't let your history boots make your heart heavy with might haves and placards not written. Just enjoy this one, I have a feeling it's going to be a doozie.'

'Yeah, you're right, Vince, let's just enjoy the day.'

We partied awhile with the moo-bop bots, our battered old, Make Milk Not War, banners held aloft until a group of distressed vegans rushed over asking us to make it clear the milk in question was soya or oat and definitely not from a cow. I politely waved my udders at them and pointed out that as a bovine I have a right to lactate should I want to. They apologised and left us alone.

All sorts of groups assembled; radical feminists pointing out the patriarchal oppression by Cadmow over the mainly female Daisybells. There were radical men's rights groups who seemed to think the attacks were a feminist agenda. Flat Earthers loudly declared the moon-cow attacks a plot by NASA to trick people into believing in the moon which they claimed was a giant hoax. Only lunatic believe in the moon was their most popular chant.

'You're Hitler you are!' yelled a left-wing demonstrator at a nearby group of far-right dudes.

'Yeah, so what if I am, I think he was right about things, well except moustaches, they are a bit weird,' replied his opposite number in the fascist camp. 'He's dead anyway so I couldn't actually be him, just shows how stupid left-wing people are.'

'I know Hitler's dead you stupid nazi,' replied the leftwing cat. 'I meant you're like Hitler only without the weird moustache, although those mutton chops and the goatee ain't exactly doing it for you. You're like Hitler come back reincarnated or something I reckon.'

'I like the sound of that, you commie idiot,' said the fascist dude. 'Me, Adam Odin Lee, the fuhrer himself, yeah hail me, hail me.'

'That's bullshit', said his colleague, 'you're not Hitler, if anyone is the fuhrer it's me, you are just a dickhead.'

'I could be Hitler if I wanted,' replied the first nazi before the pair began to fight. Within a few minutes all the far-right group were arguing about being Hitler until it turned into a nasty street brawl which the police had to break up.

We saw the farmer with his dog who seemed to just be biting people while its master waved his clack stick at our funky moo-bots.

We saw lots of regular folk as well of course including many close personal friends from demos of old and the protest community in general. Many of them were demonstrating against the recent invasion of India as you may expect groove cats.

'Drive the devil from them oh my children!' came the call of Reverend Fruit Bringer, who had just led his chanting cult into our vicinity.

His followers seemed less than entranced by the idea of encountering our gyrating mootastic groovebots whose raunch-circuits seemed to be set to overload.

'Come on my people, these wicked bovines are still tainted by Beelzebub we owe it to glory to cleanse them,' raved the reverend as he stared at the moobots moves in a distinctly lecherous manner. 'If you are too timid then I will show you the way.'

With that the reverend rushed forward, his hands outstretched into a band of our satin clad disco whirl bots. 'I will cleanse your sinful fur with hands of glorious light,' he roared grabbing one of our poor bots and molesting it with the religious frenzy of a self-righteous dirty old man.

'Keep your hands to yourself sir for I am not that kind of moobot,' shouted the moobot with a firm slap to the reverends face and a forceful knee to the groin before shoving him away.

Let me tell you funky word wranglers, when one of our groove bots gets physical you know about it. We built those mooing Mary's to protect themselves from any kind of unwanted attention, yes indeed.

The Reverend slunk back slowly and in great pain to his congregation.

'That wicked hairy harlot led me astray,' whimpered the Reverend looking pitifully at his people. They just shook their heads and looked disdainfully at this man who was constantly engaging in just this kind of activity.

We despatched the bulk of our bots out into the crowd whipping up a party atmosphere as we held back scanning the horizon for Doomsday Daisybells while trying to tune out the speeches of nearby gun advocates who wanted the right to bear arms extended to pigs, sheep and horses so they could help protect their masters' ranches.

As all this funky groovyness was going down, over in a nearby pale-shaded house the president and her teenage daughter were engaged in a bit of a heated debate on the subject of personal liberty.

'But mom,' stormed the passionate teenager, 'all my friends are going to it. Do you want me to be a social outcast or something?'

'Listen, you're not going and that is that. Apart from the danger of killer moon cows, every news channel is describing anyone consorting with dancing cows as traitors to America and deserving the death penalty,' said the President. 'What do you think the press would say if a member of my family was seen at a party attended by strange looking bovines? They'd say I was a bad mother and not fit to be President that's what.'

The girl pouted staring at the television that showed the demo-cum-party in all its funky glory. Then the camera focused in on a small detail which caused the girl to squee in excitement.

'Look mom, it's daddy he's at the party and he's dancing with that freaky moo bot. Go on dad get on down, fever out that funky groove.'

It was true the President's husband could be seen clearly dancing close and tender with one of our moo bots. Not only that groove cats, but due to the wonders of modern technology and the nosy nature of the television news industry every word he whispered softly in her ear could be heard loud and clear across the nation and around the world.

'Oh baby your fur's so soft and silky,' he began nuzzling the bot's neck and tickling its ear. 'You know I've never had a bovine before, would you do me the honour of being my first cow bot lover baby?'

'Oh god noo,' shouted the President her eyes transfixed by the slow dancing horror filling the screen.

'Well mom can I go then, if dad's there?' said the daughter in an impatient tone.

The President turned a disturbing grin on her daughter, 'of course dear you go to your precious party and when you see your father tell him from me I want a divorce and I hope he is oh so very happy with his new silky, milky moo tart.'

'Wow thanks mom, I knew you'd come round,' said the girl smiling and skipping of towards the door. 'I'll tell dad to sleep in that sleazy motel again tonight. He really likes it there.'

'Begin operation groove shield,' I told the bots as rumours of a herd of approaching Daisybells rippled through the crowd as party high fever shimmered and shifted into frenzied panic funk.

Our groove bots formed a protective wall of discoing divas between the nervous humans and the snorting, taunting Daisybells.

We turned up the music and pumped the air full of colourful smoke, silly string and sparkly golden glitter. Then the Daisybells lowered their heads, stomped at the ground and gave one final ominous snort and charged full whack at our glorious groovers.

'I can't look man, we put so much work into those outfits as well,' I said shielding my eyes as the noise of mooing Daisybells, disco cheese funk and screaming humans filled the air.

'Look Holls it's working,' said Vince giving me a nudge.

The Daisybells were in a serious funk, chasing their tails, confused and disorientated by the hypnotic beat and the mounds of silly string.

'I think all the glitter probably got in their workings and changed their primary objectives from pain to party,' said Vince.

'I always did love going glitter crazy man,' I said as a serious hand lay heavy on my shoulder.

'Holly the cow I presume,' said the scary assed special-forces dude standing suddenly at my side.

'That's my handle man, is there anything we can do for you security dude. Bearing in mind if we attack any moon cows old Cadmow will fry our brains, which is nowhere near as much fun as it sounds.'

'Yes we have been apprised of the brain ray situation by your comrade, Jane,' said the security dude, all business. 'How long can the hostile bovines be contained by your uniquely skilled forces?'

'Not long man; as soon as the glitter passes through their systems then they will be back to their killing ways. We need all these people evacuated quickly,' I said almost regretting throwing such a good party as people looked like they were having such a good time they wouldn't want to leave.

'I see,' said the security dude, displaying absolutely no emotion. 'Any thoughts on a quick and efficient way to execute that objective?'

'We could try, operation after party, man,' said Vince with a giggle and funky little jig.

The security cat turned his head slowly towards Vince, 'is that an attempt at humour son? I don't take kindly to the use of joviality, hi-jinks, satire, irony or any other kind of hilarity being used in any manner of situation especially a serious security one such as this, is that quite clear?'

'Yes sir,' said Vince as the security dude scrutinised him for any signs of mockery or nervous laughter.

'Actually I think Vince might be on to something,' I said grabbing a megaphone and giving Vince a nod.

'Come on folks you're all invited back to our place for a VIP after party,' I shouted as Vince opened a wide mouthed colourful swirling transit vortex and the partying demonstrators started pouring through leaving our disco bots and the Daisybells behind.

As we followed the crowd which included the security dude, into the vortex both myself and Vince were hit by a really nasty ice cream headache. We felt the voice of an irritated Cadmow warning us not to try this kind of thing again or we would find ourselves ground down to make a dance floor.

Chapter 12: Whip my Ass and call me Lucy

'Well whip my ass and call me Lucy, Professor,' boomed Colonel Twirl as he stood, with his hands firmly upon his hips, considering the snorting, butting Daisybell. The beast was held back by a force-field that shimmered and shuddered with every violent smash and ram from the enraged beast.

The Professor began to edge away from the military man who was suddenly brandishing his tickling stick high in the air.

'I would not feel comfortable with either of those suggestions Colonel,' said Professor Winkle eyeing the dancing tickling stick with some alarm. 'I am flattered but we should keep our relationship on a professional level and concentrate on the defeat of the moon-cows. Besides I am becoming increasingly fond of a firm-minded Scottish lady who has brought this lab and my heart under her control. At night I dream, but oh it is just a dream.'

Ignoring the Professor, the Colonel walked up to the furious bovine, its eyes glowing like red hot coals as it tried to use its deactivated laser weapons, and raised the fluffy tickling stick in anger and bitter grief. 'You robbed me of a damn fine officer today you mooing freak of nature, I aim to get you and your kind good, you hear me you bovine piece of rancid hydrogenated cinema hotdog cheese?'

The Professor came warily to the Colonel's side as he rammed the tickling stick again and again at the shielded Daisybell. 'Colonel do not torment yourself so with this creature,' said Professor Winkle slowly removing the tickling stick from the other man's hand. 'She is merely a mindless drone, with no desires or compulsions of her own only programming and some very advanced cybernetic military hardware. She is a puppet you might say. If you want revenge for your officer and justice for all human kind then we must reach the puppet masters. Then Colonel you can scourge these horn wielding moo-lords from the very face of the earth and our glorious moon.'

With that Professor Winkle and Mrs McDoon, who was listening in, began a maniacal laugh that went on and on while Colonel Twirl looked around rather uncomfortable.

Even the Daisybell stopped its frantic butting to stare in apparent confusion.

As the laughter died down Colonel Twirl considered the Professor for a moment before snatching back his tickling stick. 'Well Professor if it's the puppet masters we need to be going after, have you any thoughts on how we might get to them?'

The professor's eyes lit up and he beamed a smile so big and wild the Colonel was afraid that another bout of crazed laughter was about to erupt from the man. 'Indeed I do Colonel, indeed I do. If you will accompany me to my, glorious work bench of dreams, I will show you the wonders I have devised.'

The Colonel followed the Professor across the lab all the time alert and ready for further bouts of frenetic cackling.

'Observe, Colonel,' said the Professor activating a holo display showing a cow opening a vortex. 'the Daisybell transmits a signal when it wishes to return to a cow base, the base in question then opens a vortex allowing the bovine to return home.'

The Professor clapped his hands excitedly laughing at his own genius.

'Have you managed to locate these bases professor, because that would be real useful?' asked the Colonel getting rather impatient with the over-excited man.

'No Colonel, I have found a way to open our very own transit vortices so we can send our forces directly into the heart of the Holsteins hive of doom. Well at least some of them, a few are protected by secure passwords which we are trying to crack as we speak. If we only knew more about the foul Lord of mooing doom Cadmow such as his mother's maiden name or his first childhood pet fish perhaps. Could your intelligence people attempt to trick these details from him in the disguise of debating the best biscuits one and ones pet may have enjoyed as small children or as a calf in his case? It could be done I think.'

'To be honest Professor, I doubt very much if a twisted being like this Cadmow fellow even had pets let alone a first childhood one. Now when will the first of these transit vortices be ready for use Professor? My troops are eager to go into action and finish this war.'

'The first one will be ready by twenty-one hundred hours this evening with an additional one ready every two hours after that Colonel.'

'That's very efficient of you Professor,' said the Colonel with a flourish of his tickling stick. 'You are a tribute to the crazy-haired, wild-eyed scientist community.'

'Why thank you kindly, Colonel,' said the professor eyeing the fluffy instrument of tickle-dom with much weariness. 'I imagine you are keen to learn the secret of how I keep my hair so wild and crazy.'

'Not even remotely, professor, my father bless his soul, told me that people with long messy hair were all deviant socialised communists undermining our great nation, and their only saving grace was their bone idleness and total inability to actually organise the dreaded socialist revolution that they all dreamt of. I only tolerate your freakish foliage because you seem efficient, useful and the military have the good sense to monitor your every move all of the night and all of the day.'

The Professor shot the Colonel an enthusiastic and oblivious grin, 'well let me tell you it does not reach this level of wildness easily, simply not combing or washing the hair will not get you this mighty matted wilderness, oh no indeed it won't. I use a special mail order product known as jungle head it is formulated specially for the mad scientist community.'

Mrs McDoon rested a firm hand on the professor's arm, 'I don't believe the good Colonel is even remotely interested in your hair management routine, I know I for one certainly am not as I have mentioned more than a hundred and fourteen times and have worked hard to restrain the beating urge I feel in my being each time you mention it, maybe that has been a strategic mistake on my part.'

'Oh I am sorry my dear, I do tend to ramble,' said the Professor resting his hand on Mrs McDoon's, giving it a tender squeeze. He was rewarded with a tolerant glare and a fierce smile.

'I think you forget yourself Professor, I am a married woman if you remember. A fact I have mentioned on fifty-three separate occasions. Just because I hold no quarter with feminist types that doesn't mean I object to a strong woman quelling a rogue male's unwanted ardour with a sharp instrument to a tender spot. You know full well the spot I mean. That is often the only way to rein in the feral beast that is man's rampant lust,' said Mrs McDoon pulling her hand sharply away.

'But Mrs McDoon your husband passed away many years ago, surely you are ready to find love and tender cuddles once again, life is fleeting and we should grab what joy we can. Besides does it not say in the marriage vows, till death shall you part? Your husband's sad parting means you are free to love any tender-hearted, mad-old professor your warm heart beckons you towards.'

'Professor Winkle I sometimes think you are a man with a death wish,' said Mrs McDoon flexing her vice-like fingers furiously upon the handle of her broom her nails leaving deep clawing marks in the wood. 'As I have said to you on thirty four separate occasions, we had our wedding vows rewritten to expel any mention of till death do you part nonsense. What kind of wicked decadent phrase is that? What would happen in the heavens when all these re-married people meet up with all their husbands and wives? I will tell you what would happen, a decadent orgy of harem-soaked wickedness that's what! Is that really what the good lord wants for the righteous or is it really the plan Satan himself has concocted for the grimy cellars of his dark kingdom? And another thing me and Mr McDoon never went in for any of that sickly weak-minded cuddling nonsense either, a firm handshake was more than enough physical contact for us. Now if you want to make yourself useful you could ask the good Colonel about that little matter we discussed earlier.'

'Oh yes of course Mrs McDoon you must forgive this forgetful old romantic science wrangler,' said the professor before turning his attention to the Colonel who was in the process of walking away. 'Before you go, Colonel, we have a small request for you. The good lady here would dearly like to lead a squad into battle against one of the cow bases, in fact it is her heart's fondest desire to take down the evil lord Cadmow himself, if you could see yourself fit to grant the lady a battlefield commission to the rank of say Lt Colonel, we would be very grateful.'

Well my little laidback lassie lovers that Colonel let out a big old laugh which was in a way understandable but also perhaps a little cruel. Which we in no way endorse folks, just reporting the facts as we overheard people gossiping about them dude cats.

'I think the best thing the little lady can do to help with the war effort is to keep this place spick and span so you can do your job without tripping over any discarded inventions. Perhaps if she is really keen then knitting something for our brave troops on the front line,' said the Colonel still chuckling despite Mrs McDoon's fierce glare.

'I wouldn't be dismissing me so quickly you patronising third rate diddyman. I have hardened battle experience let me tell you, you're a fool to miss out on me.'

'You served in your country's military madam, what was your rank?'

'Well not the military per se Colonel, I was brought up on the mean streets of Glasgow which amounts to the same thing doesn't it? I also presently live in the roughest area of Los Angeles, people told me I would be killed for sure. Oh on my first day a gang of big young hooligans surrounded me waving their knives and shouting that I was on their street and wearing the wrong colour shoes. I told them I was from Glasgow, I believe in giving people fair warning. The wee laddies laughed, sneered and taunted as they came at me, bullets, knives, fists and feet a flying. I am ashamed to say I laughed at the poor undisciplined boys. They all lay at my feet a moment later crying like babies, asking what was that, what was that? That wee boys, was a Glasgow kiss, I told them.'

'Well that is a fascinating story madam it would do well in one of those mindless Hollywood movies so popular with the juvenile delinquent community my daddy always warned me to steer clear of,' said the Colonel looking rather impatient. 'Thank you for your offer madam but we have enough genuine soldiers without needing to recruit from the domestic staff.'

'You'll rue the day you cast me aside Colonel, I can promise you that!'

'Well I really must dash,' said the Colonel walking away. 'I'll certainly be reviewing your security status over the next day or so.'

'Aye and I'll be reviewing your breathing status you ignorant old fool,' muttered Mrs McDoon.

That evening back in Professor Winkle's lab, the good Colonel gathered his troops ready to go into battle as the professor's wonder machine whirred, buzzed and spluttered through its frantic firing up procedure.

'Is that freaky machine nearly ready Professor? My troops are chomping at the battle bit and that thing sounds like an old jalopy ready to fall apart,' said the Colonel as the Professor frantically adjusted the now hissing machine.

'Fear not, Colonel, I assure you this glorious machine is in prime condition and is just about to explode into life or into a million pieces if I have made any miscalculations, which I am sure I have not done,' said the Professor sounding less confident than the Colonel would have liked.

'I am not feeling very reassured, Professor,' said the Colonel eyeing both the excited science-wrangler and his straining, mildly smoking machine. 'Is it on fire?'

'It is all going to be fine, Colonel, but it might be prudent to move your troops well away from the machine,' urged the Professor as Colonel Twirl ushered his troops back. 'No Colonel, right to the back of the room I think would be best, yes by the fire door, in fact be ready with the fire extinguishers there just in case.'

The bang and bright flash of light at that moment didn't shock the Colonel unduly but the dense fog of mist that filled the lab was a little disconcerting. It was the strong smell of singed plastic and burnt wiring that began to set the normally stoic military man into a state of mild alarm. Shouts and screams from the Professor filled the room as the fog slowly cleared.

'It works, it works,' shouted the Professor, dancing for joy much to everyone's surprise. 'Behold my glorious vortex.'

Yeah groovlings that was a pretty cool vortex from what I was told, although like a lot of vortices it was a bit bland colour wise, if it had been a bit psychedelic then it would have been Christmas wine heavy gravy groovy. The one we opened in Washington was a far funkier affair.

'Let's go troops,' said the Colonel as the first squad approached the vortex.

'Permission to resume duty sir?' shouted Major Browne marching in to a sea of smiling faces. Her crutch, plaster casts and high level of weapons didn't seem to be slowing her down in the slightest.

'What in heavens name are you doing here soldier? You were nearly killed by that crazed cow,' said the Colonel. 'Not that I am not pleased to see you're on the road to recovery, your injuries were very severe. It's going to be a long while before you're better. Get back to your hospital bed and rest up, we've got this one.'

'I am nearly healed sir, I have a tip top metabolism, Colonel, my body doesn't like being sick for long,' said the Major exchanging salutes and pats on the back from the troops.

'I am the same lassie,' shouted Mrs McDoon. 'My body has no patience with injury or illness, get away you daft buggers my immune system says to all them pesky diseases. I bet you've got a drop or three of good old Scottish blood, have you not?'

'Yes my grandmother was from Edinburgh as it happens,' said the Major trying to ignore the impatient looks cast by the Colonel.

'Edinburgh is it, oh well can't helped I suppose. At least she wasn't from Berwick eh lass?' said Mrs McDoon.

'Soldier go home, rest up, that's an order!' shouted the Colonel with a smile that didn't match the tone.

'I want to fulfil my mission sir, lead these troops to final victory,' said the Major to cheers from the troops.

'You've already fulfilled your mission soldier. As far as I'm concerned you're a goddamn American hero. Now get back to bed and be proud of all you've done. Besides soldier you don't have any idea what this mission is and we don't have time to brief you. We are about to go into active combat.'

'I'm fully briefed sir,' replied Major Browne. 'I left strict instructions that all mission briefings should be fed directly to my unconscious mind should I fall into a coma so that I would be ready for action immediately upon waking. You need a strong leader to finish the job sir. These troops will follow me to hell and back, won't you girls and boys?'

The soldiers cheered, whooped and hollered, shouting 'Major Browne is our leader,' over and over again until Colonel Twirl raised his hands in supplication.

'Alright, alright you win; I guess I have no choice. You're certainly a boon to morale and I can't knock your enthusiasm,' said the Colonel. 'You can lead the troops into battle but I'll be by your side just in case. It's just a shame I can't bring the Moo-copter along.'

'I am sorry, Colonel, it was completely unfeasible,' said the Professor to scowls from the Colonel.

'Unfeasible is just another word for slack-butted-lazy-lay-in-bed loser by my book, I expect to fly my Moo-copter over the moon's surface when we take down Cadmow is that clear?'

'Impossible, Colonel, the laws of physics are not ours to command.'

'Don't hide behind the laws of physics like a trembling coward under a bed sheet Professor, those same laws of physics said a man could never fly until the Wright brothers told them all to go to hell, I suggest you do the same unless you want the FBI to look into your cleaner's links to the underworld,' said the Colonel as the squad entered the vortex.

'What am I to do?' wailed the Professor, 'it is not possible to fly a helicopter on the moon, it cannot be done, it, cannot be done.'

Mrs McDoon slapped the man hard across the face reducing him to shocked silence.

'We'll be having a lot less of that nonsense thank you very much laddie,' said Mrs McDoon looking the Professor square in the face. 'You better think of something quick smart, I don't want Colonel tickle brain rummaging through the skeletons in my closet, if you please. Perhaps I could take him for a long walk off a short gangplank. That Major might be more amenable to my plans.'

'Oh I don't think that would be a good idea, you'd go to prison and I would be all alone,' wailed Professor Winkle.

'Then make the man his Moon-copter.'

'It's not possible I tell you.'

Mrs McDoon suddenly extended the fierce looking hidden blade at the end of her broom. 'Then I strongly suggest you make it possible.' Mrs McDoon smiled at the terrified professor. 'It's amazing what wonderful creativity threats of pain and physical violence can inspire, perhaps you should do a scientific paper on it sometime.'

Chapter 13: Where no Colonel has gone before.

The squad appeared in a strange and freakish place, dazzling lights, loud rhythmic sounds and sharp, pungent odours filled the air. A misty veil half hid the many figures before them as the odd-looking creatures leapt about in some sort of desperate frenzy. At least that is how the Colonel described it later.

The squad stood, their weapons raised waiting for the orders to fire.

'Anyone care for a canapé?' said a voice as a tray of nibbles passed under the Colonel's nose, but he was unable to respond his jaw a gape, eyes staring transfixed straight ahead of him.

'I've never seen anything like this. What is going on here Major?' asked the Colonel.

'It's a party sir,' replied Major Browne tapping her feet to the funky, funky beat.

'Are you sure Major?' replied the Colonel still looking more than a little dazed.

'Yes sir, I've been to a few parties in my time. Some were a bit like this especially the ones at college,' said the Major clicking her fingers to the catchy groove tune that was playing.

Oh the groovy, funky rhythms, the cool, cool scene, the with-it, happening cats who were throwing that party must have been tasteful groove weavers indeed.

'Really, I've never been to a party, my parents always said they were for sad hippy losers and idle work-shy punks who wanted to ban the bomb and have their commie friends nuke us and take over the world,' said the Colonel looking suspiciously at the Major's clicking fingers and bouncing feet. 'Looks like brainwashing to me.'

'That's a shame sir,' said Major Browne restraining her groove for a moment in hope of calming the increasingly agitated Colonel.

'Anyway I think those two dancing cows may be some kind of fifth column who have split away from the others, rebels waiting for a cause. Perhaps we can make them into our allies.'

Then two of the coolest cats you ever did see appeared out of the mist in front of them with a tray of funky cocktails each one guaranteed to make the tongue loosen, the mind swirl and feet groove all of the dance long night.

'You cats planning on being wallflowers all night, this is a party you know?' I said offering the tray to the Colonel and the Major. 'Try the yellow one it's our own recipe, in fact we are having name the cocktail contest later, unfortunately all the names we have come up with so far have dubious connotations when we you look them up on the internet, you cannot be too careful these days.'

'We, doggone demand, your unconditional surrender,' shouted the Colonel waving his gun in our faces in a manner that was more than a little rude, especially considering we had just offered the dude a particularly refreshing beverage, crafted by my own fair hooves.

'Sorry man,' began Vince flashing a peace sign with his hoof. 'You folks will have to check your weapons at the vortex if you want to join the party. We are peace-loving bovines see.'

'We aren't checking anything anywhere son, you understand. We will stick a few shiny bullets into your no-good mooing hides if you do not surrender with due haste,' replied the colonel his manner not appearing to mellow in the face of our peaceful countenances.

'Make milk not war, man,' I said offering more supplicating peace gestures.

'I wish you'd suggest that to that damn Cadmow and his doomsday Daisybells that have been going on killing sprees all over the place of late,' said the Colonel in a not unreasonably stern manner.

'We did dude, he just tried to fry our brains. The cat's not a cool cow, if ya dig man.'

'I really don't think these are the cows we have been fighting sir?' whispered the Major to the Colonel before she addressed us cats. 'I know this is a bit corny but would you cows mind taking us to your leader? I am Major Browne by the way and this gentleman with the big gun is Colonel Twirl and if you really are peaceful then we are delighted to make your acquaintance.'

We both gave a little chuckle, 'Don't fret over the corn groovy sister, we normally live out life's beat at maximum cheese so we are cool with a classic B-movie vibe. The thing is we are very much our own bovines, we don't tend to follow leaders we just plough our own furrow along life's rich byway.'

'Have you the faintest idea of what that bovine just said, Major?' whispered the Colonel.

'Yes sir,' the Major replied, 'I have watched enough reruns of cheesy sixties television shows and humorously awful old B-movies to catch the drift.'

'I see, Major,' said the Colonel eyeing the Major's fingers suspiciously as they once again danced to the funky retro beat. 'That was while you were being brainwashed at all those parties I suppose?'

'Yes sir, it was. A lot of good times were had back then and no mistake sir,' said the Major with a nostalgic sigh.

'I'll take your word for it Major. Now can you tell me what that cow said I caught something about ploughing up a corn field and planting cheese which makes as much sense as the lyrics to this damn song. I can only assume it's in some form of code, damned if I recognise it mind.'

'From what I gather sir, they are peaceful bovines but not part of a wider group. It also appears they have been contacted by lord Cadmow and threatened with some sort of brain frying device if they actively help us,' said the Major as a drunken human staggered up behind us.

'In the name of the presidential family I would like to vouch for these good bovines,' slurred the man as he put his arms around our shoulders belching musically before staring longingly at the Major's chest. 'They are good loyal Americans and they throw one hell of party.' He continued before singing a strange hybrid of the American and Canadian national anthems.

'Is that the President's husband?' asked the Colonel.

'Yes sir and I believe that's his daughter trying to pick him up,' replied the Major as the drunken presidential spouse slumped to the floor but strangely kept on dancing as he lay on his back.

'Come on, dad, you're not twenty-two anymore,' said his daughter as she and Vince tried to help the man to his feet. 'You're not forty-two anymore either for that matter.'

'Colonel Twirl, Major Browne please stand down, we need to commandeer that vortex,' said the two black-suited secret service dudes as they flashed their identity cards and adjusted their sunglasses.

'And you two gentlemen are?' asked a continually baffled Colonel, who was reaching for the handle of his tickling stick in the way a nervous child would reach for a security blanket.

'I am agent Oakes and this is agent, Name-withheld-for-security-reasons,' began the agent giving the tickling stick a hard stare. 'I wouldn't do that sir, the secret service does not take kindly to being tickled, teased, taunted or toyed with in any manner whatsoever.'

It was true groove cats, a number of ladies at the party had taken a liking to agent Oakes and proceeded to flirt with him using the traditional tickle, tease method which when deployed by female humans is usually very effective, but when attempted on the agent it didn't go down well at all.

Also agent, Name-withheld-for-security-reasons, really was called that, apparently he had changed his name ten years before.

The eagle eyed amongst you will have noticed that I reported only one agent going through the vortex in Washington. All I can say is once the party was in full swing another agent was suddenly there as well, must have gate-crashed I guess, I cannot blame the cat it was a funky shindig and no mistake.

'What the hell is going on here, we are on a classified military operation vital to our victory in this war and I don't understand or appreciate you interfering with it,' said the Colonel to the impassive faces of the agents.

'Your appreciation or understanding is not required, Colonel, your co-operation is though. You and the Major will help us escort these two bovines through the vortex and into Professor Winkle's lab where things will become marginally clearer,' said agent Oakes indicating towards the vortex.

'Hey agent Oak tree dude, we can't just abandon our party, man. Gigs like this don't run themselves you know. We've got to look after all these good and crazy folks,' I said as the agents and the military folk gave me a disbelieving look.

'We anticipated your concerns, Holly,' replied agent Oakes. 'We have arranged for a Ms Lucy Jones and a Mr Spandex Twirl both Disc jockeys from the former club Astro, to take over the party's organisation.'

'Cool man, sounds like our party is in good hands lets head on in and meet this Winkle cat,' I said beckoning to the agents to lead the way.

As we headed into the vortex Major Browne leaned in to talk into the colonel's ear. 'Spandex Twirl, any relation sir?'

'I don't have a son, Major,' snapped the Colonel.

'I never said you did sir,' replied the Major rather taken aback. 'I thought a nephew or cousin perhaps.'

'What kind of son would change a perfectly good name such as Randolph to a weird ass name like Spandex? What the hell is a Spandex anyway? Is it like a rolodex or something?'

'Sorry sir I didn't mean to open up old wounds sir,' said the Major wishing she had kept her mouth shut.

'Tell me, Major,' continued the Colonel, 'what kind of son would break his granddaddy's heart by entering a frenzied hotdog munching contest despite all our pleading. He even used canned cheese; can you believe a son of mine would do something so sick and twisted?'

'Sir I have no wish to pry into your private family business,' replied the Major.

'And now he has taken up with those weird music industry people. I tell you Major I don't understand young people today. I only hope this war knocks the music out of them and a bit of real dairy common sense back in.'

Chapter 14: A spot of moonlight on the moo cows.

Picture the scene my little disco infernos, my good and groove filled self along with my partner in funky times chewing the cud in crazy old Winkle's lab, sitting round a big old table, munching on tea and biscuits, laying down a bit of bovine history as the frenzied Daisybell battered itself senseless against the flickering force-field.

We told them about the peaceful cow people who came from a distant star. Our people were an advanced, space-going race, spreading our peaceful ways to the less- technologically advanced, more-aggressive species such as the folks on Earth.

We told the assembled how Lord Cadmow had persuaded many of the cow people that the warlike beings were a danger to us and we were fools for not arming ourselves and ruling over the other races with an iron hoof.

We told them about the civil war that devastated our home world and caused chaos on many others including Earth.

'To cut a long story short the sour cat Cadmow and his supporters were eventually defeated and put on trial,' I said to a fascinated audience. I should have been some sort of after dinner speaker groovers. 'When they were found him guilty they put Cadmow and his cohorts in suspended animation because they don't believe in the death penalty.'

'With all due respect to your people, Holly,' said the Colonel not sounding as if he was about to say anything particularly respectful. 'They sound like a planet full of God-dang-fools. I mean you got heaping load of warlike folk and the fella with enough common sense and basic honest to god gumption to suggest you rearm yourselves; do they listen to the fella? Hell no, they declare him a danger to society. Do they execute this big old danger to society? Hell no that would be to goddamn sensible, they put him and his dangerous friends in suspended animation all together were they can escape and have another shot at power. That really is a special kind of stupid.'

'I think they were trying to stand by their principles man, you know be on the side of the angels,' I said feeling more than a little defensive.

'On the side of the idiots more like,' said the Colonel. 'What does this Cadmow want in the long run? Conquest of Earth followed by some sort cow-based galactic empire?'

'No man,' I said, 'what the bitter cat wants is vengeance. He sees our people as traitors to him and to our species. He wants an enslaved human race to build a vengeance fleet that will go and conquer our people and then build a galactic empire if he is still in a bad mood which I suspect he will be man.'

'It seems to me we have another potential problem,' said the Major. 'After four thousand years we have no idea what has happened to the cow race. They haven't been to check on their prisoners lately.

It is possible they have been conquered by another more warlike race that could be turning their warships towards us at this moment.'

'Perhaps they ended up taking up a Cadmow-like philosophy in the end and their conquest fleet is on its way,' said the Colonel in that cheery way of his. 'Not that they would have much time for Cadmow himself, dictators don't normally have much time for rivals. No they would probably kill him, blame a real or imagined enemy and then build a big old fancy as you like statue to him and have a parade in his honour.'

'Anything is possible I suppose man,' I said feeling a little down at all the heavy negative talk about the cow people. 'Although, I cannot see our people turning to the dark side, myself.'

'No man our people are peaceful cats,' agreed Vince.

'Peaceful like Lord Cadmow?' replied the Colonel

'One bad apple man.'

'Yes, your one bad apple and his rotten cohorts are causing a hell of a lot of trouble in this particular barrel, aren't they?' said the Colonel as an awkward silence descended on the room, except for the Daisybell who was emitting a series of frenzied snorts as it rammed its horns against the rippling force-field.

'There is something I don't understand, which is unusual,' began the Professor. 'If neither of you were allies of this Cadmow fellow, then why did you end up being punished along with them?'

'Yes I was wondering about that as well,' said the Major as the whole table seemed to look at us in a real claustrophobic way.

'Well man it was a kind of miscarriage of justice thing, you know man,' I said to a sea of stern faces.

'Yeah that's right,' said Vince, 'a case of mistaken identity gone too far at a fanatical fancy dress jamboree sort of vibe, resulting in a heavy un-funky ending, you know what I mean.'

'Although being woken up by cool funky happening cats did a lot to make up for the heaviness of it all,' I said trying to lighten the mood and soften the hard judgemental faces of all those at the table.

'That all sounds a little vague, can you give us some more detail?' asked the Major.

'That's all in the past man, my memory is hazy on the specifics,' I began to a sea of unimpressed faces. 'A lot of time and funky substances have passed under our respective bridges since then. Earth is our home now; humans are our comrades through the grooves and the grime. I tell you true us and that Cadmow cat are on radically different frequencies. His is rage, ours is rhythm and funkadelic tidings to all funky Earth kind, human, animal and even the flowers in the meadow man, yeah.'

'Yeah, Holly, isn't that the ever-tripping truth,' said Vince, flashing a quick peace salute.

'All that we are saying is give peace a chance...' we both sang and swayed making peace signs with our rainbow painted hooves. The Major started nodding along and seemed about to start singing until a red-faced Colonel banged his fist furiously on the table.

'That is quite enough of that,' shouted the Colonel, giving everyone quite a start, me and Vince nearly leapt out of our fur. 'Look what you've done to the poor Major, she was nearly hypnotised by your damn peace song. Another verse and she'd be holding a placard writing class and probably shouting commie style peace slogans at our brave troops instead of leading them into battle. I ain't going to lose a good soldier to a pair of bovine beatniks, so help me I ain't.'

'It's alright sir honestly, I wasn't about to become a protest singer. I was just humming along, the cows are quite good at the harmony singing in contrast to their rather dubious sense of rhythm,' said the Major.

'Major you're rambling, now take some deep breaths and read through this copy of military standing orders to clear your head,' said the Colonel before casting us a hard stare. 'Now if you bovines have finished your little sing song I need answers, serious detailed answers, not, airy fairy, blue moon Mary ones either. I need to know your exact relationship to Cadmow that caused you to be imprisoned. Also why didn't you tell us about this Cadmow character earlier, now that would have saved us a whole barrow-load of trouble? Without straight answers we won't know if we can trust you two to help us. You could be deep cover agents for the mad moon mooer for all we know.'

'Well man to be honest, you cats gate-crashed our party and seem to be asking us for help, so we don't feel the need to justify our existence,' I said feeling more than a little defensive. 'We didn't tell you about Cadmow because we had no idea where the cat was and to be honest we were trying to forget the dude.'

'Would you even have believed us?' asked Vince. 'If you had you might have tried to find him and accidently let him out. We thought it best to let sleeping mad manic moo cows lie.'

'That's right,' I continued. 'Our ability to help you is seriously limited anyway man, due to Cadmow's headache ray. We'd go all scanner funk on you cats before we could do you any good. Now if there are no further questions we'll head back to our party cats, we've got a cocktail contest to proceed over. It's not as if you folks have been great hosts, we've not been offered a refreshing beverage and you don't even have any decent music. Vince man lets go.'

Me and Vince stood up to go but so did Colonel Twirl.

'You bovines are going nowhere, Major throw these two in a cell until we get some sensible answers from them,' said the Colonel much to our alarm.

'Belay that order Major, these Bovines are under our protection,' said Agent Oakes much to our happiness and the colonel's irritation.

'Agent Oakes this is most irregular, these bovines are under my jurisdiction. We have no idea if we can trust them; they are evasive with beatnik overtones not to mention an unclear historical link to our moon-cow enemies. Hell jingo they could be just waiting to lower that force field and let the damn Daisybell over there go on a rampage, and I for one don't plan to let that happen.'

'No Colonel, we have been monitoring Holly and Vince and for well over a decade now and we can assure you they are not a threat to national or planetary security. Although we were a bit concerned about their dancing for a while but the after effects are short term people normally regain their sense of balance and eyesight within a few days,' said agent Oakes. 'Their recent actions have been directed against the bovine threat at some risk to themselves, unfortunately Lord Cadmow has now deployed a brain scrambling machine to neutralise them as a threat.'

'That's right man,' I said, 'we would love to help but if we did it would be death by the ultimate, terminal ice cream headache without any of the creamy goodness to compensate for meeting that grim old reaper cat, sorry again dudes.'

'We are hoping to do something about that,' said the agent, 'Professor Winkle, we would like you to come up with a helmet for these bovines that would block the malevolent brain busting rays? We could do with that in say the next week.'

'Hey folks I really don't think that's possible,' I said, 'that's some pretty advanced technology the cat is messing with, probably far beyond human capability for a few centuries at least.'

'Well the professor is pretty smart, we'd like him to take a crack at it,' said the agent. 'Think you're up to the challenge, Professor?'

With that the Professor leapt up from his seat and raced over to us, a look of enthusiastic glee spreading across his face as he began measuring and scanning our heads. Bursts of excited muttering and frantically excited note taking came from him as the red-faced Colonel Twirl banged a fist on the table.

'Wait just a commie baiting minute agent oak tree, this is a military operation and those bovines and that science wrangler over there come under my jurisdiction, is that crystal clear? Professor sit down, Major arrest these bovines.'

'These are direct orders from the President, Colonel, you can check with her if you like,' said the Agent handing an envelope to the still-steaming military man.

Mrs McDoon began a mad extended cackle, 'he's got you by the short and curlies Colonel and that's the truth,' she said as the Colonel snatched the envelope from the agent's hand.

As the Colonel began reading the enclosed letter the good Professor let out an excited squeal, 'Yes, yes and yes once again, I believe it is possible. A noble helmet of bovine protection will be constructed by my own divinely inspired hands, driven by my infinitely wondrous mind. Give me seven days and full access to the brains of these good cows and it will be ready.'

'You're not one for modesty are you professor?' said Mrs McDoon.

'Certainly not Mrs McDoon, modesty is a lie in my opinion, if people do not know of my genius and I hide it selfishly away how can I use my magnificent brain to benefit society if it is eclipsed and muted by false and mindless modesty?' said the Professor.

'That is good news professor,' said agent Oakes, 'may I suggest you crack on with that immediately.'

'I will still need the professor's help with our actual mission, to take down the cow bases unless you are taking charge of the military campaign as well,' said the Colonel.

'You are to carry on with the campaign, Colonel, and I am sure the professor can do both, isn't that right, Professor?' said agent Oakes to the Professors gleeful nodding.

'Oh yes indeed,' said the Professor, 'the idea that a genius as great as mine would not be able to multitask two virtually impossible projects at the same time before a hearty brunch is I must say quite, quite fanciful. Like a normal person with the typical dim lit intelligence not being able to walk and talk at the same time. Oh yes quite comically fanciful indeed.'

'You'll be doing what exactly with our brains man?' said Vince sounding as alarmed as I was feeling.

'Just a deep brain examination to find out how the moo mind functions, so potentially harmful rays can be successfully blocked,' said the professor with a rather unfortunate giggle.

'Yeah man that sounds all very well,' I said, 'but how can you block rays from a machine you have never seen, especially as you don't have a sample of the harmful mind beam in question?'

'Oh bovines have no fear I have a truly wondrous plan to overcome that minor discrepancy,' said the professor even though it sounded like a pretty major one to me.

'I plan to dress up as a rebellious moo general claiming I am turning against Cadmow. I believe this baiting will provoke the fanatical bull lord into using his brain warping on me. Of course the toxic rays will have no affect as I have a human brain but I will be able to get a sample of the beam so I can develop a successful counter measure. It will be as easy as selling porky pies, as they say in merry old England.'

The professor's statement would have been more reassuring if it hadn't been for the continued appearance of the fanatical giggling throughout. Don't get us wrong groove cats we don't have a downer on manic giggling per se but it kind of has its place. If you're hanging with a stoner cat buddy all hysterical over some bad old B-movie plot holes and painfully bad acting, then a bit of a giggle fest is cool and freshly funk-some but I would not want the same cat to start examining my brain cavity in anyway whatsoever. If you're being honest with yourselves funky readers neither would any of you.

'Why don't you dig up the big spaceship and use that to defeat the mean tempered moo lord?' said Vince sounding a bit desperate to divert the assembled folks from Winkles overly enthusiastic brain fondling frenzy.

'Spaceship, what spaceship?' asked Major Browne sounding a bit doubtful.

'Yeah that's right,' I said giving my old fella a bit of moral support in his scheme of distracting the brain wrangler. 'There is a big old powerful ship under the great pyramid in funky North Africa, Egypt to be more exact, I believe it's in the Nile Valley man.'

'Under the great pyramid you say,' said Winkle getting quite excited. 'Yes I heard the stories but assumed they were myths but I also assumed the legend of wise space bovines descending from the stars to guide humanity forward, was a myth as well but here they are talking star cows who I am sure were wise in their way before slipping down the weed-slicked slopes of hippy hedonism that ensnares and infantilises so many of the young. Yes Colonel you must dig up this ship as soon as possible.'

'That's not my call, Professor,' said the Colonel, 'I'll have to speak to the President, in the meantime keep working on those moo bonnets for these two bovines or I'll have to lock them up. It goes without saying I still expect to fly the Moo-copter during the final battle.' The Professor had gone quite pale as a look of terror froze his face in a horrified gaze. 'Don't look at me like that Professor, you were just telling us all how much of a genius you are, it's time to put your brain where your mouth is, like some kind of zombie these young folks are all into for some strange reason I cannot for the life of me fathom.'

An hour later we all sat in the same room as another squad of soldiers disappeared through a vortex. A vast view-screen showed an image of the President as Colonel Twirl reported on another failed attack on a cow base and his hopes that this one would go better.

As the conversation turned to the spaceship under the pyramids we were called forward.

'Colonel, I have been in discussions with the Egyptian ambassador and his government are very reluctant to let American troops dig under the pyramids. He claims there is no spaceship and that the presence of American forces would only damage one of the great wonders of the world,' said the President to much grumbling from our group.

'With all due respect to the Egyptians Madam President, as the United States of America is the leader of the free world then these wonders must naturally come under our jurisdiction. I strongly recommend that we send in troops quickly to secure these pyramids and any spaceships underneath or nearby.

'I'll do my best Colonel,' said the President, 'but are you one hundred per cent sure about this ship? We already have a substantial military commitment with our forces in India who are meeting stiff resistance from not only the Indians but the Russians and Chinese as well.'

'I have the information on very good authority, Madam President,' said the Colonel pointing at us, 'I can guarantee its accuracy, these whacked-out hippy space bovines have told me there is a ship and I tend to believe them. Holly why don't you tell the President what you told me.'

I shuffled nervously forward, glad to see the colonel's attitude towards me and my old fella had seen a marked positive improvement. I flashed the President, who I had voted for by the way, a double barrel peace salute and a huge funky-to-make-your-groovy acquaintance grin, my battering eyelids spelled out unicorn peace in fluorescent rainbow colours, well I was just about to address the President, you can't blame a girl for making an effort in those circumstances can you cats?

'Hi there groovy Presidential sister,' I began feeling a bit dreamy with the battering butterflies in my belly the only things preventing me from spacing out completely with the awe of it. 'I am Holly and well I must be one of your biggest fans, you're trying to do cool stuff. It's so sad all those bad cat opponents spreading fake news and setting all those vicious attack ferrets on you. Not that I blame the ferrets themselves mind, it's the way they are treated and bred that makes them inclined to attack. They are victims too in a way but I guess it's hard to see that when six of them are latched onto your noggin, gnawing away to a bone munching frenzy.'

That's when the President's eyes began to glaze over and the Colonel poked me in the ribs muttering, 'The ship Holly, mention the ship.'

'Oh yeah sorry man,' I said to the Colonel before addressing the President once again. 'That's right, Madam President, there is this big old spaceship under the pyramids, you should dig it up and declaw that bad moon cat, or should that be dehorn the bad moon cow, who knows man who knows.'

'It is very nice to meet you, Holly,' said the President, 'America and the world thanks you for your efforts against our moon cow enemies but I am reluctant to commit our forces just on your say so.'

'Mom you've got to believe Holly she is so groovy,' slurred the president's daughter putting her arm around me in a giddy way.

'The girl's right love, you should listen to her,' said the president's husband attempting a little jig with me as he rubbed his face where the Major had been forced to slap it.

'I was only being bloody friendly, Major, you should be flattered really,' he said looking over at the Major who was flashing the appropriately painful military gesture at him.

'Oh my god is that my daughter?' shouted the President, 'are you drunk? Have you bloody cows got my daughter drunk? She is only fifteen years old you should be looking after her not plying her with alcohol for God's sake.' Oh man she was fuming something toxic.

'No, you got the wrong end of the rhythm stick groovy Presidential sister. It's a contact high vibe. Your daughter just thinks she is drunk. It's been funky moo cow, mock-tails all the way. Despite our loquacious laid back outlook we take our duties as the responsible adults seriously.'

'Holly's right, honey,' chipped in the presidential spouse. 'We've all been looking out for her, she is as sober as any American teenager rocking down at a freaky party hosted by hippy influenced spaced out star cows is likely to be.'

'You what, I'm sober?' steamed the now furious teenager. 'You tricked me? I thought you were all cool. I wanted to be properly sloshed like a British teenager in one of their real ale watering holes. You guys are all super squared squares stuck at the back of an ice box like the most boring ice lolly nobody wants.'

'Sorry teenage groove sister,' I said offering a friendly hoof which was quickly knocked away, 'I feel your teenage rebel cries of frustration I really do but as one of the responsible adults in the room I could not let you get sloshed. You'll understand when you have teenagers of your own. By the way groovy sister when did the word square become cool again?'

'You say square all the time, Holly, don't you think it is a cool word to say?' asked the teenager.

'Well it is cool if you're an ageing, child of the sixties still got the groove, cat like me, but you young happening kits must have your own slang you use amongst your peers. Perhaps the words just swinging back round the linguistic ghost train to spook your parents and help you bond with all the groovy grandmas and grandpas.'

I took a breath and all the cats around were looking slightly agog and ever so slightly slack jawed.

'I thought your talk was ahead of the curve,' said the Presidential offspring her tone softening. 'I forgot you're groovy old creeker wranglers who can still party. I guess with great age comes great responsibility and you just had my back. Sorry if I was all moody Mary and stroppy Sarah on you guys.

With that she gave me and Vince a big old hug.

'That's alright sister,' I said, 'you're not the first teenager to be a bit stroppy and at least you didn't try and read us any pretentious poetry.'

The President cleared her throat, bringing us all to a respectful silence. 'I am glad she is sober and apparently starting to adult under your bovine influence I just wish you could do the same for her father,' she said looking disdainfully at her husband who had slumped to the floor and was now making several rude gestures at his wife. Some even I didn't know.

'Now let's get back to this ship, I am yet to be convinced on this matter,' said the President giving us the hard stare of truth evaluation which always looks a bit weird, even on our leader in chief.

That is when, much to our relief the special agents walked forward and addressed the president directly.

'Agents Oaks,' said the President, 'good to see you, what is your assessment of the situation.'

'Well madam President we have been closely monitoring these bovines over many years and they do come from an advanced culture with an advanced knowledge that can be of use to us. Much of that may have been diluted by their rather hedonistic lifestyle but I still believe much remains that is useful to us. If that knowledge involves ancient spaceships hidden on Earth then we are obliged to act by either taking these vessels by force if necessary or committing ourselves to a tactical nuclear strike on the Nile valley in order to deny this ship to our enemies whether they be bovine or human in nature.'

'Tactical nuclear strike, tactical nuclear strike, we want a tactical nuclear,' chanted a group of soldiers guarding the vortex generator until the Colonel and the Major stared them into silent submission.

'Well we will not be nuking the Nile Valley,' began the President to much frustrated booing from the troops.

'The funny ferret man said you'd never nuke anything,' shouted one of the soldiers, 'he was right as well, glad I didn't vote for you now. No one ever nukes anything it's just not fair. Just a few little nukes that's all we want, is that really to much to ask for?'

'I'll have you know, young man, in the early days of this war I tried to nuke the moon on three separate occasions only for the missiles to be repelled by Lord Cadmow's superior force-field technology,' replied the President as the soldiers were taken out of the room shaking their heads and muttering about politicians not keeping their promises.

'I will be talking to the joint chiefs immediately about landing troops in Egypt and I do hope that a spaceship is there. In the meantime, Professor please make haste with these moo helmets so Holly and Vince can help us fully.'

Chapter 15: A Barney with the Bull Lord.

In the moon base control room a large bed of hay held the lounging figures of Lord Cadmow, Moolock and Buttercup. They all studied the view screen with much interest.

'This sequence makes no sense Moolock,' said Cadmow turning his head in puzzlement. 'Please can you explain strange human logic behind it?'

'Indeed my Lord, first you must understand that the fans of this particular series of movies are superstitious in the extreme. They came to believe as the series progressed that the odd numbered movies held a curse which have doomed them to be very poor quality. After the fifth film only even numbered movies were produced. Therefore episode six is followed by eight then ten etc, etc.'

'If I did not know you better I would think you were joking Moolock,' said Cadmow. 'Do these humans not worry that some of these films will secretly be odd numbered despite having an even number in the title and do they not wonder about the nature of these missing odd numbered films? I have noticed the humans seem to enjoy criticising bad forms of entertainment as much if not more than enjoying and discussing the good.'

'The humans have solved this problem in their own curious way my lord,' said Moolock. 'All the odd numbered films are made by fans as amateur bad movie parodies. Imagining just how bad the cursed films in the sequence would have been. They are apparently very popular; all are now official cannon and some even having limited cinema releases. Sometimes it does go wrong when rival fan film makers make very different movies for the same numbered films. Savage online battles ensue some have even hacked into rivals' computers programming them to electrocute the owner.'

'Indeed, Moolock, the curious insanity of these human creatures never ceases to amaze, how they have made the technological advancements they have is a wonder,' said Cadmow stealing a little of Buttercup's popcorn before starting the next movie in the series.

'I believe their brains have been addled by excessive sugar consumption in recent decades, probably taken in biscuit form I imagine,' said Moolock as the screen flashed 'incoming message' in large red letters as the tannoy boomed the same information at a much higher volume than was welcome to the ears of either space cows or humans.

'You got yourself an incoming call there fella,' shouted Billy Bob from his jar.

'I can quite clearly see and hear tha,t human,' replied Cadmow.

'You should answer that then, it could be something real important, perhaps you won the lottery or us humans might have thrown in the towel, you know making you the winner and all. You wouldn't want to miss out on that would you, I mean if you don't pull your finger or whatever it is you have out and answer the call smart as you like, the pesky earth governments could give the planet to some Martian come lately sneaky space chancer claiming Earth for freaky advanced space goats.'

'Fascinating, human,' said Moolock grinning as he gave Billy Bob's jar a playful and painful blast of electricity.

As Billy Bob hollered in indignant pain Cadmow answered the call.

A freaky-looking vaguely bovine figure appeared on the screen, 'is it the glorious moolord known as Lord Cadmow to whom I am addressing?' asked the strange bovine without its lips moving.

'Do you not know the face of your own moolord?' snorted Cadmow. 'I do not recognise you, insolent hornless wretch. Identify yourself and state your business, quickly we are doing important work here.'

'I reckon that's just some human in a cow costume trying to trick you fella, don't fall for it,' shouted Billy Bob to furious snorts from Moolock.

'Yeah and not a very good one either, it's just a horse suit with plastic horns stuck on,' said Cletus. 'The right one's starting to fall off now.'

'Silence human filth,' shouted Moolock as the yokels began to holler and chuckle.

'I apologise,' said Cadmow to the figure on the screen, 'I have some half-witted human prisoners, they are so simple and stupid that not even the agonies of constant torture has managed to teach them their place in the grand bovine scheme of things,' continued Cadmow before raising his voice and turning to the yokels. 'Which is firmly at the bottom of life's putrid, rat-infested cesspit. Humans, do you understand?'

'We understand you're a real sweet-talking, silver-tongued son of a bovine,' said Billy Bob with a whistle and a roll of his eyes and much muttered agreement from his comrades.

'I quite understand my Lord,' said the vaguely-bovine-looking being with the poorly- glued horn. 'I have found the vast majority of humans to be simpleminded creatures. I apologise for not recognising you, my eyesight is not what it once was. I am Professor Winkle horn a bovine scientist of great intellect; I need to know the name of your first childhood pet for a science project?'

'For a science project you say,' said Cadmow. 'Well let me see, bear in mind I was a young calf barely off the udder. He was called lord splashy fluffy horn; he was blue and purple qwellfling. Oh he was so playful and affectionate, I used to cuddle him all the time, he so loved having his flippers scratched, yow, yow, yow, he would go. Although he would give a nasty kick when he was bored, broke my right hoof and that is when my father threw him back in the sea, I often think of that little quellfling and the soft purr he would make just before biting me with those sharp little teeth.'

'Why thank you my Lord, that is most useful,' interrupted the figure on the screen.

'Was there anything else?' asked Cadmow.

'One more thing,' said the now single-horned being on the screen. 'I am defecting to the human side and am rebelling against you. I have heard you have a lethal headache-inducing machine but I am certain my bunker will protect me from its deadly rays. You can try and use it on me but it would be pointless as you would fail and just look a hornless buffoon or should that be bull-foon? I mock you, ha, ha, ha; I mock you, ha, ha.'

'You are most unwise to rebel against me and even more unwise to mock me,' said Cadmow with an evil laugh. 'You will now suffer and die as an example to other arrogant mock happy fools.'

Lord Cadmow activated his machine with a hearty laugh. The figure on the screen reached for his head as he operated a console in front of him. 'Oh gosh the pain oh the agony, I so wish it would stop golly yes I wish the pain would stop,' he said in a very unconvincing tone.

'Now you will die, traitor,' snarled Cadmow, turning the machine to higher and higher settings.

'That's it, good, good, if I can have a little more unbearable agony, Lord Cadmow, that would be great,' said the being on screen apparently forgetting that he was supposed to be in terminal pain.

'You insolent wretch,' bellowed Cadmow, turning the dial. 'I will give you full power and you will suffer properly damn you.'

'Wonderful, that is it, I have it. I mean oh yes that really does smart, so much suffering, et cetera, et cetera.'

'You should be dead now, are you not?' asked Cadmow.

'Oh yes sorry, goodbye cruel world, it is a better thing I do now et cetera, et cetera. For I now die,' he said apparently slumping onto the floor before somehow terminating the communication link.

'Did anything seem a bit fishy about that, my Lord?' asked Moolock to heckles and jeers from the yokels.

'Yes Moolock, such an intelligent bovine wanting to rebel against my glorious self, that is odd but I suppose great genius can bring with it great arrogance and overconfidence. A shame to lose such a great mind but an example must be made of all traitors; he could have been a great boon to the cause, such a shame, such a shame.'

'Those two really are a special kind of stupid,' whispered Billy Bob. 'The porch light might be on but no ones been home in a good long while I'd say.'

'Yeah ain't that the truth, it's what they always say, too much television watching addles the brain.'

'We shouldn't be complaining none too much about it though,' said Billy Bob. 'That's exactly the level of dumbass skunk butt crazy we need from them for humanity to win this war.'

'You foolish deluded humans, it is us who are winning the war,' said Cadmow, 'in fact a final decisive and quite glorious victory is at hoof.'

With that Cadmow and Moolock began to laugh in a way that cackled with manic malevolence or so they thought at least, groove cats.

'Well you deluded pair can believe whatever you care to,' said Billy Bob. 'Let's see if you're still cackling when your brains are crackling in that big old electric chair built for two.'

'Two, humans, will Norhlick not be joining us at our execution then?' asked Moolock.

'Hell no good boy,' laughed Billy Bob, 'that two-faced son of a tax collector will have defected as soon as he sees the war going the way of humanity. He will be telling all your secrets in order to save his own neck from the chopping block.'

'Moolock do not laugh, they are mocking Norhlick with their lies,' said Cadmow as Moolock let out an almighty booming laugh.

'I believe the human is only stating the blindingly obvious my Lord,' responded the still laughing Moolock.

'Have I missed one of our glorious lord's wondrous jokes?' asked Norhlick as he entered the room with a tray of tea and biscuits. Norhlick let out giggle of fake almost spiteful laughter as he glared at all but the moo lord himself. 'Please treat my humble ears to this mirth beyond measure.'

'We were, as the humans say removing a quantity of liquid waste product from your body in order to create humour,' said Moolock. 'At least these three humans were, I was just going along for the ride.'

Norhlick looked confused as he passed out the tea and biscuits, 'sounds like a most useful operation, yet I felt not even a tickle, is that normal? Or is that perhaps the joke?'

As everyone sat back and enjoyed their tea and high-quality biscuits the entertainment for the afternoon arrived courtesy of the human resistance from good old reliable, despite being much abused, momma Earth.

'Well butter my butt and call me a biscuit, ain't them some pretty colours?' said Billy Bob as the room filled with the bright lights of a dozen or more swirling colourful vortices.

'I always say if you're going to create a proper inter-dimensional vortex you need to make it big, make it bold and most of all make it proper colourful so you either want to go through it real bad or you know the folks paying you a visit ain't messing around, one thing I cannot abide is dull and sloppy pan-dimensional visitors. First impressions count and I just know those vortices are going to provide us with professionals who mean business,' replied Jim Jam Jimmy clapping his hands as the troops poured out.

The three yokels hollered and cheered their approval as the troops of many nations began exiting the wormholes, firing their weapons at the bovines; some demanded the surrender of Cadmow and his cohorts, others didn't bother with such delicate procedural niceties.

Well my little electric cool aid karma cruisers the cheering of those yokel cats began to become more muted as it became obvious the weapons were having no effect. Internal shields absorbed the wave upon wave of bullets and explosives that came against them while the internal lasers laid waste to the majority of the invaders.

Cadmow clapped and snorted with glee dancing around the room as one of the surviving soldiers, his face in a snarl of rage, started ramming the force field with his shoulder. 'Damn you, damn you,' yelled the soldier.

Cadmow tapped the other side of the force field, 'why don't you just go back through your little vortex before I blast you, I'd prefer not to have anymore mess you see and you won't get through, go on get, going human,' said Cadmow making shooing gestures at the soldier. 'Shoo, human, shoo, on your way now. Skedaddle if you please as these idiot humans say.'

'I can't, I can't,' said the soldier now almost sobbing with distress. 'I promised my girl your horns; she wants to make some real pretty jewellery with them. I don't want to let my girl down, I promised see and she will be real upset.'

The soldier, tears pouring down his cheeks pulled out a hacksaw and starting to saw at the force field, 'please Mr Cadmow sir let me have your horns, please sir, for my girl, I don't want to let her down, please. You don't need them for your protection or nothing what with all those fancy lasers and things you got. I haven't got anything fancy like you, I just got my girl and I loves her see, please hand those horns over sir, it would mean the world to my girl and she means the world to me Mr Cadmow sir.'

As the soldier sobbed into the force field another two of his compatriots rushed across to the first. 'Leave those horns soldier, I promised them to my girl, you find your own.'

All three solders began crying and fighting while shouting about the love they felt for their romantic partner back home that they had promised horns as tokens of deep-felt love and affection. More and more soldiers who had made similar promises joined the fray to the bemusement of Cadmow.

'Fall back, to base and regroup,' came a booming voice from the many vortices. The surviving soldiers who were still sobbing and fighting stumbled back through their relative vortices dragging their dead and injured comrades with them.

With the soldiers gone as one last act of the defiant human spirit, the vortices spat out a large quantity of explosives which promptly detonated. With that the vortexes disappeared.

'Leave the shields on until all that dust has settled,' said Cadmow as a lone figure appeared through the mist waving a white flag.

'Don't be shooting at me non laddie,' said a steely Scottish voice. 'My name is Mrs McDoon and I have an offer and a challenge for the great leader, known I am told, as Lord Cadmow,' she looked at Moolock in a quizzical way. 'Is it perhaps your good self?'

Moolock laughed heartily, 'no human it is not me, it is an understandable mistake though. I am General Moolock the cruel and highly intelligent power behind the throne.'

'It isn't me either, human,' said Norhlick.

'I never thought for a moment it was, laddie,' said Mrs McDoon. 'Now if you are making the tea, I like mine very strong, very hot and with only the tiniest dash of milk. Don't be putting any sugar or lemon anywhere near the thing, if you value your wedding tackle that is. You got all that now?'

'How dare you,' said Norhlick marching over to Mrs McDoon. 'I will make you pay for your insolence.'

Norhlick attacked Mrs Mcdoon with a hidden blade which was easily swept away with her broom as were his other attempts at violence on her person. He lay at her feet as she jabbed her broom at his face in irritation. 'Now get away from me you annoying little windy-arsed fleabag.'

'I think you should make the human her tea Norhlick,' said Moolock, 'she has provided us with some entertainment so deserves some hospitality and refreshment before she is finally despatched, which she assuredly will be.' Moolock's evil stare and grin at Mrs McDoon was met with a dismissive shake of the head.

'I wouldn't be counting your corpses before they've croaked, laddie, I may be getting on in years but I am as feisty as they come and notoriously tricky to kill,' said Mrs Mcdoon looking from Moolock to Cadmow who was raising from his seat to loom over her.

'I am Lord Cadmow,' boomed the bull lord with a rather theatrical snarl. 'It is my glorious hooves that will bring your doom and wring your puny neck, after you've had your tea and biscuits naturally.'

'Of course you're the great fellow himself,' she said looking Cadmow up and down. 'It should have been obvious you're the boss, ruling these folks with an iron grip no doubt. I was a fool not to spot the clear signs straight away; I must be getting daft in my old age.'

'I see, you naturally recognise the bearing and nobility of a great leader, I thank you human, I am pleasantly flattered by your admiration,' said Cadmow smiling broadly and puffing out his chest with pride as he struck a pose of superior pomposity.

'Well not exactly laddie,' said Mrs Mcdoon. 'Only a fella in a fearfully strong position of leadership would get away with walking around looking like a confused psychedelic circus strumpet clown. Everyone is too afraid to tell you the old midlife crisis routine is just making you look daft, desperate and a bit of a greasy laughing stock, no offence laddie, you may even be able to turn things around but I fear things have probably gone too far. You've not tried to form a rock band with a weirdly cheesy name such as; old guns or senior studs, have you? There is no going back after that laddie, no going back at all.'

'I pity your obvious jealousy human,' said Cadmow with a laugh and a snort. 'My associates also suffer from the same sort of fun hating envy. I am happy with my funky new look, my sexy new lady and my rocking new electric guitar, they're all the rage you know. Perhaps you should get a life as the young folk say. Make it quick though for I will be taking it very shortly.'

'It's got to that stage has it laddie?' said Mrs McDoon with a knowing nod of the head. 'In that case I'll say my piece and see how the land lies. I challenge you lord Cadmow to armed combat, not lethal mind just to a clear victor emerges. Should I win ...'

'Which you will not human,' boomed Cadmow, 'you may be brave, foolish or both but you are doomed. Your life will end this day in noble combat, do not think about tomorrow for you will not see it.'

Mrs Mcdoon fixed Cadmow with a steely gaze. 'Power is no excuse for rudeness, now as I was saying should I win I will offer myself as your ally in exchange for the noble land of Scotland for which I will be queen and I want a hundred of your cyber cows which will be called Marauding Morags made naturally from the finest highland cattle to keep order and clean the streets of all the sub human vermin that infest them. Scotland and its people will be free and independent you can do what you like with the rest of the people of the world. Do we have a deal?'

'Why not, human, but remember when you lose which you will, death is all you will receive. Until, ah here is Norhlick with your tea, while we drink it you can tell me about this Scotland place you are so keen to rule. I do not care in truth but it seems like the hospitable thing to do, feign an interest in my guest's obsessive ramblings, if they are suitably dull it sharpens the appetite for their final culling.'

After they had finished their tea and biscuits the indulgent Cadmow leapt up and offered his hoof to the good lady which she took before rising to her feet.

'I'll be using this wee broom for the battle,' said Mrs McDoon brandishing her broom as a staff weapon, knives suddenly extending from the ends. 'I suggest you select your own and do it quickly, least I start and end the battle without you.'

'Moolock pass me my horn staff,' said Cadmow as a mighty battle staff with large sharp horns emerging from either end was thrown across the room into the eager hooves of the battle-ready stamping Bull Lord.

The two combatants circled each other, jabbing and taunting with their weapons.

'Now you shall die noble yet foolhardy lady,' said Cadmow before suddenly lunging in with a certain death strike.

'Oh I don't think so laddie,' she replied partly blocking and partly dodging the blow, before replying with her own skilful jabs. 'I intend being alive for some years yet, I may even outlive your good self.'

'Ha human you have skill but your arrogance will surely be your undoing just as the many candles that surround our hay bed and the highly flammable nature of both this kimono and the pungent all over body wax which I spread thickly across my hide to stay young and arouse the high passions of both myself and my energetic young lover will surely be mine,' said Cadmow, going in for another blow.

Mrs McDoon blocked his blow, 'Too much information, laddie, we're supposed to be fighting not fornicating. Now take my advice son focus on the battle and ignore any wayward messages bubbling up from your wedding tackle, if you know what's good for you.'

Their weapons clashed again and again as the battle dragged on and on. As minutes became hours with no victory in sight, everyone else in the room went back to watching the television except the yokels who were happily betting on the fight and offering odds to Phil and various cow generals Phil was apparently in contact with.

The fight carried on deep into the night. As everyone retired to bed the pair still battled on, their blows, blocks and witty fight banter still ringing through the air.

As breakfast was served the next morning neither of them appeared to weary. 'I also offer a cleaning service at a reasonable rate, you could use that with all these bodies cluttering up the place,' said Mrs McDoon.

'We could certainly do with someone to keep the place clean,' suggested Moolock as Phil handed out breakfasts, 'our present human servant makes more mess than he should be capable of.'

'It's not my fault,' said Phil, 'if you lot didn't leave the bodies of your enemies all over the place it would be easy to keep the place clean and tidy. A body is a heavy, awkward thing to get rid of never mind several dozen, then there are all the stains left behind by all the rancid life juices, you just can't get that stuff out of the carpet. Now all the bleach has run out I'm fighting a losing battle I really am.'

'Have you tried bicarbonate of soda, laddie? I always add a twist of crab apple blossom for freshness. Some others use lemon but I say they're damn fools and as for those that use incense well there is no reasoning with those happy clappy new age nitwits,' said Mrs McDoon as the two combatants took a brief breakfast break.

'Sounds a bit old fashioned,' said Phil handing Mrs McDoon her hot salty porridge. 'Anyway this weird flavoured soda won't move all these heavy bodies will it? You know there will be loads more before this war is finished, probably hundreds and it's not fair me having to move them all by myself. I was diagnosed with slothful sod syndrome but no one here cares they just threaten to make me do a moonwalk without a spacesuit if I don't shift the decomposing rancid corpses double quick. I'll probably do myself an injury and then you'll all be sorry.'

'No, human, we will not shed a single tear,' said Moolock. 'Now Mrs McDoon how is your porridge?'

'Oh, laddie, the porridge is bitter like a twisted old maid snarling with spite at a loved up young couple and it's as hot as the scolding steam that rises from the devils foul Jacuzzi itself. It tastes just right, compliments to the chef,' said Mrs McDoon eating with great enthusiasm.

'Our battle has given you quite an appetite,' said Cadmow tucking in to his own meal with equal gusto. 'I am surprised you are still alive to be honest.'

'I am a tricky one to kill, laddie, many have tried and been quite shocked when they found my blade at their throats and a last gasp of breath departing their dying lips,' said the lady with a disturbingly nostalgic burst of mirth.

'I am prepared to agree to your demands if you provide us with a professional level cleaning service,' said Cadmow. 'As soon as you start clearing these corpses I will give instructions for the construction to begin on your Daisybells.'

'Sounds like a fair arrangement,' said Mrs McDoon, 'only they won't be called Daisybells, mine will go by the name of Morag, Marauding Morag's. Named after a wee calf I had a soft spot for as a child. When I was young and daft with sentimentality, I even have a tattoo of the creature in a spot on my body no other person has ever seen not even my late husband. May his time in heaven be spent in hard righteous labour like it was in life. Of course I never encouraged him to gaze upon my naked flesh. In the early years of our marriage I occasionally caught him staring at my body in a wanton and nay lustful manner, I forgave him of course because men even the best men can be weak and foolish in the presence of the female form but I made a point of slapping him hard across the face every time that look appeared in his wandering eyes.'

'Then we have a deal, human. I would appreciate it if you start removing the corpses as soon as you have rested,' said Cadmow.

'Oh they'll be no need for any of that,' said Mrs McDoon, putting down her empty porridge bowl and starting to stack the first of the corpses. 'I've had my three hours sleep for the week and I won't be bothering with any more of that idle nonsense until this place is shining fit to bring out jealous fits of rage in them silly super cleaners they have on the television nowadays, amateurs the lot of them.'

'Excellent,' said Cadmow, sounding rather bemused. 'Now Phil as soon as you have finished washing up the breakfast dishes, help the good lady with the corpses.'

'Do I have to?', said Phil, 'those corpses look really heavy and anyway the way she is flinging them over her shoulder I don't think she needs any help.'

'Do as you are told, human,' said Cadmow with a gaseous snort.

'But I'm a prisoner of war, isn't it against the Geneva Convention to make me work or something,' replied Phil sulkily throwing the breakfast pots in the soapy sink water.

Moolock flicked back soap suds that had splashed all over him. 'Human, we are wicked and cruel overlords who see you as part of an inferior species of annoying halfwits. Strange as it might appear we do not feel bound by any foolish human treaties.'

'Yeah but I do everything around here,' whined Phil, 'get those jar fellas to do something for a change, all they do is stand around in their stupid glass jars making stupid comments all day. Didn't they kill an old girlfriend of lord Greasy horn, surely a bit of hard labour would be appropriate from them.'

'Hey fella,' shouted Billy Bob across the room, 'I'll have you know we work real hard each day, we use our brain power and real-world experience to either assist or undermine the efforts of these bovine overlord types, depending on who exactly is doing the interrogating naturally. As far as folk's killing other folk's romantic partners is concerned, well we have already apologised for any unfortunate confusions on our part. Who is to say that one or more of us fellas were not romantically involved with ladies working at this very base and have now been killed by the Moolord himself who unlike us has found himself what I am told is a very attractive young lady bovine friend as well as those very erm individually styled if a bit too revealing kimonos.'

'They are wet, human,' said Moolock, 'I am not having them drip all over the place, all this horn grease causes to many slip hazards around here as it is. We let you live human; you have done very little but take advantage of our good nature and hospitality. Now we have employed the services of a professional then perhaps we can let you go, on a nice long moonwalk without a spacesuit, what do you think human?'

'I think Mrs Mcdoon needs some help,' said Phil going pale with horror before rushing off to Mrs Mcdoon. 'How can I help Mrs McDoon?'

'Oh laddie, just carry these two wee tiddlers for me,' said the Mrs Mcdoon throwing two bulky bodies in his direction, crushing him to the floor.

'Great, no problem always happy to help,' Phil murmured from the depths of the corpse pile.

'Moolock, who is it that calls me Lord Greasy horn?' asked Cadmow.

'I am sure I have no idea my lord, I am sure I have never used such a disrespectful nickname,' replied Moolock looking rather sheepish.

'I would hope not, Moolock, anyone who did would not only be insolent in the extreme but ignorant of modern style and well-known markers of masculinity. A well greased horn on a bull is a sure-fire sign of true bullishness. The grease of a true bull if you will, can I tempt you with a pot?' said Cadmow.

'I will resist that temptation my lord,' said Moolock, giving an unimpressed sniff at the pot and a raised eyebrow at the slogan which read, the greasiest bulls frolic in the greenest meadows, 'I will keep my horns as they are if it's all the same to you. I have always lived by the simple belief that a dry horn is a happy and more importantly a productive horn.'

'Suit yourself Moolock, but you are missing out on the attentions of frisky lady bovines,' said Cadmow taking back the pot of horn grease and applying a little to his hooves. 'Of course you don't care that much for romance do you, Moolock?'

'I once had a practical arrangement with a highly intelligent female for a while so as not to let our superior genes go to waste, it was well planned, executed with upmost precision, with a positive outcome and absolutely no wax, grease, chest spray or ill- fitting gaudy kimonos were required,' said Moolock with a haughty snort.

As the yokels hollered their approval for Moolock having a relationship in a way that made the word practical sound like it was a euphemism for sordid act of lust, Mrs McDoon shouted over the din. 'Oh, laddie I nearly forgot, have you tried digging up the ship under the pyramids?'

'Ship, human, what ship?' asked Cadmow and Moolock together.

'Those two hippy dippy moo for nothings, Holly and Vince were advising the military powers that a big spaceship was buried under the pyramids presumably by your people. You should make haste if you want it, the Americans are busy digging up the Nile Valley as we speak,' said Mrs McDoon.

'Human, are you certain of this?' said Cadmow.

'I only know what Holly and Vince told the military, it could have been one of their drug-crazed hallucinations for all I know.'

'If there is a chance this ship exists then we must have it,' said Cadmow. 'Despatch an army of Daisybells immediately.'

'Yes my lord I am doing so now,' said Moolock turning to a console. 'We must deal with Holly and Vince as well.'

'Oh yes, Moolock, I will deal with them now, once and for all.'

Chapter 16: New bonnets for the moo cows.

'Oh I do wish someone would rescue my beloved from the clutches of that moo-crazed maniac, but no one seems to care,' worried Professor Winkle as he made the final adjustments to the moo bonnets. 'She could be subject to the most terrible torments, oh my heart worries for her so.'

'I am not risking more of my troops to rescue Mrs McDoon. She seemed more than capable of looking after herself,' said the Colonel pacing the room, taking deep breaths and occasionally glaring at the Professor and at us. 'Let's get those helmets finished, then we'll take back the moon from that damn Cadmow.'

We sat still as the moo-bonnets were fitted, on a big screen in front of us reporter Josephine Barnstorm was giving her own take on the latest turn in world events.

'As we reach day seven of the Egyptian pyramid siege, where brave American forces try to carry out their top-secret anti-cow mission in the Nile Valley while fighting against wicked cow-loving forces of Egypt and her evil allies who deny American soldiers their right to occupy these wonders of the world which surely are the property of all of humanity and not just the selfish Egyptians. How did they even get these pyramids? Stolen from America perhaps? Has our President given away too much by offering to give them shiny new pyramids of steel and glass to replace the shabby stone ones in our way? Surely if any people deserve pyramids it's the American people. Plus we have shocking revelations about a long history of cow worship dating back to ancient Egypt and the cow goddess Hathor. The question tonight is how widespread in the world is this cow collaboration network and how do we defeat it? Is America being too soft? What's your view?'

With the moo bonnets settled on our precious noggins, the good Professor held a mirror before us so we could see the hideous things more clearly.

'These might save our lives but who is going to save our street-cred?' said Vince.

'We could always paint rainbows on the horns and tie coloured ribbons to them, start a craze, like hula hoops for the head,' I suggested trying to see the positive besides the life saving angle.

'Yeah groovy sister, we could sell them and make our fortunes,' suggested Vince already reaching for our portable emergency crafting kit, we carry for just those kind or fashion emergencies.

'If you do successfully market them, I would be entitled to a substantial cut,' said the Professor. 'I have a very good lawyer should you disagree.'

'Let's quit all this fashion talk shall we,' said the Colonel removing the mirror and looking us straight in the eyes. 'My daddy didn't care for fashion and neither do I, now let's quit this bullshit and get down to some bull-beating brass tacks, if that's fine with you bovines?'

We both politely nodded in the affirmative and avoided telling him that we could tell he didn't go in for fashion.

'Right that's good, now you've got your reassuringly hideous protection helmets are you both fully committed to helping us?'

'Of course man,' I said, 'anything you folks need, we are happy to help.'

'Good, now you're to work with the professor here, to bring down all those force-fields and lasers in the various bases especially the moon base.'

'Sure we'll get right on it,' said Vince and my good self.

A crowd was gathering round us, admiring our moo bonnets and shouting out ideas for projects.

'We've gathered up a lot of Daisybell parts,' said Major Browne, 'could you build more of those rock and roll ninja moo bots, like the ones you had in Las Vegas?'

'Sure,' I said, 'I could work on that and Vince could do the lasers and force fields.'

'Hold your horses, Major,' said the Colonel 'I'm not comfortable with putting more of this mind-warping popular music out in the world, it could brainwash our own people, we could end up with a nation of mooing communists.'

'Sir the brainwashing rock and roll will be under our control, it will be us brainwashing our enemy, any of our people in the vicinity could be issued with ear protection,' said the Major.

'Alright, Major, I will take that under advisement, gather the parts, recall Jane and her moobots then I will inspect the ear protection myself, if I think this rock and roll is within safe tolerances then I'll give the green light.

'Thank you, sir, Holly, you're with me,' said the Major.

'Wait up a minute,' said the Colonel. 'I have one more question for you two bovines.'

The Colonel gave us one of his piercing stares and waved the tickling stick in our faces like a party clown on a funky dance drug.

'Ask away man, our minds are at your disposal.'

'The thing is, our troops are meeting stiff resistance in the Nile Valley, they have demolished the pyramids and dug very deep, very wide holes looking for this ship and so far nothing,' began the Colonel. 'Now I need you to confirm for me that your people buried a spaceship under the Nile Valley and I want a precise location and depth of this ship. We need to get that thing out darn quick before Cadmow cottons on and sends in his damn no good Daisybells.'

'Nothing to do with our people man,' said Vince sounding a bit embarrassed.

'What?' snapped the Colonel.

'Yeah it was these little grey critters playing some freaky game of interstellar hide and seek,' I said as the colonel's face started to go a funny shade of red. 'We saw a show about it on the U.F.O, channel, they said Elvis was on the ship because they've got a place called Memphis in Egypt just like where he came from in Tennessee.'

'Are you saying that we have just invaded Egypt and demolished the pyramids because of something you two saw on the goddam U.F.O. channel?' snarled the Colonel clenching his fists so tight the tickling stick snapped in two.

'We thought it was worth a chance man,' said Vince in a mellow tone that didn't seem to be calming the Colonel down very much. 'You know those conspiracy cats might have got it right on this one. Those freaky dudes are due; I mean it's the law of averages, like a stopped clock being right, twice a day and all that.'

Colonel Twirl's silence was disconcerting, but not as much as his wild stare and deep focused breaths.

'Perhaps the Egyptians moved it to another valley,' I suggested helpfully, 'what about the British Museum, they have loads of stuff from Egypt. Has anyone thought to ask them, it might have been put into a big storeroom and...?'

'It would be best to stop talking now Holly.' It was Major Browne, patting the Colonel's shoulder and encouraging him to take those deep, deep breaths. 'Now relax Colonel, you're in your safe, calm place. On the farm, the big old farm, you're churning milk and making cheese.'

'Cheese, Major, is it, is it...? began the Colonel, sounding like a spaced-out kid, half nervous, half wonderstruck.

'Yes Colonel, it's the real dairy deal,' continued the Major in a soft soothing whisper. 'Your daddy's watching and he is oh so proud, so very, proud.'

'Do you like the cheese daddy?' asked the Colonel in an alarmingly childlike voice.

'Oh yes Colonel, your daddy says the cheese is real fine,' whispered the Major. 'He says your cheese is the most American thing he has ever tasted, better than; thanksgiving turkey, peanut butter and jelly sandwiches, homespun county fair taffee and even cherry pie baked by a homecoming queen on the fourth of July.'

With that the Colonel suddenly stood ramrod straight, saluted and began to sing the American national anthem.

'We'll get agent Oakes to explain things to the President and the joint chiefs, sir,' said Major Browne beginning to lead the Colonel away. 'After all if it had been left up to you in the first place those two cows would be in custody now and we wouldn't have had to invade Egypt or knock down any of the ancient wonders of the world at all.'

'Should we lock up the moo cows and throw away the key, Major?' asked the Colonel sounding strangely uncertain of himself.

'No sir, not just yet, let's see if they can bring down those force fields first,' said the Major. 'See if they can be useful to us before we throw them in prison.'

A heavy and uncomfortable silence fell on the lab for the few hours following the revelation, me and Vince kept our fashion free heads down and our funky chat strictly on mute, while we worked on our assigned projects.

The Colonel soon returned to his relatively normal state and took great delight poking agent Oakes with his now mended tickling stick as the poor agent explained the new reality to the President, the joint chiefs and the Egyptian ambassador.

Suddenly on the big screen appeared the snorting image of Cadmow himself. 'Holly, Vince, you fools have betrayed me for the last time. You will die fast and I will watch to make sure, not like these foolish movie villains,' laughed our nemesis.

'Nice to see you as well man,' said Vince. 'Hey that's a cool guitar you got there, why don't you play us a few chords before you turn our brains to fried dough balls.'

'What sort of fool do you think I am?' said Cadmow pressing the button that would send a ray of terminal brain-boiling doom in our direction. 'I will play while you fry.'

With that he picked up his guitar and started to play. The tuneless, cruel abuse of cheesy pop classics assaulted our ears as wild sparks of electricity covered our moo-bonnets setting all the little bows and fancy ribbons alight.

As we ran about the lab, frantically screaming and trying to put out the flames, Cadmow mooed with joy, assuming we were dying painfully as the result of his machine. Once the flames were out our suffering continued as the music got steadily worse.

'Operation counterblast, now,' shouted the Major.

A vortex opened suddenly and two huge speakers were wheeled out into the lab. These funky sound blasters were linked directly to our party sound system. The party we had left to come into the lab was still in full swing and our trustee D.J buddies were blasting out the latest rock country fusion classic called; Devil dancing bovine butt kicking blues.

It was a catchy and more importantly loud little number that filled the lab with noise. Some more delicate souls such as the Colonel and the Professor immediately reached for ear protection. Some folks are just philistines man. If someone showed them a beautiful rose they'd probably cover their eyes so they didn't have to look at it, cutting out their tongues to spite their ears, sad but true of so many grooveless grouch smiths in this world.

'We've got him on the run, Major,' shouted the Colonel rushing towards the view screen, tickle stick raised in full attack. 'Take that you Lord of mooing misrule.'

With that the Colonel jabbed his stick at the screen. 'Dance, dance, yes, yes dance for your uncle Twirly.'

On the screen, Cadmow, still strumming at his groove staff, leapt to his feet and began gyrating and jumping around the command centre like the oldest swinger in town drunkenly clearing the dance floor at a whacked-out wedding disco. It gave me a real hunger for wedding cake and free champagne.

Cadmow worked up a proper frenzy, sweat and chest oil spraying everything in sight. The manic bull Lord reached a crescendo and began to smash his guitar towards the control room screen as a glorious climax of his frenzied funk out.

'I'll take that my lord,' said Moolock relieving Cadmow of his instrument before it did any serious damage.

Now some of you reader cats out there may be thinking my attitude to Cadmow's style and attempts to play the guitar despite a lack of talent as rather hypocritical. After all I am an ageing hippy who still likes to rock up at funky night clubs on a Saturday night with a dancing style that some jealous José's can be quite critical of.

Well, guilty, as charged man, my only excuse is that old sour cat Cadmow is the villain and I don't have too many qualms about laying on a double standard vibe to a cat that has caused so much chaos, besides when I do these things it's with style.

'Moolock why are you interrupting my good cheer and celebrations are you not delighted at the death of those two freakish idiots,' said Cadmow pumping the air with his right hoof fist, while humming, we are the champions.

'Apologies my lord, I thought you were in danger of damaging the delicate instrument panel that allows us to wage our glorious campaign of conquest,' said Moolock holding the guitar as far away as possible from the frenzied bull lord. 'Besides the buffoons live.'

'That they do, Moolock,' said Cadmow, finally taking a moment to peer at view screen. 'You two idiots are supposed to be dead, why have you failed in that simple task?'

'It's our funky new metallic moo bonnets,' I said doing a little twirl. 'Do you like them man?'

I had upgraded the bonnets from hideous helmets of horror to groovy gray matter guardians in light of them saving our sirloin from the fire.

'They were created by my own genius hands,' said the Professor rushing forward to put out the last of our head fires and examine the moo bonnets for damage. 'They held up better than I expected. I thought there was a good chance one of them would short out and electrocute the wearer.'

'You thought what, man?' me and Vince said, feeling more than a little freaked out.

'I calculated a forty percent chance one would fail but not both, there was only a very small chance of that. One of you was almost certain to live and we only really needed one of you so there wasn't any problem.'

'You have such a sensitive bedside manner, Professor,' I said as the oblivious man poked, prodded and rammed his screwdriver into the bonnet and occasionally my delicate head as well.

'No matter,' said Cadmow. 'You are welcome to the rambling fools. I almost pity you humans with your new horn-witted allies. I have been told by my new cleaner a Mrs McDoon that a mighty starship is buried under the pyramids. I have despatched Daisybells to retrieve it and then you will meet your doom.'

'They tortured me something barbaric so they did,' said Mrs McDoon rushing towards the view screen. 'I fought them all night so I did but it was all, to much for me to bear in the end.'

'I thought you defected and asked to become my ally,' said Cadmow.

'That's right, laddie,' whispered Mrs McDoon. 'I'm just hedging my bets, after all you're prancing about with your electric guitar, those two are plotting against each other while on the other side they've got two hippies with their heads alight, a pompous fool with tickling stick and an eccentric professor whose inventions are always on the verge of blowing up. I honestly have no idea which way this is going to go.'

The Professor ran frantically to the view screen. 'Oh sweet lady, I am relieved to see you. How are you? How have they been treating you? Have they hurt you my sweet?'

'I've just been telling you, they tortured me something awful you great deaf wazzock.'

'Oh my, oh my I worry for you so, my dearest lady,' said the Professor beating at the screen in distress.

'You're sailing very close to the wind, laddie, I am a married woman if you've forgotten and nobody's dearest. Even my late husband would not have used such sickly sentimental language in my presence,' said Mrs McDoon angrily shaking her broom at the view screen.

'Oh, Cadmow, please let her go. You've got what you wanted from her, now release the innocent, delicate flower.'

'Stop your fussing man. I've got a wee bit of cleaning to do before I go anywhere. These cows are dirty creatures, blood stains on all the floors and that sticky horn wax in the strangest of places. I don't know what they've been doing with it but it's a demon to shift. I've got no time for all your morbid waffle mugging, I got work to do, good day to you, professor.' With that she stalked off complaining about the bovines walking hay into every room.

'As I was saying,' began Cadmow looking a little bemused, 'I will get the spaceship and you will all be crushed once and for all beneath my mighty war hooves.'

Moolock wiped the Bull lord's sweat and wax-soaked brow as Cadmow stared at us waiting for the looks of dread and terror to sweep our faces.

'Surrender your world to me while you still can feeble Earth maggots,' continued Cadmow rather uncertainly as smirks appeared across the faces in the lab.

'What are you wretches laughing at, has fear driven you all to giggling madness, what, what is it, speak to me for Cowdon's sake.'

'There isn't a ship under the pyramids man,' I said to looks of disbelief from Cadmow.

'You lie, perhaps you hope I will send my Daisybells elsewhere and let you have this glorious prize. This feeble deception will fail and I will have it. Why are you still laughing at your own destruction, it is wrong, you must cower in fear before your mighty Bull lord.'

Cadmow stared at us in a mixture of rage and panic as we all continued to laugh our little hearts out.

'The ship was something Holly and Vince heard about on the UFO channel,' said Major Browne.

'That's right boy, little green men from Mars and something or other to do with that rock and roll singer, Elvis, if them aliens took him why can't they take the rest of the damn music types I want to know,' said the Colonel while rubbing Cadmow's image with his tickling stick.

'Is this true?' asked Cadmow staring at us intensely.

'Well they were gray and didn't really have an obvious gender,' I explained, 'oh and they came from Sirius B, but everything else is broadly true man.'

Suddenly it was Cadmow's turn to laugh, and well he certainly made a banquet out of it. He laughed long and hard until some of us started checking the time wondering if we should terminate the call and get back to work.

Then the laughing turned into a broad grin as the Bull lord stared at a point just over our shoulders and the grin got even wider.

'No ship under the pyramids eh,' he said as we all muttered in boredom and embarrassment that this was indeed correct.

'Then I will have those ones,' bellowed the Bull lord pointing at the television screen on the wall behind us.

As we all turned around we saw the news images of a small fleet of space ships approaching earth.

'Hell's teeth fellas it's them damn good for nothing space goats,' shouted Billy Bob from his jar. 'Someone needs to give them the bums rush, real quick, like, because I ain't taking orders from no goats. Cows is bad enough, but goats is just plain nasty, I ain't kidding around none here either, goats are mean no matter how well you treat them they just butt you and butt you and just for good measure they butt you some more.'

Billy Bob would have carried on in a similar vein but a little bovine electric shock therapy made the fella lose his thread. He was just about able to suggest Cadmow's paternal parentage was in serious doubt.

As we watched angry politicians and pundits demanded the ships be blasted back to various fictional planets from well-known science fiction and fantasy shows.

We heard Cadmow recall his forces for an attack on the ships before terminating his communication link with us.

'What the hell is that critter saying,' said the Colonel, 'if they are demanding our surrender then contact them and say we will fight them on the beaches and the hills just like that Churchill fella did.'

The news channel was now showing a transmission from the fleet. On the screen an angry bovine Captain was bellowing and banging its hoof in apparent frustration or maybe fury, it was hard to tell for sure.

'Hang on a minute, man, the bovine language seems to have evolved quite a bit over the centuries besides the cat's accent is troweled on a bit thick,' I said straining to hear the meaning as every human eye stared at me expectantly.

I brainstormed a minute with my old fella until the Colonel started clearing his throat and waving his fluffy wand of mirth in my general direction.

I quickly gave our translation before the frenzied fluffer got to my very ticklish fur.

'Ok, first of all something about a faulty translation machine trying to transmit messages in so many languages. The Captain thinks humans will assume they are invaders while the first officer disagrees, this is a bone of contention between the pair as it has caused problems on previous missions,' I explained to mutterings of irritation rather than gratitude from those assembled.

'Anything else, non-translation-related, Holly,' said the Major rather impatiently, 'such as; the reason for their visit, hostility status, intentions that kind of useful thing.'

'Yeah, the Captain is just getting to that. They are very angry with us, very angry indeed. They accuse us of deliberately releasing a dangerous criminal. They think we want Cadmow to help us get some sort of, space empire going. They warn us that he is dangerous and will turn on us sooner or later. We must turn him over to them immediately or else there will be big trouble.'

'They're welcome to him as far I'm concerned,' said the Colonel. 'Someone get a line to that ship, we need to make them aware of our situation.'

'Sir the President is on the line,' said one of the communication officers. 'She wants a translation, so she can decide whether to blast them straight to hell or open up a inter-species dialogue all civilised and friendly like.'

'Soldier tell the President what this bovine just told me,' said the Colonel.

Suddenly the communication screen filled with the image of the cow captain still rather annoyed but with the translation machine now in working order.

'Humans, you will pay for this attack upon our peaceful ships,' shouted the Captain.

'Now listen here, Captain, despite the fact you have illegally entered our atmosphere with your ships we have resisted the temptation to blast your fleet straight to hell. Which is very restrained of us and frankly better than you deserve!'

'How are we supposed to accept your peace talk when you are using the prisoner Cadmow and his cohorts of wickedness to attack our ships from your very own

Moon base,' said the Captain suddenly pointing at us despite our best efforts to blend into the background. 'I see two of them in your base now.'

'It was a miscarriage of justice man, case of mistaken identity type thing man. Punished for a crime we didn't commit,' I said.

'Yeah that's right,' chimed in my old fella. 'Stitched up like kippers we were, banged up but we aren't bitter man. An apology would be kind of nice though and a funky parade for us helping beat sour cat Cadmow would be even groovier.'

'For your information Captain,' said the Colonel shooting us an irritated look. 'This prisoner Cadmow took over our moon base and has been attacking us with an army of cyborg bovines he calls Daisybells. He has caused us nothing but trouble and we would very much appreciate it if you took him and his little friends into custody followed by a swift execution. As far as these two are concerned, they are our prisoners and we have promised them a full pardon and asylum on Earth should they help us. Thus far they have been as useful as chocolate coffee pots but we hope they may be able to aid us in taking back our moon base.'

'Well human, taking prisoner Cadmow into custody is proving rather difficult as he is presently leading an army of renegade cow generals and Doomsday Daisybells in an attack upon our ships. They have boarded several of our vessels and are very reluctant to leave. Perhaps you could attack this moon base of yours and deprive the criminal you carelessly let out, of his current base of operations.'

'We will be launching a fresh assault on the moon base, Captain, just as soon as these two get those force fields down,' said the Colonel looking at us expectantly. 'I'll be expecting my moon-adapted moo-copter as well. We need to adapt the Robo-Elvis bots for moon surface conditions as well.'

Before anyone could answer the Colonel's looks of impatient expectations, a funky whirling wormhole appeared with fifty fierce looking Daisybells visible on the far side. Ahead of the charging doom bots were Jane and her fellow Elvis dance bot riders heading straight towards us on their battered groove bots.

'Come on Jane, you can do it,' I shouted. 'Image you're trying to be the first at the bar so you can be served by a cute new barman all your friends want to bag.'

I am sure I saw her speed up when I said it as well. We cued in some appropriate chase music and the demon riders crashed into the lab.

'Holls it's great to see ya girl,' said a breathless Jane leaping from her steed and into my outstretched hooves ready for a big old welcome home hug.

'Now where is the cute barman,' said Jane as the wormhole began to slam shut.

The wormhole was almost closed when a cheeky Daisybell stuck its snorting head through the gap. It butted and snorted at us as we all rushed forward and pushed it back through the wormhole allowing it to close.

'Jane it's good to finally meet you,' said the Major rushing over. 'Are you alright, we have a medical team coming down to see to your people and engineers to patch up the moo bots. I am Major Browne by the way and that is Colonel Twirl.'

The Major indicated the Colonel who was now talking to the cow Captain and the President in a funky joint on screen meeting.

'I'd be careful of the Colonel by the way,' continued the Major. 'He is mainly alright but don't mention rock and roll, American cheese, hotdogs and most of all give the Man's tickling stick a wide berth if you know what is good for you.'

'I am fine thanks, Major,' said Jane.

'I thought you'd be all shuck up,' shouted Vince examining Robo ninja Elvis bot.

'Oy, didn't you hear the Major,' I shouted, 'no cheese in front of the Colonel.'

'She said no American cheese,' shouted back Vince, 'I can assure you my cheese is the real dairy deal groovy sister.'

'It certainly smells like it man.'

'Ask if she gets space sick, Major,' shouted the Colonel. 'We need her to suit up for the lunar taskforce ASAP.'

'I think she needs to rest up a bit first man,' I suggested giving Jane another hug.

'Is that right, Jane,' shouted the Colonel, 'do you need rest? We've got a big battle coming our way, the final battle of this war in fact it would be a damn shame for you to miss it, given all the hard work you've put in so far.'

'Don't worry Colonel,' replied Jane, 'I don't get space sick and I'm running on adrenaline, caffeine and the sound track to the movie Flash Gordon at the moment. So suit me up and point me moon-wards.'

Me, Jane and Vince gave a quick blast of Queen songs from the movie Flash Gordon with the Major joining in until the Colonel waved his tickling stick at us until we stopped.

'Save it for the victory party Holl,' said Jane.

'Now what makes you think we have been planning one of them Jane?' I said as Jane raised her eyebrows and shot me smirks sharp enough to cut through concrete.

'Okay, okay, Jane, yes we have big plans for the victory party. It will be on the moon and it will be so wild the folks on Alpha Centuri will be phoning up to complain about the noise and why they weren't invited to the galaxy's biggest shindig.'

As we bounced around ideas for the party the Major cleared her throat. 'Right, back to work everyone, we won't get to have a victory party until we win a final victory.'

We dashed in a hurried but still cool and breezy fashion back to our work places and made our final preparations for the battle to come.

Chapter 17: Battle of the Mooncows.

'I'd make an appropriately rousing speech, but it's a bit loud in here,' shouted the Major, as she tried to compete with moo-copter's frantic rotors and the painful straining groans coming from the vortex generator as it fought to maintain three gloriously colourful wormholes without exploding.

'It's alright, Major,' I said from my seat in the hovering Moo-copter, 'most of us have been listening to our own personally-tailored inspirational speeches generated by the funky new, go-into-battle, app.'

'As long as we've got the right mood music during the action, that's what counts,' interrupted Jane. 'I've got, Ride of the Valkyries and other operatic battle blasters as I am feeling classy. What about you, Holls, what have you got in your play list; Queen, Status Quo, Orgy Banter?'

'I've got a Weird Al, Gilbert and Sullivan mash up because I'm feeling kind of classy too,' I said as the Colonel climbed up the rope tail before swinging into the moo-copter next to yours truly.'

'Let's go everyone,' said the Colonel as soon as all of us going on or above the moon's surface had firmly secured our space suits.

With that my juicy jacked in Jezebels the whirlwind at a desert disco that would eventually be known as the battle of the moon cows began. The operational name for the battle; my daddy was right about mustard too damn it, was how the Colonel would always refer to it, but he was the only one.

Major Browne, Vince and a large group of soldiers headed through one of the ground level wormholes. Their team would be responsible for taking back the moon base, once they had neutralised the force fields and lasers which we felt could be done pretty swiftly.

Jane and the robo ninja Elvis crew headed through a second wormhole next to the first. Their mission was to deal with the wild herds of Doomsday Daisybells that roamed the moon's surface, waiting to be called upon as agents of chaos and destruction.

Thirdly were us moo-copter cats, high in the air facing a wormhole above the one Jane and her crew had just gone through. The Colonel would be co-ordinating the battle high above the moon's surface from our funkally enhanced moo-copter.

'By Jingo it actually god darn works,' exclaimed the Colonel as we flew above the moon surrounded by a huge bubble of air that allowed us to move around as we would on Earth. 'Professor you must be real proud of your achievement, allowing us to fly this bird over the moon and standing up against those pedantic finger wagging laws of physics.'

'I do feel proud Colonel,' replied the Professor over the radio, 'it is further evidence of my genius, of my superiority over the mundane lumpen masses who live their lives in a haze of drunken mediocrity. At the same time, I feel dirty; I have soiled and sullied the sacred laws of nature themselves. All of Neptune's oceans cannot wash this stain from my soul, I may never feel clean again. Is this how Oppenheimer felt? Am I now the destroyer of worlds as well? Oh woe, oh woe is me, my greatest achievement, perhaps mankind's greatest achievement is also my greatest shame. Out, out oh foul spot...'

'Don't be so damn dramatic Professor,' replied the Colonel. 'You did a good job and that's the bottom line besides these laws of physics sound like a gang of un-American losers, holding our great nation back the way they do. When this war is over I intend talking to the President about a war on physics. I reckon a tactical military strike, hard and fast would show these so-called laws of physics exactly whose boss.'

As the professor's weeping faded away we flew low over a snorting herd of Daisybells. Far below Jane had started a conga line spinning the herd into a frenzy.

'How you holding up, Jane?,' I called over the radio.

'Just great, Holly, I've never felt so alive, the way things are going those Daisybells will be disco ready in time for the slow dance lunar eclipse smooch off.'

'You're kicking up a lot of dust, Jane,' cautioned the Colonel as the delirious jiving Jillaroo's kicked up their dancing hooves and whole heaping helpings of sticky lunar sand.

'Right oh, Colonel, I'll ease up a... oh god, oh god, what the hell,' the last part was a desperate series of screams as Jane's fate was obscured by a wave of vast eruptions from the surface throwing up huge clouds of moon dust and rocking our world and the Moo-copter for all it was worth.

'By Cowdon's ever mooing grace and the pale of purity what was that?' I gasped as pilot brought us finally under control.

'Jane, Jane, do you read me?' said the Colonel over the silent radio as I gazed down at the slowly clearing cloud of dust that hid the fate of my good and brave friends and their robo Elvis bots.

That silence seemed eternal although it was probably only twenty seconds or so before we heard that radio static be swept away by the dulcet but distinctly distressed tones of Jane.

'Oh god what the hell was that,' said Jane sounding fully freaked out.

'Are you alright, Jane?' I asked trying to keep my own terror from showing.

'I'm in one piece, Holly, but that blast nearly took out two of my moo bots,' said Jane. 'What was it, a pat mine?'

'Keep calm, Jane,' said the Colonel moving the moo copter to the head of the Daisybell herd. 'There is a field of pat mines all around you by the look of things, pull back and we'll try and lead the herd away from you and further into the mine field while you regroup.'

'Thanks Colonel,' replied Jane still sounding a little panicked.

'Don't do anymore conga's, Jane,' I said watching the huge eruptions exploding from the herd far below. 'Try the birdie song or a bit of break dancing.'

'Will do, Holly, I am pulling back and will regroup in ten minutes at groove position two. What about me counter attacking with the dizzy disco Elvis hound dog remix?'

'That sounds groovetastic, Jane, just don't do *The Time warp*, that could set off more mines.'

Jane acknowledged my warnings as we flew further on, leading the butting and snorting Daisybells across the erupting moon surface. Each blast enraged the deadly herd to a frenzy as well as shaking and knocking the moo-copter something wilful. All the calming mellow moo mantras I had been taught by the many gurus I had consulted over the years flashed impotently through my terrified brain.

'Are you alright, Holly?' asked the Colonel clearly noticing the way I desperately gripped my seat.

'Hanging in there, Colonel, thanks. Cool as a cucumber, just a little concerned for my friend, Jane, down there in the thick of things,' I told the Colonel not wanting to burden the man with the news I was as freaked out as a cat down a well of angry puppies.

'Normally I'd use the tickling stick to boost morale in situations like this, Holly, but it's just not possible in these damn space suits,' replied the Colonel.

'Oh well never mind, Colonel.'

'This is Major Browne to Colonel Twirl we have secured the control room sir,' crackled the radio.

'Well done, Major,' replied the Colonel. 'What about the rest of the base, is there much resistance?'

'Considerable resistance sir,' replied the Major. 'Cow Generals and Daisybell forces are dug in throughout the base and there seems to be a lot of booby traps. Pushing on slowly sir. Fortunately the international forces have arrived although they keep arguing about who should be in charge. Up to now I have used the threat of the tickling stick to keep them in line.'

'Good work, Major. As soon as you can get the laser cannon back online we could do with a little help taking out these Daisybells.'

'We are working on that sir,' replied the Major, 'Cadmow did a good job disabling the offensive systems before he left to take out the moo ships. It may take some time and as I said we are meeting some heavy resistance, we've got our hands full with that.'

With all those pesky pat mines going of left right and centre not only were we being constantly jostled like a festival crowd at the bar during a super quake but all that stick- happy moon dust was obscuring our view something wicked.

'Visibility severely reduced sir,' said the pilot, 'this air bubble is a positive dust trap and the radar has only limited range.'

'Shake it off, soldier, we need our vision clear,' suggested the Colonel as the pilot began taking evasive action.

'Large object heading straight for us sir, I think it's the lead moo-ship. Brace for impact.'

'Captain what the hell is going on, change your course immediately. You're on a direct collision course with our back yard', yelled the Colonel as dazzling set of ship lights glared through the thick haze of dust that hung all around us on our dust trap and now probably death trap of an air bubble that made our scientifically dubious jaunt possible even though it really wasn't.

'Yes foolish humans and traitorous bovines it is I the bringer of your doom, my course is set, your only choice is to crash and then die on the cold dead moon below, while you no doubt look at mother Earth in the sky and pine for your family who will soon be joining you in death unless they join me in my reign of vengeance and conquest, either way I win.' It was the cruel bellows of Lord Cadmow who had by the looks of it taken command of the biggest, best armed moo ship in the fleet.

The Colonel managed to get off a frantic volley of the moo-copter's weapons just before we were hit ourselves by the moo ship and a barrage of manic laughter that serenaded our rapid and ungainly descent headlong towards the moon's surface.

'Brace for impact,' shouted the pilot as I wished in my terrified way that I could hear my Vince's sweet moo one last time, because I was damn sure we weren't going to get out of this alive. My fears felt vindicated as Cadmow's evil cackle leapt once again from our headphones.

'Pathetic Earth maggots thank you ever so much for falling so conveniently into my little trap, now please do me a favour and die, quickly now, pop your clogs eh.'

We sat for a second in our ruin of a copter now without our protective air bubble. We had our spacesuits which were undamaged and a good supply of air but as we stumbled out onto the moon surface we realised how vulnerable we were. Pat mines all around us; a huge herd of Daisybells looking on in the distance and Cadmow now apparently in full control of at least one of the deadly moo ships.

We tried our radios frantically but static was the only reward we received for our efforts, except of course for the channel of cackling, snorting hate from radio Cadmow and his bad trip lunar playlist.

'I wish I had my god darn tickling stick, I'd show that barn bothering son of a cheese string,' muttered the Colonel as both he and the pilot fired their weapons impotently at the buzz happy ship that passed overhead at terrifyingly close range for the third time.

'Why isn't he using the weapons, man?' I asked as the ship went in for yet another round of the scare the fur off coolest cow on the scene game. It seemed to be working as well my little cinnamon rolls, my wits had pretty much departed and my fur wasn't going to be far behind I was sure.

'He must have only partial control of that ship, it means we still have a chance, Holly,' said the Colonel as we aimed our weapons at the advancing herd of Daisybells. Using the fuselage of the fallen moo-copter gave us the illusion of protection as we crouched behind it. An illusion that became increasingly transparent as the snorting herd raced our way.

Suddenly a glorious beam of light leapt out from the direction of the base causing the Colonel to raise his fist in triumph.

'Nice shot Major,' yelled the military dude ready to declare victory as the mean old moo ship shuddered, its shields sparkling and growing briefly dimmer.

'Again, Major, hit them with another blast of glory light,' urged the Colonel gesticulating for all he was worth at the ship. No further beams of freedom came though, despite our prayers and wishes in those endless moments.

With a snort and a bellow in our disappointed ears Cadmow turned the now recovered instrument of torment towards the moonbase.

'Let the Daisybells finish them, while I destroy that base,' said Cadmow.

'But Cadmow, we should watch their deaths,' we heard Moolock plead, 'did we learn nothing from the humans mindless entertainments. If we leave them to die out of view they will surely find a ingenious way to escape and perhaps defeat us, for is it not written such in the movies and the whole culture of those halfwit maggots, they will come up smelling of roses if we do not watch and actively prune them from the universe ourselves.'

'Nonsense, Moolock, we have taken too much of their nonsensical culture seriously as it is. Those on the ground will be trampled under the hooves of justice we will raise that base to the ground, just as soon as you have full control of the weapons systems,' bellowed Cadmow.

'The weapons will be on line in a few minutes my lord.'

'You have been saying that for quite a while, Moolock, now please get on with it.'

The radio went deathly quiet then as I guess Cadmow must have realised he was transmitting on an open frequency and decided to cut us off in our darkest hour. The silence of the grave lay heavy on our dust-slicked helmets as the pilot gazed across the bleak lunar landscape, like some moody cat in an overly dramatic beat style poem. The only thing missing was a black sweater and a pipe.

'Look who's coming to complain about being eaten for dinner,' said the pilot as a frantic stampede of Daisybells stormed towards us.

'Jane, Jane, can you hear my voice? Are you still alive mellow sister?' I mooed desperately to a deathly radio silence, hoping against hope that Jane, my good and always funky friend was out there somewhere with a plan or at least with a pulse and a fighting chance to maybe pull a last dash chance rabbit of cutting it a bit too close for comfort victory out of the magical hat of hope and dreamily-deluded optimism.

As the Colonel raised his weapon and muttered an angry defiant curse, I watched something white being waved from a Daisybell that was pushing its way rapidly to the front of the advancing herd.

'Don't shoot,' yelled Jane over the radio, I've tamed these Daisybells. They'd be eating out of my hand if we were back on Earth and they weren't robots.

'This is no time to be getting new pets, Jane, no matter how sad and cute they looked in the store,' I said as Jane came into view, riding her Daisybell towards us for all she was worth.

'Well what can I say,' said Jane finally pulling up in front of us. 'I've always had a soft spot for bovines and these seemed to be neglected by their owner so I took them in, can I keep them mom, can I?'

'It's good to see you, Jane,' I said as she leaned down for a hug.

'You too, Holly,' said Jane as I looked round at a large semicircle of docile-looking, Doomsday Daisybells as they nodded their heads and tapped their feet to some groove we could not hear.

'What did you do to them, Jane?' I asked as the Colonel began to examine the Daisybells more closely.

'I'll tell you what she's done, Holly,' said the Colonel, 'she has brainwashed them using rock and roll, turned them into draft-dodging, peacenik, hippy dropouts who won't want to fight for anyone let alone Cadmow. Nice one, Jane.'

'Well sort of Colonel' replied Jane, 'but not exactly.'

Jane told us how she had been thrown from her ninja Elvis bot and on to the back of a Daisybell. Clinging on for dear life as it bucked and leapt in a wild moon fury, Jane had fought desperately to link into the bombastic bovine's computer system where she tried to influence its core program with music; finally managing to update its herd program with an experimental teenage rebel virus she had been working on with the Professor.

'The result was they no longer wanted to follow orders anymore and were bored, looking round for teenage kicks,' said Jane, 'so I gave them rock and roll, disco, punk, heavy metal, pop, rap, the lot and they want to follow us now. Climb aboard, Holly, and let's teach these cats how to party.'

As I jumped aboard a seriously rhythmic Daisybell I saw the Colonel wearily mounting a groove steed of his own next to Jane.

'Exactly what am I meant to do, Jane?' asked the Colonel.

'Just hold on, Colonel. Your Daisybell will follow the herd which I will be leading. Try and sync your communication system with the Daisybell and sing something groovy to it.'

'I don't know any rock and roll songs, Jane,' said the Colonel. 'Is the singing strictly necessary?

'Try some traditional, folk perhaps Colonel, or country, even just whistling the *star- spangled banner* would do it. Singing will keep her calm; they aren't used to being ridden.'

'No problem, Jane, I can manage that,' said the Colonel beginning a patriotic song about a sad trucker who loved the roads and wanted them covered with American flags.

'On no you're with me hun,' shouted Jane as the pilot headed to a separate Daisybell.

'Now hold on as tight as you like now,' Jane said rather saucily as the eager pilot leapt on behind her.

'Get a room, sister,' I muttered as we began our charge across the lunar landscape towards the moon base and the deadly, so far unconverted, herd of Daisybells that lurked menacingly next to it.

I looked around for the other ninja Elvis bot riders from Jane's team and saw them sprinkled throughout the herd, spreading those good vibrations that rippled round us like the funkiest of festivals, just with that stick happy moon-dust instead of mud threatening to clog up the works.

Jane led us all in a swaying groovetastic sing out, as we rode arms joyfully waving in the airless void as we steered that funky freewheeling herd towards the base that sat surrounded by most of the Daisybells as the Cadmow-controlled ship hovered above with the bull lord threatening our people with all manner of uncomfortable and distressing deaths if they didn't surrender to the inevitable power of Lord Cadmow.

While the newly boogietastic Daisybells we rode were fully converted by the teenage rebel virus, the vast herd just up ahead most definitely were not, and man those bellow happy horn wielders looked as mean as they come.

We heard over the radio Major Browne desperately trying to contact the various ships captains for help but it turned out they were all battling hard to stop Cadmow's forces taking control of their respective ships to be much help.

The two herds stopped nose to nose, ours suddenly surly, disaffected and looking around for either a protest or a party, pondering no doubt on the fairness of it all. The others were mean, angry and ready to attack, they out-numbered us massively.

'What's happening, Jane,' shouted the Colonel. 'Are they nearly brainwashed yet?'

'They are fighting it, Colonel,' shouted Jane the tails of our opponents wagging aggressively as they lowered their heads and stamped the ground in horn sharp rage.

'I am going to have to do it manually,' shouted Jane, as she leapt in the air, did a funky low gravity summersault and landed firmly across the back of an angry Daisybell that bucked and snorted with rage as Jane clung on.

'Be careful groovy sister,' I whispered crossing all my hooves and in my mind my horns as well.

'Move the herd forward,' shouted Jane as she fought to introduce the full rebel teenager virus into the resistant herd, as they tossed her for all she was worth.

'How am I meant to do that exactly,' I said getting quite exasperated at my failure to coax any movement at all from my stubborn Daisybell who was telling me in no uncertain terms that I could not tell her what to do and that I wasn't her mother.

'Tell her it's a parade, Holly,' shouted the Colonel, whose section of the herd was trotting eagerly forward. 'If that doesn't work tell them the other Daisybells are the police trying to stop them getting to a rock and roll star they really like.'

I leaned in close to my Daisybell and told her as sternly as I could manage that she was forbidden from going to the parade all the Daisybells ahead of us were attending especially in the clothes she had on. She defiantly trotted forward reminding me as she did how I couldn't tell her what to do.

As our two herds merged the teenage rebel virus began to take full affect, rebellious teenage attitudes started to ripple out in huge waves of stroppy defiant cool.

'We have to work fast,' shouted the Colonel as the cow-ship began to pass low over the herd.

'Yes, Colonel,' said Jane, 'if you can get me on the ship I can turn the Daisybells there.'

'How are exactly do we do that, man?' I asked.

'Me and Holly can take the rest of the converted herd into the base and turn the Daisybells there,' said the Colonel ignoring my question even though it seemed quite pertinent to the situation.

'You'll never take us alive damn you,' shouted the Colonel into the radio. 'We'll fight you to our last ounce of strength. Humanity will be victorious our spirit will prevail.'

'Will you please shut up human,' said Cadmow over the radio. 'Your gibbering nonsense is clogging up this frequency and we have important business to conduct.'

'Freedom, freedom we will resist,' yelled the Colonel as I began humming *La Marseillaise* like in that funky old movie Casablanca.

'Why aren't you trampled under the hooves of doom? Die just die and get off the line.'

'It's your damn Daisybells,' said the Colonel. 'They are thinking for themselves and have decided to bring us aboard that ship as your prisoners, I think they want to impress you like a cat bringing in a juicy mouse for its owner, but we won't let them, do you hear me.'

'Sounds a bit fishy to me my lord,' said Moolock. 'Let's just blast them as soon as we have the weapons back online.'

'And when will that be exactly Moolock?'

'Hey cool and groovy moo sisters what's happening in daisy town?' said Jane to her section of the herd.

'It's a bit boring, I wish there was something to do,' replied the Daisybells.

'How do you fancy a visit to a cool spaceship, like the one making low and scary passes over our heads right now?'

'Boring with a capital b,' muttered the Daisybells. 'We're not nerds, we like to go to concerts not conventions.'

'Well you're in luck then,' said Jane, 'aboard that very ship is a cool just about to be the biggest thing ever, bull band, lord Greasy Horn and the snorty Moo Boys. Yeah and they are filming their first music video now. We could go and watch them and perhaps get a private show, us all being their biggest fans, who liked them before they were properly famous, which is always a mark of being cutting edge and the coolest of the cool. How about it ladies, are you up for it?'

'Lord Greasy Horn and the snorty moo Boys?' muttered the Daisybells doubtfully.

'I think I've heard of them,' said one of the herd. 'Cadmow is the lead singer and he plays the guitar.'

'Oh yes I've heard of them too,' confirmed another herd sister, 'Moolock is the one I like, he's the snorting moody one, so cool.'

'I like Norhlick', piped in another, 'he's the sneaky one, I'd love to sneak up on him one day.'

'Well I have a radio link to Cadmow. Why not tell him you like his music and want to watch him play,' said Jane as the Daisybells began to giggle with excitement.

'Cadmow are you there? Can we talk to Cadmow please.'

'This is Lord Cadmow, who calls me at this busy time.'

'It's us your biggest fans, the Daisybells. We love your music it's so cool, especially your guitar playing it's just so on trend.'

'You Daisybells enjoy my music do you? Well you were all designed to have good taste. Would you like a signed copy of my album or perhaps a lock of my fur for your scrap book?'

The Daisybells let out a squeal of delight. 'Can we come aboard and watch you play those cool guitar riffs, please Cadmow we're your biggest fans, we truly are.'

'Well as you've come all this way,' said Cadmow, 'why not, but I only have time to play a few songs not a complete set. You see as well being a funky cool musician I am also busy conquering the lowly human maggots, and they are rather stubborn when it comes to surrendering.'

The Daisybells made excited oh and ah noises as the excitement rippled through the herd.

'I advise against this course of action my lord, it could be some sort of trick,' advised Moolock.

'Nonsense, Moolock, my fans need me. It would be wrong to deny them the pleasure of witnessing my sweet, sweet style in person. Now open a vortex and allow my followers in.'

'Take half the herd, Jane, we'll liberate the moon base,' said the Colonel

'See ya later, Holls, don't start the victory party without me,' said Jane leading her substantial herd through the groovy swirling vortex.

'Good luck Jane,' the rest of us shouted as we lead our equally substantial herd on towards the airlock which was deep inside enemy territory.

'Yes sir I understand,' said the Major sounding extremely doubtful as we explained the situation to her. 'I'll open the airlock straight away, sir, if you're quite sure and haven't just gone moon cow crazy with battle fatigue.'

'I am as sane as Holly here, Major, now open that door that's an order,'

'Well you've certainly put my mind at rest, sir,' replied the Major as the airlock opened and we poured in.

'What the hell have you done to my precious Daisybells, you'll pay for this,' screamed the voice of Cadmow over the radio as we swarmed through the base converting Daisybells and defusing booby traps left right and centre.

'Jane must be winning all the ship-based Daisybells over,' I said as we continued through the base.

'With a bit of luck the cow peoples forces should take out the Cadmow's generals easily now,' said the Colonel as we heard the Major opening up a second front with the forces she had at her disposal.

The Daisybells showed no interest in fighting themselves but fortunately without the Daisybells, internal force fields and lasers there were only a small force of Cadmow's generals to deal with. Between us the Major and the various international forces we made short work of liberating the moon base from them.

As we headed towards the command centre we came across a strange looking group of what we assumed were Daisybells. They were much shaggier than the average Daisybell with much bigger horns.

'I cannot convert them, Colonel,' I said, 'I've tried everything.'

'So have I, Holly, they must be a new breed resistant to the teenage rebel virus,' said the Colonel as a familiar figure leapt aboard the leader of the strange new herd.

'Or perhaps they're not Daisybells at all laddie,' said Mrs McDoon raising her broom in defiance. 'These wee lassies are Morag's and they're made of sterner stuff than those lily-livered creatures. No my beasties have the spirit of noble teenage Scottish rebellion; they want Scotland to be free and decent. Their hearts are spurred on by the music of the Proclaimers and the poetry of Robert Burns. But don't look worried none, that Cadmow has clearly lost so I'll be on my way and trouble you no more.'

With that she opened her own vortex and led her proud herd through it as the lady herself serenaded the beasts with patriotic Scottish ballads.

In the years that followed there were many sightings of Mrs McDoon and her Morags throughout the land of Scotland, with many odd and curious legends growing up around the legendary patriotic herd.

Without their Daisybells Cadmow's generals were quickly defeated, some being taken into custody aboard the cow ships for return to the cow home world, others fell in combat against the forces of Major Browne.

'Good to see you, Major,' said the Colonel as we were welcomed back into the command centre by a cheering crowd of troops.

'You too, sir,' replied the Major with a salute and a big grin. 'Nicely done you really saved our bacon, sir.'

'It's Jane we need to thank, Major, her rock and roll virus really brainwashed them good.'

That's when my fella ran through the crowd as I swung down from my Daisybell. 'Holly babes thank Cowdon you're alright,' said Vince swinging me round in a frenzy of soft moos and grassy nuzzles. That might not sound good to a human but let me tell you to this cow it was heaven.

After clearing some space in the control room, mainly by releasing the Daisybells back onto the lunar surface where they partied to their hearts content, we released the yokels from their jars and started wondering where Jane was.

Suddenly a vortex opened, Cadmow, Moolock and Norhlick raced out with Jane and a small herd of Daisybells in hot pursuit.

As Jane waved hello and me and Vince ran to welcome her back all guns swung round to point at Cadmow and his crew.

'Hold it right there, boy,' shouted the Colonel. 'It is my duty to order your immediate surrender or my troops will open fire, but quite frankly there is no point in bothering as I intend to make sure you get the goddamn death penalty for your war crimes against the human race. Your people made a big mistake in letting you live, I don't intend on repeating that mistake.'

'No human,' laughed Cadmow reaching out a greasy grasping hoof. 'I will not surrender to you or anyone else.'

'That's all I wanted to hear,' said the Colonel opening fire.

But despite the bullets flying towards them the three renegade bovines continued to laugh as each and every bullet bounced of some sort of protective energy field around them before tinkling gently to the floor.

'I intend for us to escape,' said Cadmow grabbing his spare guitar, a packet of chocolate digestives and a large pot of extra silky horn wax. 'One day if my plans go well we will return and make your worthless species extinct and rid the universe of you pathetic gibbering freaks.'

With that the old sour cat crew disappeared in a flash of blue light.

'Oh what a sell out, treating his fans like that,' muttered the Daisybells that had been with Jane. 'To think I liked him as well,' snorted each Daisybell in turn before strutting off to form their own bands that would just be about the music and definitely not about pandering to popular musical fads of the corporate music industry.

'Where are our prisoners?' said the captain of the lead cow ship as she emerged from the vortex flanked by a retinue of armed guards and senior officers that didn't look like the kind of bovines you would want to mess with.

'Well,' repeated the captain impatiently as everyone stood in an embarrassed silence, looking at the floor.

'They got away, man,' I said as Vince nudged me and told me not to draw attention to us. 'Yeah in a big blue flash of light.'

'How could you let this happen? They must have been right in front of you,' berated the captain as one of her crew scanned the area with some funky scanner before whispering in her ear.

'They were aboard your ship, with all its advanced technology, surely you could have caught them there, captain,' said Colonel Twirl as me Vince and Jane disappeared through the vortex back to Earth in order to transport all the victory party goodies as quickly as possible before someone said we couldn't have one.

Chapter 18: The victory party and beyond.

The victory party was as you might expect a funky affair. The Daisybells danced strictly on the lunar surface but from time to time a few of us donned spacesuits and boogied on down with them.

Lots of medals were dished out and every media channel in the world wanted to interview Jane who was too busy dancing with the cute helicopter pilot. We did have to drag her away from an angry encounter with Josephine Barnstorm who was pretending she always knew we were the good guys really.

We told the media and a distressed Professor Winkle that Mrs McDoon had fallen in battle against the Daisybells. Unfortunately the reporters at the party kept describing her as a great all American hero from Glasgow Montana. Making up all manner of stories about the town and state. They even claimed the states motto is; if you pee on the mountain you better listen for them hooves. Which I am sure isn't true but the reporter claimed it was something to do with aggressive feral goats, objecting to the unhygienic habits of tourists.

It seemed that the Cadmow crew had disappeared into an alternate universe. Colonel Twirl spent most of the party discussing with the cow ship captain plans to send an expeditionary force into the multiverse to finally hunt down and capture the bull lord and his allies.

We managed to reconcile Colonel Twirl and his DJ son Spandex. When the Colonel was told how many communist countries had banned western rock music and American movies during the cold war, the Colonel was able to see his son's chosen career in new light.

The yokels managed to get their pictures taken with three attractive young women sent by a modelling agency to add a bit of glamour to proceeding. 'These are our new model girlfriends, aren't they fine,' the yokels keep shouting as the young women nudged them in the ribs pointing out they were not and never would be romantically involved with them.

Late on in the party a silver flying saucer turned up outside. Apparently it was one stored in the British museum since the nineteen thirties when it had been found buried under the Nile valley. The little silver alien that emerged from the craft loved Elvis and wanted to show us its Elvis tribute act and beg a lift to Sirius B from the space bovines as its interstellar drive was broken.

We let the cat do its show and the being was pretty funky and was so popular it was invited to do some shows in Vegas when they rebuild that town.

The space cows told us we were now exiled to Earth, although they couldn't find a record of what we actually did, we seemed quite annoying so we could not return to our home world and all its funky purple grass. A shame but we have come to love Earth so never mind I guess.

As the party wound on late into the night a vortex opened and from it crashed a big old pickup truck with three young fellas armed with shotguns on the back. As the shotguns were pointed at us a feisty looking older woman leaned sternly out of the passenger window.

'Listen up people,' she began, looking around the room. 'The names Bendle, Ma Bendle, my prize cow Buttercup was recently stolen and I have tracked her to this location. Return her to me now and we'll say no more about it. If you have objections to that please take those up with my boys back there.'

Well man we all quickly located Buttercup and helped her into the back of the pickup as quick as we could.

'I was wondering something, Ma Bendle?' began Vince.

'What's that son, you curious about something?' said Ma Bendle fixing Vince with a piercing stare. 'Curiosity killed the cat you know? I don't suppose it would do a bovine much good either. Ask away if you feel the need but I reserve the right to offend by telling you to mind your own goddamn business.'

'I just noticed Buttercup seems very anthropomorphic, she applies horn wax, eats popcorn with her hooves and makes a damn fine martini which are not skills found in most ordinary cattle I've met,' said Vince with an eye on the shotguns.

'That's an interesting story so I will tell you,' said Ma Bendle. 'On my bottom field where Buttercups herd grazes, back in the fifties the government did some weird top secret nuclear experiments on that land. Then come the sixties we let spaced out hippie's camp there. Those beatniks grew funny herbs which they fed to the ancestors of Buttercups herd. They sung weird protest songs and filled their heads with all manner of political and philosophical nonsense. Ever since that time cows on that field have had ideas above there station. Does that answer your questions?'

'Yes thanks, Ma Bendle,' replied Vince.

'That's good, now I'll be leaving you good folks in peace, it was most amenable doing business with you,' said Ma Bendle turning the pickup back towards the vortex. 'One last thing, Cletus, if I catch you anywhere near my land, my cows and most especially my granddaughter you'll be getting a visit from my boys here you understand?'

'I don't know what your implying, Ma Bendle,' said Cletus. 'I was just being neighbourly like.'

'You'll soon understand what I mean when you're picking buckshot out of your sleazy butt, boy so just think on now,' hollered Ma Bendle as she honked her horn and disappeared back through the vortex.

One year later.

One year later we were watching the movie of our battle with Cadmow. Oh man it was a bad movie. They called it, invasion of the killer cows. Cadmow was a cackling flatulent loon wanting Earth's supply of milk and Hay. The movie version of Cadmow used a freaky pat ray to drown cities in slurry. He was defeated by an eccentric farmer who was in the habit of bringing his cows into big cities and going to nightclubs with them. It was these funky cows that turned the Daisybells into groovy party animals. The film ended with a funky bovine-inspired festival on the moon itself. Cadmow being run out of the base when funky rave goers take it over.

'This film sucks big time man,' I said after twenty minutes, 'we should split now.'

But Vince thought it was hilarious so we stuck it out till the lights came up, and the credits stopped rolling.

As the lights went up we looked round in horror as every seat was occupied by a killer cow clone, of either Cadmow or Moolock. Their eyes all shone red with evil delight, as cruel cackles erupted from them.

'Heavy man,' I said.

'Yeah, with cheddar cheese on sister,' replied Vince as we huddled close.

Then those freaky clones took their masks off and it was just kids dressed for the movie. The kids pointed and laughed at us because we had come as the least interesting characters in the movie apparently. What cheek.

'We should go and check out our club, Holly, I hear they have finished rebuilding it,' said Vince.

'Lead the way, man,' I said following Vince out and into the night.

Let me tell you a funky night was had by all.

Goodbye groove cats, and remember, your mind is like a parachute it only works if it's open. Stay mellow and chant those moon cow mantras every night.

The End

About the Author

Rodney Milton is a fifty something worker in the food industry and lives in North Wales in the United Kingdom. As part of his offical midlife crisis he has chosen to write daft stories about space cows. He is a member of the left field creative writing group in Chester as well as the Chester science fiction and fantasy bookgroup.

Milton Keynes UK
Ingram Content Group UK Ltd.
UKHW050204250324
439991UK00013B/1532

9 798215 626252